WHAT DEATH
TAUGHT
TERRENCE

THE STING

Critics deliver
Thoughtless blows,
Their impact solid and lasting.
With not much more than
A condemnation of the prose,
A paragraphs-long linguistic blasting.

As a writer,
Thoughtful and careful in construction,
Sure to have my musings
Torn apart—
Every punctuation mark,
Every word choice,
Every conscious decision as to voice,
Each contraction or conjunction—
Demolition without compunction,
I ask only this of the critic
Intent on the sting.
Before you end another promising career
As it begins,
Might you *read* the damned thing?

WHAT DEATH TAUGHT TERRENCE

A Novel by
DEREK McFADDEN

KENBOSKI & SEIDENVERG BOOKS

ISBN: 978-1-7333963-1-8

For my parents, grandparents, and great-grandparents. You believed in me and my talent. And you raised a dreamer who—proudly—never stopped dreaming. If you stop dreaming, you stop living.

For everyone who believed in this book.

And for everyone who wonders if putting their words to paper is the right thing to do.

It is.

D

MANY TIMES MISTAKEN

If anyone believes,
Erroneously,
That God, who is to have brought forth
Heaven and Earth—
While His angels sang
An untouchable harmony—
Birthed them by mistake,
May I, with an implement
I hope will never shy
From *my* truth,
Humbly advise:
Let a prayer be sent,
From this poet's pen,
For all who wish it meant
For them;
Anyone who requires proof.
Up into the universe's
Roofless expanse.

That those who have yet
To discover their gifts,
Given out of love,
Not by chance,
Shall have the option to
Call for help from up above
When their lives seem rent
Or devoid of direction.
Knowing that call will be met with:

"Do not fear life.
There is no such thing as perfection.
I am with you.
You might feel alone,
At times even crazy.
But you are safe,
Under my protection,
And nothing can be accomplished
Without faith.
Like your parents before you,
And theirs before them,
You come from a God who is many times
Mistaken.
Yet you are so far from a mistake."

1

DEATH, PART I

TERRENCE MCDONALD IS 55. THE YEAR IS 2045.

The TV is on, and I'm on the couch, leaning as far back as I can. My heavy, indecisive brown eyes—their lenses blurred ever since my tumultuous, too-soon entrance into the world—flutter between open and shut. I am half-watching half-listening to a football game on a Sunday afternoon. *Was that the doorbell?*

"Who is it?" I call out, expecting to hear my daughter, Megan's, voice. These days, she is the one person who visits me. The *only* person who knows I'm making my home in this little oasis fashioned from wood felled by my own hand.

"Terry, it's Mom. I'm here to help you move."

My mom? That's not possible. She's…

Wait. To help me move? Oh, God.

I rise from the couch and glance back at my lifeless body. Five-foot-eight standing up, but now it's slumped over, grayish-blue. A few stray locks of the hair I inherited from my father, still mostly pepper-black, spill over into my unseeing eyes.

Shit. I still had more I wanted to do, damn it! Was it my cerebral palsy? We've co-existed forever. Has it somehow—in its slow, indirect way—finally done me in?

I turn back around toward the TV, and I see my mom materialize in front of me, a concerned look on her face.

"Are you okay?"

"No, of course I'm not okay!" I scream. "So… is that it then? I'm dead, just like that?"

She doesn't say anything, but her silence says everything.

"How? How did I die?"

Mom puts her hand on my shoulder like she always did when I was a kid and I was upset and needed some time to calm down. "You don't remember?"

"No, Mom, I don't remember. If I remembered, why would I ask?"

She is silent for another beat. "If you don't remember… then it's probably best if I stay quiet for now. My job is to take you Home."

"I am home," I shoot back.

"You don't understand. Where I'm taking you… this is a different kind of Home. This is the place where you'll find out what happens next."

"Is there any way around this? Any way at all?"

These words are as close as I've ever come to arguing with my mom. That's because arguing with her does not come naturally to me. And, considering the life I have, I never thought I'd hear myself plead for it.

"No, Terry. I'm sorry, but there's not. You know that, if there were a way, I'd tell you what it was. But this has been decided."

I pull away from her. Am I frightened? No, not exactly. But I am… disheartened.

Before I can go too far, she takes my hand. "Come with me, Terry. I love you."

It's been so long since Mom said those words to me—*I love you*—that I'd forgotten how true and convincing they sounded in her voice, and how much I missed them… and her.

·   ·   ·

Without warning—and without the white-light-emitting tunnel I experienced as a kid—we're not in the cabin anymore, and I find myself in a house so familiar I am comfortable in seconds. The smells are familiar. The floorplan. The art on the walls. This is a replica of the home I shared with my wife, before she got sick and I moved into the cabin.

"See, it's not so bad," Mom says. "I picked it out and furnished it myself. Just for you."

It *is* a nice place. Much nicer than I'm used to these days, that's for sure. Not that I have anything but a vague idea where we are.

Now that I've calmed down some, it isn't just this new house I'm appraising. I'm also getting my first real good look at Mom in twenty years. Hers is a face looking as youthful today as it appeared in the photograph announcing her entrance into womanhood—taken in her eighteenth year. I remember seeing this picture in a family album decades ago.

"You've got all the comforts you're used to," Mom explains. "Along with a couple you might have forgotten about."

"So this is where I'll be living now?"

The frown on her face hints at the fact that things aren't that simple. "Well, that depends on your appointment, but I sure hope you will. Your father and I are just down the street."

"Dad's here?"

"Yes, he made it." She smiles. She'd told me as much before. Years ago, on her final day. She'd said it twice, in fact. I'm not sure I'd believed her either time.

"My appointment?"

"Everyone has an appointment when they first get here."

"What happens? Who is the appointment with?"

"I can't tell you, Terr." Mom takes a seat in the first of three chairs arranged in front of my large television screen. This is the only liberty she's taken in the design. The original home had two chairs in front of this television, because two was enough for Mattie and me, but I sense Mom gave me the extra seat in case I should have company over. "Those who have been through their own appointments, like me, are expressly forbidden from sharing any details with newcomers, like you. Each appointment is different based on the soul and the life it concerns."

"Ah." Now I'm nervous. And not just because I get the feeling at this moment that Mom is spouting some section of a well-rehearsed monologue. I wonder if, at this appointment, *everything* in a person's life is considered.

"Yes, *everything is* considered," Mom says.

I shoot her a confused glance. *Did she just read my mind?*

"Oh, I'm sorry. We don't often use *spoken* words or languages here. I mean, we *can*. And we will, especially in cases when explanations or announcements need to be delivered to a large number of people. God prefers spoken language Himself. But it's more common, for those who have been Home a while, to communicate telepathically. I thought that was what you were doing."

I shake my head.

"Well, in a few days, once you're feeling acclimated, let me know. You can call me on this." Mom produces what looks like a cell phone. "That's a direct line to me and me alone. When you're ready, I'll come and pick you up and take you to your appointment."

"Okay."

But first, she thinks, *get some rest. You look terrible.*

I am a little tired, but what do you expect? I'm dead.

"You're getting the hang of our telepathy already." She laughs, gives me a hug. "I've gotta get back to cook your father's pot roast, or he might go a little nuts."

Sounds like Dad. A hungry Carl McDonald means an irritable, hard-to-deal-with Carl McDonald (I was going to say *hard-to-live with*, but the word doesn't fit).

Mom pats my shoulder and disappears. This new Home is going to mean some big adjustments for me.

·   ·   ·

I'm going to guess it's taken me the better part of three days-spent resting and recuperating from life—to convince myself I'm really dead and, secondly, that I'm ready to face whatever might be in store for me. I have to guess at how much time has passed because, as it turns out, this new home of mine, furnished by my mom, does not include a clock. Not one. I only discovered this flaw after she departed, so there was no way to readily remedy it. Stores specializing in timepieces aren't plentiful in the afterlife.

Wait, that's not true. Maybe they are. I don't know what lies beyond these four walls yet. I've barely moved since I got here. But I am as pre-pared as I'll ever be for my personal appointment, so I pull out the cell phone Mom gave me—an older model ubiquitous in my childhood—for just this situation. It doesn't require dialing. My connection to her is immediate.

"Terry?" she says.

"Hi, Mom."

"You're ready for your appointment?"

"I guess."

"Okay." She pauses, a bit too long for your run-of-the-mill pause. Something's bothering her. "Okay, I'm glad to hear it."

"What's wrong? You're gonna pick me up, right?"

"I was planning on it, but it looks like your Grandpa Jack needs to be picked up today."

"Oh, you mean he's—"

"Yep."

"I'm sorry, Mom. Boy, he lived forever, didn't he?"

She laughs. "Pretty darn close. I'm just glad he got to go out the way he wanted; peacefully, in his sleep. Anyway, your dad and I have to be there for him, but I'm sending your old friend Charlie out to you. He'll get you where you need to go, no problem."

Charlie. How nice it will be to see him again. It's been a long time. This isn't the only thought I have upon hearing Charlie will be here soon, but it's the only thought I feel comfortable sharing, in case Mom can read my thoughts through the phone as easily as she could standing in the same room.

"Okay, thanks. Tell Grandpa Jack I say hi."

"I will. And you call me when you and Charlie get to your appointment. Otherwise, you'll have me worried."

"Sure thing."

We hang up, and I wait. There's the sound of tires churning gravel and then a knock at the door twenty minutes later… I think. I answer it.

"Charlie Ewell's limousine service." He smiles and nods toward a jet-black vehicle closely related to a town car that's parked nearby.

I step back. Blink. Once. Twice. He's still there. My mind doesn't know how to make sense of this.

It really is Charlie. Well, of course it is. Mom told you he was on the way. Yet despite my mom's assurance, there is this part of me that snickers at most religions, labels them NOT FOR ME, and I never warmed all the way up to the idea of Heaven. Therefore, even after seeing *Mom again*, I doubted my old friend Charlie would show up. *You're telling me Charlie will be here! Charlie? Yeah, right.*

Just like I couldn't bring myself to argue with her—*Charlie can't possibly be on his way, Mom!*—I can't deny it now.

"It's you," I say.

"Sure it's me," Charlie says, as though he's just shown up to my most recent—*and last?*—birthday party, cheer on his face, a gift in his hand.

"Like, *really* you."

"Yeah. It's really me."

"How?"

"I know it's a lot to take in when you're new," he says, "or when you've just come *back*. I was so glad when your mom called and asked me if I would pick you up. I've missed you so much."

"Same here," I admit. The initial shock of seeing Charlie is ebbing slowly, like adrenaline leeching out of my bloodstream after an earthquake.

"It's so good to see you, Charlie." We enfold each other in a backslapping, how-have-you-been hug.

When we're apart again, he says, "And you, Terry. It's just now dawning on me how odd this circumstance is."

"True. But under what other circumstances *would* we see each other?"

"Good point. In one of your dreams, maybe. You ready to get going?"

"Sure. Is there a set time we *have* to be there? My mom always said it's better to be early than late, no matter what the occasion."

Charlie throws his car keys in the air, catches them, as we make our way down my temporary home's front steps.

"Don't worry about time anymore," he reveals. "Time is a human invention. It is seldom kept here."

"That would explain the lack of clocks."

"Which always throws newcomers off. And don't be nervous. Sure, no one who's been through an appointment can tell you what *your* appointment will be like. That's because appointments are unique to each soul, but they aren't to be feared. Your appointment is a place where you will get the chance to ask questions and learn." Charlie flashes a quick grin. He opens one of the back doors for me, and I see that in the car rides an elegant woman. "Terrence McDonald, this is my wife, Patty Ewell."

Patty turns in her seat, puts out her hand. "It truly is a pleasure to meet you, Terrence. I've heard a lot about you."

I give her my hand but can find no words. I've never met Patty before. She passed away the night I made Charlie's acquaintance.

THE WAITING ROOM

So empty,
Even when it's full,
So sterile and small,
I try to resist its downward,
Depressive pull.
Here I deeply fear
A new peril's call.

2

THE APPOINTMENT

I never figured the waiting room would be tiny, but this one is just that. So *much* smaller than anticipated. Tiny doesn't begin to cover it. It's a cubbyhole.

I am surprised, too, at the lack of decorations heralding the coming holidays on Earth. I guess I'd thought the absence of time in this dimension would be temporarily ignored, no expense spared. A lighted tree ornately festooned, a menorah prominently displayed. A wreath, poinsettias, mistletoe. And maybe these touches would foster the illusion that the place was bigger than its square-footage. The blank white walls prove me wrong.

My cell phone rings.

"Mom?"

"You made it."

"Yeah, Charlie dropped me off. I was just reaching for my phone to call you."

"I knew I could count on Charlie," she says. "So you haven't been sent into your appointment yet?"

"No. But it's better to be early than late. Isn't that right? You taught me that, Mom." I take a sip from my can of Coke. Charlie had it waiting in the car.

"It's certainly not a lesson your father would have taught you." She seems pleased that I give her the credit for my punctual nature. "Too bad it doesn't apply anymore."

I can't argue with her there, and the smile in her voice brightens my mood. "Mom, I'm curious. Why aren't there any decorations in this place?"

"Because no belief system is valued above any other," she explains. "Not here. All holidays are celebrated here, in concert with their earth-bound counterparts. The lack of décor in that waiting room is simply a way to respect all faiths by honoring none."

The red-haired receptionist—attractive in an earlier epoch—suddenly begins giving me the evil eye from behind the counter about three feet in front of my chair. *Get off the cell phone.*

Is it too loud for her liking?

"Mom, I gotta go. Tell Dad hi for me."

"Will do."

"Love you." I flip my phone shut.

As soon as we hang up, the receptionist calls my name. I approach the counter.

"Is this your first time here?" she asks. Her voice is flecked with the smoke she inhaled twenty years ago, and I know without being told that she *could* have traded in her spent lungs for new ones, but she kept the wrecked set to remind her of a lesson learned.

"As far as I know."

Her eyes narrow. Apparently, there are two things off-limits in front of this woman. Cell phones and sarcasm. "Okay, then, Mr. McDonald. Go through that door." She points just to the right of my current position. "And then enter the second door on your right."

"Second door on my right," I repeat, trying to commit the phrase to a memory that has been failing me of late.

"M-hmmm."

"What do I do once I get there?"

"Sit and wait."

The same thing I've been doing. I'm getting pretty darn good at it. "Okay."

I find the second door on my right without any trouble and turn the knob, but before I can enter, telepathy interrupts.

We're waiting for you, Terrence, it says.

Who's waiting for me?

We're your panel. It'll be our job to determine your place in the after-life. We're at the end of the hall.

The receptionist's instructions must have been in error. She has numerous appointments to keep track of, I'm sure. Countless souls to direct. It's understandable.

To the end of the hall I go.

.   .   .

The three beings seated across from me at the conference-room table wear shimmering white robes. Their identities are unclear, each of their faces shrouded by a pallor that matches the robes. Their lips and eyes lack color, too. Their voices are pleasant but offer no clues. Among this group, nevertheless, there *is* a clear leader.

"What would you say is your overall impression of your life, Mr. Mc-Donald?" the leader asks.

"Huh?"

"Would you say you were able to do everything in your life that you wanted to do?"

The answer is not worth verbalizing. Anyone who came into contact with me for more than five minutes near the end knows this. Not to suggest many people did. My existence had degenerated into lonesome days during which I found myself comforted only by the clack-clack-clacking of my wife's old typewriter, handed down from her mother. The nights and their silence were worse. Finishing the manuscript she never completed but always dreamed of publishing kept me as focused as I could be when the sun was up, and that wasn't very focused at all. As for my own accomplishments—or lack thereof—here I am, a supposed writer, who never published a word. I spent the better part of my life in a profession I loathed.

"Of course not," I say.

All three of them frown. They share glances, a telepathic conversation I'm not part of. Shimmering Robe Two, the one seated in the middle, speaks next. "Mr. McDonald, our job as we sit here is to determine a proper occupation for you moving into the next phase of being. To do this, we take into account the life you led, your disappointments, happinesses, hurts, guilt, pain."

I'm silent for a moment before wondering aloud, "So what will I be doing, your honors?" *Was that polite enough? I think so.*

Shimmering robe three: "It was polite enough, but it wasn't what you really wanted to say, was it?"

Oh, crap, I forgot. These guys can hear what I'm thinking. Shit. Probably shouldn't swear in this setting.

"I'm sorry."

"It's okay," says Two. "Panels hear every kind of thought imaginable, and that includes the occasional barrage of profanity. We're trained to expect it. Believe it or not, it helps us to do our job. The Boss believes meeting like this is the most effective way to pick vocations for the many souls who come before us."

"The Boss?"

"I think you know who that is," says the leader.

"So what was it you really wanted to say to us?" asks Three, seated on the far right. "Your intent was certainly not to ask what you would be doing. Besides, we'll tell you that. We wouldn't withhold such important information."

"Well, based on my life, as you say your judgments are, I feel like I'm in the wrong place. Like I've failed in my existence. I've felt that way for a while now. Like I may not deserve to be here."

I can tell they understand this impulse.

"A lot of people feel that they don't deserve to be here when they first arrive," offers Three.

"They do?"

"Yes."

"But it usually wears off," Two chimes in.

Usually. Good to know.

What if it doesn't?

"Mr. McDonald?"

"Yes?"

The leader eyes me with... is it suspicion or concern?

"Terrence, are you all right?"

Concern.

Am I all right?

"M-hmm. Just a little… overwhelmed."

"That is to be expected." Clearing the throat. "It's a requirement at this stage in our work with you that we disclose a few important facts."

"Which are?"

"Firstly, we are not the only judgment panel. Truth be told, there are millions. The judgment panel you are assigned upon death is made up of a group of souls whom the soul awaiting censure knew in life."

"Are you telling me I know you? All three of you?"

"You did," says Two. "In different capacities, and to varying degrees, throughout your life."

The leader speaks again, "We will reveal our identities later in the process. For now, our faces and voices will remain hidden from you so that we may judge your words and actions without being influenced by your feelings for or against us."

Three jumps in. "The Boss feels this new format gives the judgment process the fairness it used to lack. Before the institution of what The Boss calls "The Prior Encounter Rule", all judgments were made by folks the soul had wronged."

"Hell was getting pretty full," says the leader.

I shudder. Is that a joke? Sarcasm? Whatever's behind it, the comment reverberates in my mind like gunfire in an echo chamber. It terrifies me. Hell may have been pretty full once, but perhaps it isn't full enough *now*.

And when the panel speaks of Hell, are they speaking of my ultimate destination? Where I truly belong? I half-expect so. Part of me believes I am destined for this fate. The part of me that hates *me*. Meanwhile, another faction of my persona, quiet but persistent, lobbies hard for a different panel altogether.

We can do better than this. It whispers, to avoid detection. *We can find a panel whose members aren't quite as sarcastic, a panel that will take its task more seriously.* I'm not sure this is true. I haven't gotten the slightest hint that the panel isn't serious about their task, and everyone I knew in life was sarcastic at times. But we can try.

I want to talk to The Boss.

Not that I think anything will come of my unspoken appeal.

Until something does.

·　　　·　　　·

The leader interrupts our appointment, having received a telepathic message not unlike the one that brought me to this room, and the other two panelists are asked out into the hallway.

Who might the message be from? I wonder.

Soon, the leader returns. The others are in tow, silent partners.

"Mr. McDonald, it seems there has been a *minor* mistake."

"How's that?"

"While we are your judgment panel, *you* were supposed to first have a meeting with The Boss. Visits with Him are exceedingly rare. But it is foretold in your life's chart, and so we must honor it. Please forgive me. The mistake was mine."

The apology accepted, I return to the door I was originally instructed to open prior to being sidetracked. Inside is a facsimile of my childhood bedroom. Everything is as it was back then, from the smell of Dad's burning incense wafting through the house and permeating all nooks and crannies, to the flowered bedspread I detested that my birth- mother, Lisa, insisted upon. Once my true mom, Chloe, entered our lives, I thought she might suggest a different design, but she never did.

It is all as I recall it. Which is easy enough. The majority of my adolescence was spent here.

A MEETING WITH THE BOSS

Everyone asks for a meeting with "The Boss."
They ask when it's cold outside;
The world trembling under a bitter white frost.
They ask when an extended heat-wave,
A symptom of drought,
Keeps away the rain,
The white frost,
And dries everything out.
Or when an expected loved one,
Forever lost,
Never arrives via train.
They ask at Christmas.
When that same beloved relative isn't there.
And look back,
Wishing for just one more holiday shared.

3
MEETING GOD – THE IMPERFECT CHAMELEON

When I convinced myself I should discuss the merits of my panel and do my best to reason with Him, I had no idea I would actually get the chance. The appointment with my panel made me nervous, but the prospect of meeting The Boss Himself leaves me light-headed. I may pass out (Is that a possibility here?). I'm shaking like a scared puppy ripped from its mother for the first time, a rough pair of hands surveying its soft fur. *Will I meet doom in these hands?* I have no way of knowing, but I sure hope not. I have no way of knowing what He will look like, either.

He appears in front of me, and as I stand before Him—about ten of my own paces and five normal steps to the right of the twin bed—in this bedroom I never thought I'd see again, he is a dapper-looking, suit-wearing older gentleman. Skin dark as pitch, with a smile white as gleaming ivory.

Charlie. The husband of Patty, the love of his life, who was dying the night I entered fatherhood. Charlie, The provider of limousine service when time no longer governed.

"Sir?" I start. I am uneasy, aware of whose ear I hold.

"Terrence?"

"Sir… I… why do you look like Charlie?"

"Does it distract you?"

"A little."

"I tried to pick someone who would make you feel comfortable. If I remember right, the impact of your meetings and time spent with Charlie never left you."

"He was like a second father to me," I agree. "But I sure didn't think God would look like him. I thought God would be… perfect."

"Your first lesson in the afterlife, Terrence: Even God isn't perfect."

"Really? 'Cause that's gonna piss off a lot of people who live their lives latched onto the idea that You are."

"Let them be pissed," says The Boss. "I tried My best. I worked so hard to fashion a world we could all be proud of. What the hell happened? I feel like I've lost control." He stays quiet until asking, "Do you know who I blame?"

"No. Who?"

"The zealots. The extremists. The people who believe they were created in my image."

"A lot of people believe that last one. Those first two, I can understand your being miffed with them. Are you telling me we weren't created in Your image?"

He shakes Charlie's head. "I am electricity. I am water. I am dirt. I am fodder. I am the things you want to say, the things you should let lay. I am your scars. I am your tears cried over drinks in bars, or on a sun-dappled wedding day."

I understand. "You're everything."

"Yes. Everything *except* biologically human. I left that to you and yours. Perhaps it was a mistake." He takes a deep breath. "So what did you want to see Me about?"

You can do this, Terrence. He's just like you. Only… He's God. "Sir, I wanted to talk to you about my panel?" It's a question, not a statement. "I wonder if there's any way I might get a different one? Different judges? There are millions of panels, after all. It's not that I dislike mine, but I get the feeling a fresh start might be beneficial for—"

"Nope." Short, and sour as a rotten lemon. I never knew words could have a physical taste. There is no anger in this one, just finality.

So much for reasoning with Him. I sense He has more to say to me, though. Our meeting is not over.

"Put simply, the reasons I'm here with you—the reasons you aren't still conferring with your panel like so many in your position," He says, "those reasons are twofold and have nothing to do with your own desire to switch panels, or with your prayer… that's what it was; a prayer… to meet with Me. You're a new arrival. Those things aren't exactly common, but they aren't unexpected, either. They're by-products of fear and uncertainty."

"Okay." It is the most not-okay *okay* that's ever passed my lips.

"Please allow Me to offer you a little background. Then I'll tell you the story of how it is that we've ended up here together."

"Sure, God, tell your story. It's not like I'm doing anything else. I'm a captive audience."

For me, sarcasm is a coping mechanism. I'm doing my best to cope with the situation I find myself in, but I'm not sure any mechanisms will quite suffice for *this* job.

"I would like to believe, Terrence," The Creator tells me, "that the afterlife might actually be perfect. I had this illusion about Earth once, too. That I'd birthed something infallible. I've come around to accept the error in My thinking, on both fronts.

"There are many, many things that make humanity imperfect. One of them is time. There's never enough of it on Earth. So time was one of the first variables I excised from the afterlife, back when I still thought the afterlife could achieve the perfection Earth would never see.

"It was brought to My attention, around the same time we did away with *time itself* up here, that the appointments souls go through upon returning to us were being judged unfairly. I'm sure your panel discussed this."

"They did," I confirm.

"Enemies judging enemies. What a disaster! I thought it would work because I believed in the goodness of humankind. I believed in my creations. And I believed, erroneously, that most humans subscribed to the theory that everyone should do unto others as they would have done unto themselves. I thought I'd infused humanity with enough kindness and compassion to ensure this outcome. I was wrong. People chose to punish their enemies with everything at their disposal, and things got… out of control.

"We had to make some changes. That was clear. Hell isn't a fun place, Terrence. It's not supposed to be. But an overcrowded Hell is unmanageable. One of the changes agreed upon was The Drawing."

Even though I know He'll tell me, I feel compelled to ask, "What's The Drawing?" I want Him to know I'm listening. That He has my full attention.

"Roughly once every Earth-century, a drawing is held to determine in whose review I will personally take part. My involvement *does not* supersede a panel's authority. It's really meant as a way for me to make certain everything's running smoothly, and then I'll sometimes make changes based on what I observe."

"And so you're saying I was chosen in the last Drawing?"

"That's right."

"Wow, I feel kind of special." I can barely suppress a look of triumph.

"You shouldn't," God says.

"What's that?"

"You shouldn't feel special. At least not because of The Drawing."

"Why not? Everyone living on Earth is in The Drawing, right? You put them all in the hopper. And, this time around, I won! Why shouldn't I feel special?"

God uses telepathy for the first time. *I can see this is going to take more work than I'd thought. Do you think your cerebral palsy makes you special?*

"Maybe," I hedge. Somehow, I know the answer; I just don't want to say it.

"It doesn't. The fact is, everyone on Earth has some form of palsy. Only most people don't know it, and some never will."

I must look dumbfounded. It is definitely how I *feel*.

God plows on. "Before you went to Earth, Terry, you asked to speak with Me upon your return."

"Upon my return? You mean when I died?"

"Right, when you died. We call it 'coming back' or 'coming home.' Sounds better. Not everyone coming back asks for a meeting. In fact, very few souls *ever* do. Usually only those who expect to live exceedingly difficult lives, or those who feel they'll need to go over what they've learned as a sort of debriefing, and they want to do it with me. For this second group, to which you belong, Terrence—though you might argue that, at times, you belonged to both groups, and I wouldn't deny it—meeting with a panel won't be enough, and they know that going in. Only those who request a meeting prior to leaving Home are entered into The Drawing. The stipulation requiring their entrance is written right into their lives, as it was written into yours, and you were fully aware of it. Earth is so overpopulated that to put *every* living human into the next Drawing wouldn't be efficient. I made an executive decision to do it this way.

"Now, Terrence, it is important that you understand you are completely within your right to ask Me any questions that may come to your mind during this meeting and the review process. A judgment panel's decision is something of a one-way street. They decide, you abide. A life review is different, and it is even more so when I am involved first-hand. I want you to come away from this review with as complete an understanding of your life as you can possibly get.

"The first lesson in the afterlife, one that everyone learns—whether they want to believe it, that's a decision each person must come to individually—is how I am imperfect."

"I'll try to keep that in mind."

He barely acknowledges my words. Puts up His hand. *I'm not done.* "Your second lesson in the afterlife-"

"There's a second lesson?" *When does the review start?*

"There will be many lessons," God says. "Most of them will be covered in the review. But you'll have to understand these initial lessons before we can truly get going. They show you how things work here. Bear with me, alright? I've got a lot to get through with you. It would really help me if you would show some patience."

I nod. Patience isn't a quality I possess in abundance, but when the God you've known forever only on a shaky faith appears to you at life's end and asks you to show some patience, you commit yourself to the cause.

And you tell yourself, *Show some damn patience.*

"The second lesson is easier for me to verbalize than it might be for some people to grasp." He drapes a big Charlie-arm over my shoulder. "Will you come sit with Me, Terrence?" With the other hand, He points out two empty seats about ten feet away. These took the place of my bed without me noting the change.

They're the kind of chairs that recline and have cup-holders, the kind that'll give you a massage should you require one. I want to say no, I won't sit, I won't hear His rationale for allowing the world's maladies to persist. But that chair calls to me, and we do sit, He with a groan, I with the pains of age beginning to catch up with me. My right knee aches sharply... and perpetually. My left shoulder yelps whenever I try to lift it too high for its own good.

"I thought, when you got to Heaven, all pain was supposed to be eliminated." Expunged like a bad memory that's overstayed its welcome and disappears in a purge of the unnecessary.

"Yeah, well, this isn't Heaven. Not yet, anyway. This is a waiting room, let's call it. As good a place as any to begin thinking back on your life and what it has meant. But first, if you'll allow Me, I'd like to explain why I chose not to create a true devil."

Whatever you wanta do is fine with me. This is your show.

"The myth of the devil began," God starts, "as a way of keeping the peace on Earth. He was the pitchforked embodiment of evil, a persona I was pretty proud of myself, for thinking him up. If you stepped out of line, you could be sure he'd handle you when your time came. You'd have to answer to Me, of course; God, the all-powerful, but also to him. He and his "fires of hell" were much scarier, anyway."

"You could have *actually* created him. Why didn't You?"

"I could have created him, sure. Given him a residence here in the afterlife. A body and a soul. I could have sent him down to Earth, if I'd wanted, but I didn't need to do any of that.

"By the time I came up with the devil-myth, Terrence, we'd already been through several versions of Hell up here. The Hell we've settled on now is simpler than those that preceded it. The truly evil souls—everyone knows who *they* are—I'm okay with them getting the original fire and brimstone. That seems fair to Me, and that option remains available. Then there's another category of Hell. This division is made up of the souls who believe they've lived unfulfilled lives and, therefore, do not deserve a trip to the afterlife. They choose to remain behind in a kind of *personal* hell."

Like me. That's where I belong.

"No, Terrence, not like you. If you truly felt you didn't deserve to be here... you're not an evil person, so you wouldn't be here. You'd still be down on Earth."

I give Him a quizzical look, but I don't say anything. I need more than that, and He knows it. He'll explain.

"I know you're not the biggest fan of ghost stories, Terrence," He says.

After all these years, there it is. Confirmation. He *did* pay attention. As a kid, I hated camping trips and telling ghost stories by the fire before bed. (I loved making s'mores, but every camping trip guaranteed a ghost story or two.) I always woke up in the middle of the darkest nights shaking with fear, certain the ghost from that evening's tale would jump out from under my pillow, grab me, and pull me out of my life and into some shapeless black void. I'd spend the rest of eternity occupying haunted houses. Trapped forever.

"Ghosts are real," God says. "They inhabit one of Earth's dimensions. Not the same dimension humans occupy, mind you, but an adjacent one, and quite often humans can perceive them. Most ghosts don't want to remain on Earth, but for them doing so is a kind of personal punishment, sanctioned by Me. These ghosts don't feel they *lived* completely; they didn't learn all of the life lessons they were meant to, leaving their souls unfulfilled, so when the white tunnel of light comes to take them Home—you remember the tunnel, don't you?" I do, but I think it more important for Him to continue uninterrupted than for me to deliver confirmation on this point. "When it comes, they fight it, like fighting against a river's strong current. They'll remain down on Earth, staying close to the people they knew, the people they loved, until they've learned all lessons they were meant to learn. This could take years. Or, for some unfortunate beings, it might not happen at all. These are the saddest cases, where—even after watching over their loved ones—a soul could not glean all the lessons they were required to learn. This means they'll never see Home, or their families, again. You might think this a terribly harsh rebuke, but it is far from the harshest.

"And, with that, I'd say we're just about ready to start the review, Terrence," God says.

I want to say, Thank God, with my usual sarcasm. I settle for, "Thank You," with none of it.

"You're welcome. Besides reminding you that you can stop the review at any point to ask questions—no question is off-limits—there's just one preliminary issue left to cover. A panel will always ask its subject—and, in this case, as the head of the Drawing, I'm asking you—to please make all efforts to discern what the overriding lesson of your life was."

The overriding lesson of my life. I let that thought take a prominent place in a mind out of whose windows now hangs a weathered No Vacancy sign.

"Everyone has an overriding lesson that trumps all others," says God, "and everyone's lesson is different. At the end of this review, I'll need you to tell your panel what your personal lesson was. If you can't, you will not be permitted into the afterlife."

"Where will I go? Back down to be a ghost or something?" *That wouldn't be ideal, but it wouldn't be so bad.*

"No, I'm afraid not, Terrence. As per your original contract, which you signed before going to Earth, should you fail to grasp your overriding lesson, you will cease to exist, in any form."

"Why would You implement such a punishment? Cease to exist, in any form? That means… no afterlife, no ghosting, no nothing."

"That's right."

"That's awful!"

"It was a parameter insisted upon before your contract could be signed."

"Why did You insist upon it?"

"I wasn't the insistent party, Terrence. You were. I would never insist on such an irrevocable punishment.

"Those who agree to go to Earth have a sizable say in the consequences set forth in their binding documents. You were so afraid you'd miss the big lesson of your life, and so committed to ensuring you didn't miss a single one, that you wrote the cease-to-exist provision in yourself. I protested, everyone who was there protested, but you would not budge. 'If I don't do it this way,' you said, 'I might not learn anything.'

"I know it's a shock, Terrence. But, if you can—it's going to be difficult, but if you can—put any thoughts of the contract out of your mind for now. We will get back to it, I assure you. But first… the review."

A PERMANENTLY TARNISHED GEM

When one's body betrays them,
If you're not used to it—
Think athletes,
Beautiful people,
And the lot—
It can serve as the first sign
Of tarnish on a gem,
Leave one wrought with contempt.

When you're used to the betrayal, though,
You know time spent complaining
Is a waste,
And you barely bother to vent
Your frail frustration to anyone,
In any place.
Acceptance is the grail you chase.

4

ARE YOU GONNA TAKE THE PAIN AWAY?

"How does this review work?" I ask.

"We plug in everything we know about you and everyone you know—which is *everything*." God is noticeably proud of this fact, winks. "Then we are able to extrapolate from all of that a soul's exact thoughts and feelings from any situation at any time in their lives.

"During the review, you will see—and sometimes be transported to—different scenes from your existence. You will also hear many voices, including your own. This might be a little strange for you at first, since you didn't speak aloud any of the narration you'll be hearing yourself say. It makes some people uncomfortable."

"I can handle it." I feel my body tense. This isn't cerebral palsy but something much more universal. I clench my fists to keep them from shaking. My whole self goes numb, and I fight the numbness with all I have. *You can do this, Terry,* I tell myself. *Never trying means never failing, but it also means never succeeding, either.* Dad used to say that, didn't he?

"Let's start with the surgery. Are you okay with that, Terrence? Are you okay if we jump right in?"

"Yes."

I hear myself agree. With that, the pain of a young, palsied body knocks me out of my chair to the ground. *I didn't know we were going this far back! I thought you said we were starting with the surgery.* I'm two years old. I can't walk. All I *can* do is crawl. My hands are balled up in fists clenched tight not of my own doing. I try to open them. The left hand protests vehemently. But, with a shot of pain that says, *I'll let go, but you're gonna pay,* it relents. The right isn't so forgiving. At two, I don't have any concept of time, but looking back I must have spent a good two hours alone in my room (my parents thought I was amusing myself with toys, and any time I wasn't crying at that age acted as a respite for them; I was, after all, *so damn colicky,* as Dad put it). I wonder why. I willed myself to get that hand working. I gritted my teeth through the different levels of agony. Level one: bearable. Level two: bring on the tears, but fight. Level three went past tears and into my memory bank. *No matter what you do, for the rest of your life you'll remember the day your right hand's solid fist made its last stand.*

A chill runs the length of my four-year-old body, now ambulatory. When the chill reaches the middle of my back, it is no longer a chill. It has converted into something else, something familiar, and it actually *hurts.*

The pain I associate with my childhood returns. My legs on fire. This pain is specific to me. I know it will pass, but it always takes me back to a hotel room where Dad and I stayed one night when I was four years old.

.   .   .

"Why are we here again?"

"So the doctors can help you, chief." Dad tousles my hair and kisses me on the forehead, part of his tucking-me-in routine, one he performs each evening, no matter where we're laying our heads.

"Help me how?"

He's on his knees at the side of my bed, and we're eye to eye when he replies. "They're gonna fix your back so you can walk better."

When I walk, my hips swing wildly outward; a useless motion my parents have been warned—and I've overheard but never discussed—could result in my being confined to a wheelchair for the rest of my life, if corrections aren't made. My hips can't take the strain. "And you won't hurt as much."

To me, "not hurting as much" means getting to spend a never-ending day in a faraway carnival full of rides and cotton candy, clowns and elephant ears.

I don't need promises the pain will go away. A mention that it might while Dad and I wait for morning in a California hotel room, and I'm sold.

Constant pain shooting through my legs has been my evil twin for-ever. I'm ready to get rid of my twin. And if I can't get rid of him, maybe I can convince him he doesn't need to hold my hand anymore.

"Dad?"

"Hmm?"

"Can we say our prayer now?" Another part of the nightly tuck-in.

"Sure."

Our prayer is one Dad came up with. Mom's favorite prayer is differ-ent ("It's more religious than us guys are," Dad says). Dad's is the only one I know well enough to say perfectly.

"Dear God," I start. He repeats what I'm saying, and I slow my speech so that we are exactly in time with each other, at least for the part of the invocation that never changes.

"Thank you for this day. Keep the bad dreams out. Keep the good dreams in."

Now to the blessings. The wording of each blessing differs slightly, depending on my mood and the hour of the good wishes. The later a prayer is held, the shorter its blessings.

During this go-around I say, "God bless Dad." My father smiles. "Mom." He looks away, and this bothers me. "The doctors, the nurses, and, God, bless me, please. I'm scared."

"You don't need to be scared, buddy," Dad says. "Whatever happens, I'll be right beside you."

"You can't be with me in the operating room."

"No. That's true. But I'll be in to see you the minute the doctor says I can. Can you be strong for me, Terry? If you'll be strong for me, I'll be strong for you."

"It's a deal," I say with a yawn.

After our prayer, I may not *look* scared anymore, but I can't help *feel-ing* scared as the lights go out. In the darkness, I can't wrangle a wink of sleep, and neither can Dad.

·　　　　·　　　　·

The doctor is wearing a white coat, and he's down at my level, in-troducing himself. People really like to get down on my level when they think they're going to tell me something important. I'm on a table covered with crinkly white paper, wearing only underwear.

"I'm Dr. Clayton," he says.

"I'm Terrence," I say.

He laughs, glances Dad's way, and winks. "Yes, I know all about you, Terrence."

"Are you gonna take the pain away?"

"Do you have pain in your legs?" There is a glint in his eye. He puts his hand to my left leg above the knee and gently squeezes.

"My legs have a headache," I tell him. "All the time." I know what's going to happen next. He'll look at me all funny, the way grown-ups always look at me.

The doctor jerks his head back, and his face says, *This kid's pretty sharp.*

"We're going to do something about that headache. For now, let's check your reflexes, shall we?"

After the doctor bangs my leg with a hammer, I'm led into a small room. It's me and a bunch of men in white coats in there. I only have one friend in the room; a stuffed animal who's been allowed to have the same surgery I'm having. "We can do that," the doctor said. "He looks like a pretty tough bear."

I look down at my friend the bear and say, "This might hurt, but be brave for me, okay?"

I want to cry for what's on the other side of constant pain. It might be something worse. One of the white coats tells me to put my face up against a round thing that reminds me of a telescope but isn't. I can see an uninflated balloon inside it. Is the balloon red or purple?

"Do you see the balloon, Terry?"

"Yeah."

"Can you blow it up for me? Take a deep breath and blow into that tube there."

"M-hmm." I blow.

I'm asleep in no time.

·   ·   ·

I wake to a white-hot pain in my back. A pain so powerful that, where there should be a scream announcing it, there is nothing. I am mute.

A single tear rolls down my cheek.

One of the doctors says, "Your dad wants to see you. Is that alright?"

I nod.

"Hi, hon."

Since I'm turned away from the door, lying on my stomach, I can't see Dad. But hearing his happy voice is enough to send me into a rage. This is his fault. He's the one who put me here.

"Get out of here!" I scream.

.   .   .

Now my adult voice takes over, remembering, the context of a life lived fully behind it.

Though Anger and I used my pain to bond, the anger subsided with time. The surgery was an experiment, Dad told me, but it worked. I started down an epic and winding path through physical therapy sessions with women I swore were put on earth to hurt me.

They came to my home and stretched my leg muscles so that I could walk more easily one day, but each exercise was like having a piece of my body pulled apart and put back in a different place. In between visits, through a year of recovery, when I wasn't trying to convince my body to sit upright, which it never liked doing, I would lay shirtless on the couch, open spine exposed, waiting for a scar to come.

Eventually, it did. The scar was long, and there was a real tall-tale behind it, but it was my own true story. When anybody asked to hear it, I told it to them. Those most interested were my new friends in Ms. Dryden's kindergarten class.

My life was not painless after the operation. There were follow-up appointments and a lot of poking here and pushing there, and the carnival wasn't quite what I'd been told it would be. I wasn't allowed on all the rides, either. Safety concerns.

The pain was around throughout my life, but it didn't hurt as much. Dad was right. It wasn't constant anymore. It came and went and bothered me most in those times when I felt like I didn't have control of a situation.

Times like now.

THE REVIEW

"Looking back on the surgery, Terrence, you must have thoughts on it you wish to express to Me." God is my old doctor, and our surroundings have transformed into the office where I first met the man who cut me open.

Where I sat atop his white-papered table, underwear my only shred of privacy, while he checked my reflexes. *Shitty, as usual, I imagine he wrote in his notes.* God's chair is still a chair, but mine is the white-papered table itself. Thankfully, I get to keep all of my clothes on this time, and hence my dignity remains intact.

So this is what He meant when He said I'd be transported to different scenes from my existence. He wasn't kidding. In this case, I have truly been transported. Unlike the surgery, where the closest I got to being there again was to relive the pain while watching the scene unfold before me, this time I'm a physical participant. The constraints of palsy are upon me once again. The heavy legs. The lack of coordination. And, unique to me, the eyes so adept at not being any good.

.   .   .

"It hurt like a son-of-a-bitch, that's my initial thought." I let my lips turn up at their corners. They slide back into place without any effort on my part as I go on. God has a look on His face that says, *Anything else?*

"It's the first time I ever remember being truly angry. I was angry with Dad. At You. I was furious that no one stepped in and saved me from the pain before it was too late."

"Are you glad you had it done? I think that's really what I want to know. Was the surgery a benefit to you?"

"Sure, I'm glad. And, yes, it was. I walked a little differently than everybody else my whole life. but I *walked*, and considering what might have happened if the surgery went undone, I believe it was worth it."

"Is there any part of you that's still angry?"

"Am I angry at you? No. Not for the surgery. Maybe for the *underlying issue* that caused me to need the surgery."

"The palsy?"

"Of course the palsy." I lower myself off the table and onto the ground (As a child, I remember virtually hopping off this table. I don't hop anymore. My body hasn't allowed me to hop off tables or out of chairs and into a standing position for decades. Yet if I tried it here and now, the hopping, it would work. I'd hop with more ease than I've ever done anything.) and head for the doctor's office door.

Reaching for its silver lever-knob, I look back at Him and say, "But I'm also angry at my dad."

"Your dad? Why?"

I tell Him why, and as I tell Him, each circumstance I bring up plays in full all around me. Wherever I focus eyes legendary for how unfocussed they were, there is a version of me and a version of my father.

"He never treated me like a normal *person*. He never let me feel *worthy*. When he was sober, he treated me like I was made of porcelain. I was the breakable son he *had* to protect. He wouldn't let me do anything for myself. Cooking, cleaning, choosing the clothes I'd wear each morning. I couldn't even pour a bowl of cereal on my own. He knew better, and that was that. When he was drunk, he was a different person altogether. He didn't care what I did, as long as he could get his hands on his next bottle of whatever. On my tenth birthday, when I went up and down the halls proclaiming, 'Six more years and I'll be driving', a smashed Carl McDonald yelled out, his voice flat, slurring his L's, 'You'll never drive.' Admittedly, this wasn't his call. It was the state's. But blame is more easily shoved off on one person than it is given to an entire state. It's easier to make him the evil culprit than to howl against a faceless bureaucracy. And so I did."

"Terry, come back here and sit down, will you please?" God's doctor says. "I have something I need to tell you."

I return to the paper-table against my better judgment. *Hurry this up, okay? I know there's not any time where we are, but I've always hated this room, with its exam table, its foreboding skeleton of a human body that worked better than mine ever had against one wall, and the more we talk in here, the more I am re-acquainted with the impression that I am trapped.*

"Having to tell you how you'd never drive was one of the hardest things your father ever had to do," God informs me.

"If it was so hard for him, why did he seem so eager to tell me? Why did he shout it out at me and stop my celebrating dead?" I glance over at one form of my dad, delivering the terrible decree from the living room couch on that fateful day, and I want to give him a solid punch in his already red face.

"From his perspective, Terry, it was like ripping off a Band-Aid. He knew he'd have to tell you sometime, and the fact that you were looking forward to driving gave him what he saw as his best opportunity. You might wish he'd been a little more sensitive, but when alcohol had control of him, sensitivity took a bit of a vacation."

"Despite his personal failings—as a man and as a father," I allow us to move on, "he was regarded as a success. A son wants to surpass his father's success, he dreams of it, but he'd settle for simply *equaling* it. I don't know if there was any one day when I realized this, but by the time I was twelve, I knew I'd never get to where my father had gotten, no matter what field I chose to work in. Armed with that knowledge, I grew to hate him—and myself. I'd never do enough, nor would I be *normal* enough, to make him proud, or to satisfy either of us.

"Can we go somewhere else, please?" I ask God. "I gotta get outa here. This place is making me queasy." I'm more than ready to leave it far behind.

A LITTLE LUCK

Heaven is a perfect place.
But—much like life itself—
The afterlife is not.
We spend our lives in an ongoing race
To ensure ourselves a spot.
Only to find when we arrive—
Worn-out—
On the other side
That the race we've run,
The break-neck pace
We've kept up
Guarantees nothing, and
Without some serendipity,
We're still stuck.
The afterlife is as much a bureaucracy
As its predecessor.
To navigate it,
We're gonna need a little luck.

5

UNTIL YOU REACHED MAN

"Do you believe I created the world in seven days, Terrence?"

The sensation of changing locales broadsides me: I could be riding ninety miles an hour down a steep hill, a pit-of-the-stomach jaunt on a brakeless bike, no idea where I'm headed. Then we're in the office of my old philosophy professor, seated in the two chairs he kept beside each other at his desk. The professor and I met like this too many times to count.

It might as well have been the man's home, this little room. There was a small closet where he stored a week's-worth of clean suits; a TV, a radio, and a microwave he used to heat up his lunches. The only thing the little room lacked was a bed, but the leather couch against the wall to the side of his desk was a fine stand-in.

"I thought *I* was supposed to ask the questions."

"You *are*. But this is a question on which I've never received a firm answer, and I'd like to know what humanity thinks."

"I'm supposed to speak for all of humanity? I can't do that."

"Just this once, if you would."

"Then can we get back to the questions that matter to me? This is *my review.*"

"I promise."

"Okay. Well, I think creating a world in seven days is a tad ambitious, even for You," I reply. "But I believe science and religion were meant to work together."

"Which means?"

"Which means You utilized evolution when creating the world. Being God, You knew one life form would lead to another, and then another. And so on and so forth. Until you reached Man."

He nods, His hands resting together on the professor's lap, as though He's just finished a long bout of clapping and they need to rest. His nod is not a *you're right* nod. More of an *I see* gesture. "Man, as a whole, seems to think I enjoy watching him struggle. But it's not that I find pleasure in treating humanity like some kind of parlor game," He informs me. "No, that's not it at all. What I am is tired. Worn-out. Drained."

"Uh-huh."

"And… I need a break."

Alarmed, I blurt, "A break? But you're God!"

"Sure. But, Terrence, we've already discussed how I'm not perfect."

We sure have. "Then why allow the rumor that You are to perpetuate itself?"

He reclines in His chair (which is now the professor's chair) and lies back.

What am I, some kind of "psychiatrist to the deities"?

"Because it's what a certain segment of humanity needs from Me, and that's one thing I *can* do; become pretty much anything people need me to be."

Besides human, I tell myself.

"Besides human, right. You're catching on. Now, what do you say we get on with this review?"

•　　　•　　　•

He and I are seated now in the food court of a mall I frequented in my youth. Not the best place to while away a weekend, but not the worst, either. It is non-descript save for the Christmas decorations adorning every inch. Carols play above us.

"You know," God says, "I wasn't the one who gave you life."

"What?"

"Well, I *was*, but only in the strictest sense. And it was then that you put in your formal request to meet with Me afterwards."

"Bureaucracy is big even in the afterlife, is what you're telling me?"

He can't help but snicker at this. "Unfortunately." He straw-sips an Orange Julius that just appeared before Him, then He looks back up at me. "You want one of these?" He asks.

"No, thanks."

"You wanted to use our conference as a sort of de-briefing, you told Me, and that's when I had you entered into The Drawing." God tosses his now-empty cup, aiming for a black garbage can just over my head. He comes up inches short. The cup grazes rim and stays out, hits the floor, but He doesn't let the miss fluster Him. "Before you went to Earth, Terrence, you signed a contract to live the life you were given, just as everyone else does. I was there to notarize it, and to ensure that you agreed to each and every facet."

"Even the-"

"The palsy? Yes. In fact, you insisted upon including the palsy."

"Why… why would *I* do that?" I'd thought this had been His call, His error. If this was how His world worked, I could explain away the palsy by saying, "It was God's mistake." In private moments, especially as a kid, I often thought, *I* am a mistake.

"The palsy was a challenge. You wanted to learn, and you felt palsy was the best way for you to do that."

Now it made sense, my request for an audience with God. *How had a palsied life changed my being? My soul?* I'd want the answer, at life's end, and only my creator could give me that answer in full.

· · ·

We go to The Hall of Records. God says He wants to show me something. He's the guide. I'm in the role of curious tourist. Our transportation is instantaneous.

"Do you remember this place?" He says.

I have been here before. I know it as sure as I knew in life that my legs would be unsteady and shoot sharp pains up through my back when I tried to use them too soon after a restless night's sleep. "Sure. I dreamed about it when I was a kid."

"That's right. Well, *mostly* right."

"I've never forgotten it. I lost most of the memories it gave me, but I carried the feeling that dream left me with through all these years."

"That's because it wasn't a dream."

"It wasn't?"

We find a table in this massive library, the cathedral of *all* libraries. I'd prefer an inconspicuous spot off in the corner, but God selects this table, out in the open. Soul after soul move past it, their motions fluid, their human bodies discarded. They check their joints for flexibility, their minds for sharpness, and are pleasantly surprised. Of course they are. They're new arrivals—some haven't even had their appointments yet, but they are out exploring nonetheless. That's crazy to me. How are they not just as tired as I was? Exploring was the last thing on my mind. A few are waiting for their own rides, like the one I got from Charlie, or their own telepathic pages, and were told to do their waiting here. Each and every one passes by God. Never even giving Him a second look. They don't know who He is.

"No, it wasn't a dream," He says. "Definitely not."

"What was it then?"

"It was a visit, and a reminder of your life goals. You may not remember this, but you prayed for guidance. One night—one of the many when your parents were fighting—I heard your prayer, and we brought you here. You were still young and impressionable then, and we figured a quick refresher course would stay with you. That, even if you lost the specific memories, the essence of the experience would remain within you, so that when we needed you to call on it, you would be able to do that."

WOULD YOU GO BACK?

If you had a time machine
Would you go back to before birds had wings?
Witness a Ruthian homerun swing?

Maybe meet up with the dinosaurs,
Hear their primal,
Prehistoric roars?

More likely,
You'd be curious to see
Your parents before they
Took their posts
At which they played your willing hosts.
God-like figures with the power
To plant seeds.
Animate budding flowers, and
Command you, involuntarily,
To breathe.

6

CONVERSING WITH THE CLUSTER

TERRENCE MCDONALD IS 6. THE YEAR IS 1996.

I am floating above my body.

Anyone who comes into my room will think I'm sleeping. But I'm not. Not anymore. I am leaving. Where am I going? I don't know.

I glance at my right hand. It is lighter than a hand has any right to be. I can almost see right through it, and it's glowing. I flex it, expecting it to stop short like it does when I'm awake. Thanks to cerebral palsy, it never moves as it was meant to. But this night, it does everything I ask and more.

All of my joints, always held hostage by palsy, are free. A tunnel appears directly in front of me. Warmth and excitement hit me, and I begin to move toward its white light. I feel like I'm flying.

Once I'm in the tunnel, it closes behind me, and I move down a short, straight hallway leading to two doorways. They're twins, those doors. I'm not sure which one I should open, so I try the door on the left first. It opens easily enough, but once I'm inside I realize I've made a mistake. The room is dark and warm, almost hot.

I am only six, but I know I need to get out of here. I turn in the air, like an acrobat, and make a fast exit.

(My voice changes here. It becomes deeper, more authoritative, older and wiser alike. A man retelling a never-forgotten moment from his early years. I'm not surprised he's taken temporary control of the narrative here. Formative as my visit was, my younger self wouldn't have the words to describe what I'm about to see, but younger me will be back, literally in no time.)

I enter door number two and float into a room filled with light; the source being a sky whose color humble blue can only aspire to. I cease floating and make a soft landing before a long, steep flight of golden stairs. The architect should have broken it into several flights, but no such luck. Then I get to my feet and begin to climb.

The ascent is tough and steeper than I'd expected, even under the direction of my new, more flexible body. I'm already tired a third of the way up. To my left, as the climb continues, there's a river. Though small, it moves fast, and its water is clear. The air is icy on my face. It's like diving into a frosty winter morning without a coat. I like it.

This is Paradise. *My paradise.*

For a split second, it's as if I were never born at all, as if I never left this little piece of perfection. Memories buried by living—tucked away in my soul's invisible marrow, for safekeeping—flood back to me. At the top of the stairs, I turn right. *Head for The Hall of Records*, something tells me, and I know The Hall of Records will be the biggest and greatest library I'll ever see. If I took a left, I would come to the most immaculate park. My favorite place to sit and think. Ponder. A place I search for on Earth but can't find.

(Younger me returns just before I enter The Hall, as I somehow knew he would.)

I step inside the building, The Hall of Records, and find the woman at its circular front desk. "Hi. I'm Terrence Mc—"

Before I can get my full name out, she puts a finger to her lips. "We've been expecting you, Terrence," she whispers. "Please find a seat."

"Yes, ma'am."

I choose a table on the left side of the library. To the right, there is about twenty feet of carpeted space in front of a staircase with carpeted landings on every floor. An identical staircase is behind me. They wrap around and meet in the middle. On my left, my post is bordered by a bookshelf whose height measures a centimeter or two shorter than the building itself.

Within moments, two men approach me. They remove five or six volumes from the nearest bookshelf and set them out in front of me. One of the men seats himself across from me on the table's opposite side; the other man comes to stand next to me.

"What are all these books?" I ask.

The man across from me removes a top hat, revealing a full head of brown hair, and offers a slight bow.

"These books are yours."

"They belong to me?"

"In a manner of speaking," says the first man's partner. He is bald, no hat. "You're going to help write them." He pulls out a chair, seats himself next to me, and begins inspecting one tome in particular. The first man stays standing where he is.

"When? When will I help write them?"

Top Hat: "When you get older."

"How do you know?"

Bald Man glances at me. "We're the curators."

"What does that mean? Curators?"

"It means we're supposed to know these things."

They leave together, beaming. Top Hat saying, "We leave you in capable hands. We'll see you again, Terry."

"Come with me, Terrence." A young woman speaks. I turn toward her. She has long black hair, a pleasant, milky-white complexion, and a smile. She has come up behind my chair, her footsteps unheard. I take her arm, and she leads me out of the building and past Pondering Park.

"Where are we going now?" I ask her. "And, not to be rude—I know I'm a guest here—but what do *you* do?"

"What do I do?"

"Are you another curator?"

She shakes her head. "I'm your spirit guide," she says.

"What's that? Are you like my guardian angel?"

"No. Not quite. A spirit guide is what humans might call a conscience, or that first instinct that pops into your mind in trying times. I do all I can to steer you in the right direction. I'm the voice you hear, but can't quite place, when you wake in the night from a terrible dream. It's far away and you recognize it, barely. I'm the intuition you want to ignore but find you can't. That's my job. That's what I do. God, who has my job on a much grander scale, and your guardian angels… they did talk to me, though, and we came up with a plan."

"A plan for what?"

"Tonight, as you were falling into sleep, you asked to be shown what your life means."

I did.

"Dear God," I said. "Please help me. Sometimes I'm all that keeps my parents from fighting, and I don't like when they fight. Is that why I'm here, God? I need to see why I'm here."

My parents are together; married, living under the same roof, eating their breakfasts and dinners at the same table, but they are unhappy. They fight all the time. Stopping these fights is my responsibility. I made myself the referee.

"We can't show you everything, but we've agreed to show you a few of the reasons why you went to Earth."

I'm not quite sure what she means, but I thank her, anyway.

We enter a cream-colored building, smaller than The Hall of Records, its look a bit old-fashioned. A white-haired doorman smiles and holds his door open for us.

"Hi, Roger," my chaperone says.

"Patricia, good to see you," says the doorman. "Who've you got with you today?"

"Terrence McDonald."

He nods. "Terrence… welcome."

"I'm just visiting," I tell him.

"I know," he says with a smile and tips his doorman cap. "Visitors are always welcome."

Sconces light a long, narrow hallway. Patricia leads me to a large, white-painted door at the hallway's end. In the tiny room behind the door, six people stand huddled together. A few I know. Others are strangers. But they're busy talking to each other, and none of them notice me.

Patricia takes me over to a corner. "Terrence, what do you think of time travel?"

"It's cool."

"I'm glad you think so."

"Why are you glad?"

"I suppose you could say this room is kind of like a time machine all on its own, and it will be helpful if you believe in the possibility of time travel. Do you see those people over there?" A slight head-turn towards the huddle. "They are preparing for new lives, Terrence. They've come here to build their charts."

"What? That can't be right. I know them. A *few* of them, anyway. They're living their lives right now."

Patricia chuckles.

Then it hits me like an arctic blast. Chilled truth.

Time travel. Patricia and I have time-traveled. To a time before I was born. To a time before most of the people I know were born.

Patricia leans down to make eye contact with me. "Before you entered your own life and body," she explains, "you met the people who would influence you. In this room. If you don't recognize someone in the group, it's because you haven't met them yet in the mortal world. Together, you worked on all of your respective charts. And then, when the chart-building was done, you saw them off."

"Saw them off?"

"Yes." She is leading me towards the cluster. "Since they were born before you, it was your job to wish them luck and say good-bye as they entered their mothers' wombs."

When we're just about even with the group, all of their conversations—I'm pretty sure there were two or three going on at once—cease. Someone steps out of the crowd.

"I'm your Grandpa Jack," says a man wearing a baseball cap and a tan.

I told you I was going to show you a few of the reasons why you went to Earth, Patricia thinks. *Well, Jack's one of them. Everyone here is one of them. That's all I can tell you right now, though, Terrence. Any more, and this visit won't have the impact it's supposed to.*

"I haven't met you yet," I tell Jack.

"You will. In fact, we're gonna be good friends."

Something doesn't add up. "How could I not have met you? That doesn't make sense. If you're one of my grandparents, I should have met you by now."

"You're a smart cookie." He taps me affectionately on my head. Atop it, a baseball cap now rests. "I'll see you soon."

I take off the cap and stare at it, open-mouthed. I show it to Patricia, who pats me on the shoulder. *This has to be a dream,* I decide. *Things don't just appear out of nowhere in the real world.*

Jack steps back, and a handsome African-American man, his appearance faultless in a blue-gray suit and matching tie, steps forward. "I'm Charlie. Wonderful to meet you, Terrence."

"Mhmm," I say reflexively. But I barely hear Charlie.

My gaze is on a young man. I think I know him from somewhere, but... "Dad?"

The room falls silent.

"Hello, Terrence."

"Is it really you? You look different than I'm used to."

"Yes, it's me. I'm here to thank you for agreeing to be my son."

"I don't know what you—"

Just go with it, thinks Patricia. She stands behind me, beaming. *Just go with it.*

"You're welcome."

Good.

"I know I won't always be the best father to you, but thank you for being my son through it all."

"What do you mean?" He's not making sense. "You're a great dad."

"Please know that you mean the world to me and always will. I'm sorry we won't really get to know each other."

The others lead Dad away before I can reply. Is he crying?

"I don't understand." I turn to Patricia, hoping she'll let me in on the hinted-at secret.

You're not supposed to understand. Yet.

I watch Charlie, followed by Grandpa Jack, then Dad, as they enter a colorless round portal just big enough to fit their adult bodies and disappear.

"Where are they going?"

"They're going to *live,* Terrence," Patricia tells me.

Once the men have gone, two ladies walk over to me.

"Hi, Terrence," says the elder of the two. "I'm Mattie. I'll be your wife."

"And I'm Megan," says the other. "Your daughter."

THE REVIEW

"That dream was more than a refresher course, wasn't it?" The dream-memory ended, I am once again with God in the Hall. It is no longer full of souls. In fact, we are alone.

"It was more," He allows. He is still my philosophy professor, now working on a new Orange Julius. Is he allowed to drink that in here? Who would reprimand Him?

"A refresher might have been: 'You will be a writer, Terrence. You decided before going to Earth you wanted to be a writer. That is one of the reasons why Carl McDonald, a true lover of words, is your father in this life.'

"But my dream went further than that." It's strange telling God something He already knows, but it sets up my question of: "Why?"

"You dealt with people—children you knew well, and even some adults—who made fun of you. The kids did their bit every day at school. The adults gave you backhanded compliments whenever you accomplished anything. 'That's so impressive, for someone with your struggles.' 'With what you go through, it's almost hard to believe you could... ' God didn't need to complete that exclamation. I'd heard it, or something like it, so many times that it was complete in my head. "The kids tripped you when you walked the halls. They chuckled when they saw you slowly reading a book. 'You read like a type-writer,' they said. 'Hey, everybody. Look! Watch Terrence read. He looks like a typewriter.'" I specifically remember this incident. How different and outsider-ish it made me feel. Everyone turning to look at the kid whose eyes were so bad he read six inches from the words in his book, and when I finished with one line of text I'd jerk my head down to the next. I was in third grade. "They doubled over with laughter when they focused on your limping gait. You took a lot of grief, Terrence. This isn't even to mention your parents' ugly squabbles. We—your spirit guide, Patricia, your angels, and Myself—we wanted to assure you that there were reasons for it all, and you shouldn't lose hope. The best way we could think to do that was to show you that you were meant to be a lover of words and phrases, a writer, and you were *meant* to be exactly who you are."

"Why introduce me to Jack and Charlie and Dad and the others?"

"This was entirely Patricia's call, but she thought it might do you good to meet those people so that, whenever you saw them again in life, you would be reminded, subconsciously, of your visit and all that it meant."

God rises and begins pacing around the room. Up one aisle, down another, but he keeps me in sight the entire time. "I've always wondered… do you think we did the right thing? Did the essence of it all help you through your life?"

"It did."

"Oh, good. I'm so glad to know that. That was the plan. We're not perfect up here, but we try."

"I woke up determined to become a writer, and not just *a writer*, but a damn good writer."

TURNING POINTS

Turning points aren't always plain.
This can sometimes be a shame.
Looking back,
You smile to yourself,
Internally exclaim,
How did I get here?

The entirety of the way isn't clear.
But you're glad
For the currents
That carried you.

Then there are other points;
Not profuse with pride,
That yet strain and puncture
The mists of memory,
So fine,
To stand alone as massive, colorless, Profane
Monoliths to
Unforgettable,
Terrorizing
Pain.

7

I WANTED TO MAKE SURE HE HEARD

THE REVIEW

A younger me—fifteen or so, the cracking-amidst-puberty voice a clue—speaks next. Along with the voice, a vivid scene forms. Its colors so crisp, the smell of a new and overcast autumn day so precise, and it is all accompanied by all the feelings I felt then.

TERRENCE MCDONALD IS 15. THE YEAR IS 2005.

I wake to a reality I've avoided facing. There is no oak tree in our yard. There never was. When I was a little kid, I used to dream about trees and, in my dreams, they were always oak, because I liked the sound of the word oak, and they were always tall enough to climb. Not that I ever tried. I was afraid.

Then, one night, I dreamt I finally got up the courage to climb the largest oak in the state, its branches swaying in the gentle breeze outside my window.

The dream started out really cool. Me: confident. Telling myself as I walk out the front door, *You can do this. You will do this!* And I did.

But it didn't end well.

While celebrating my triumph (what had I been worried about?)—*coming up just* short of basking in it—I teetered and fell from the tree's highest branch. I broke both of my dream-legs, and it confirmed something important. Even if there were an oak tree outside my bedroom window, beckoning to me, I couldn't climb all the way to its top. I couldn't climb it: Period.

Cerebral palsy made that decision, not me. The words *cerebral palsy* make my skin crawl. I've tried to deny its hold over me, mostly over the right side of my body (meaning there's a slight lean to the left when I walk), but all areas are affected. For as long as I've lived, I've tried to ignore it. But that's hard to do. The fact is, to those who hear the phrase but can't picture the manifestation, it means simply: damaged.

I'm normal! I insist to myself.

Okay, I'm not normal. No one is. But I'm close.

To me, not normal is never being able to climb trees, while everyone else scales them effortlessly. I feel like I missed out on so much. The tree was a symbol of the things I can't do, and a symbol of the thing that causes my pain.

The next day, not long after morning's light faded the nightmare, I was in a room filled with plaster of paris, getting fitted for my first pair of leg braces. The first of many pairs. My legs screaming with palsy-ache, and the adults talking about me as though I weren't there at all. As though this wasn't my life they were discussing, just a fascinating science experiment.

I wanted out of that room. To me, it felt no bigger than a closet. I wished life or fate or God, or whoever it was that controlled everything on Earth, could give me just one day of being able to discuss the lives of those adults like they were fascinating science experiments.

·   ·   ·

God and I have had our share of shouting matches about palsy. What my parents would call "discussions" when they started having them and talking divorce. But our matches are pretty one-sided. He never responds, which makes me angry. Furious.

I'm the one to open our exchanges every time, usually with some-thing like:

"Why did you choose me, God? Why me for the palsy? Why not one of the kids who trips me in the halls, laughs when I fall, and treats me like I'm nothing? Those kids could use a lesson or six in humility, and what better lesson is there than cerebral palsy?"

The conferences often grow in volume and feeling once God refuses to respond, and it was during one of these "discussions" last fall that I uttered my first ever swear word.

"Damn you, God," I said. "Damn you. Do you hear me?" I wanted to make *sure* He heard.

·   ·   ·

From the first time I took God's name in vain, we move with alacrity to a May Sunday night, its sky grape juice purple. Dad and seven-year-old me stand beneath it and talk about the cabin. He clutches a bottle of beer in his huge right hand.

"We'll be like the pioneers," he says.

"Except with TV," I say.

"And we'll build it together. You and I."

"Yep."

He slaps his other hand onto my shoulder. Hard. "It'll be in our family for generations," he says. "You'll tell your kids you helped their grandfather put it together."

"Like Lincoln Logs but with real wood."

He smiles. His breath smells like a swamp. "We'll start building it tomorrow. How does that sound?"

"Great."

I appreciate Dad's attempt at cheering me up. I'm feeling like a shut-in. Besides going to school and limping across the playground, enduring recess, I've gone nowhere and done nothing all week.

"Give those legs time to rest, son," the doctor advised at my last check-up. "You ask a lot of them."

To Lisa, my biological mother, this meant making sure I was in bed by seven-thirty, my legs raised up on pillows. Bored out of my head.

·   ·   ·

I should have seen the cabin talk for what it was. A pipe-dream. Not a welcome distraction, but a drunken proposal that would never happen. It was not unlike some of the ideas that would slip into Dad's addled mind after a hard day's work and an evening of getting smashed even harder.

Whenever Dad came home from the neighborhood bar, after Monday's half-price happy hour or Friday night darts and—drunk—made the declaration that he was going to run for city council "to clean up some of the crap that's going down in this no-good, one-horse town," Lisa would nod and point out his dinner on the table, now ice-cold. He'd already eaten, knowing he wasn't getting a hot meal at home.

She'd refrain from screaming at him, but she'd mutter, "He's a lost cause. Why should I waste my breath?"

Then she'd go to bed. Maybe complain of a migraine. This was their custom.

.   .   .

It's the Monday afternoon following our cabin conference. Rain is falling in what Dad calls "the steady Seattle way" outside. And that sound won't let me ignore how much I need to go to the bathroom.

Here at school, there's a rule in place called "The Buddy System." If you need to go to the bathroom, it says, first tell a teacher and, second, find a friend willing to go with you. This rule also applies to after-school daycare, where I am now, and I think the thought behind the system is that there *has* to be safety in numbers. It is the answer for Stranger Danger.

Connor is my best friend. A lot of people make fun of me—I'm thinking of Shannon Selby; she's been bullying me since we started school. I don't know why.

"Why can't you walk?" "I bet your parents wish you were never born." Sometimes, when we're at recess: "Hey, Terry, wanta race me? I bet you I'll win!" She always has a group of girls around her, ready to laugh at what she says, even when what she says isn't that funny. "Why do you have pencils in your desk? It's not like you *need* them. It's not like you can use them."

But Connor doesn't do that. I've known *him* since preschool. Connor stands up for me when he hears Shannon say mean things. tells her to shut up.

He and I head into the boys' bathroom. I spot a free urinal (they're all free; we're alone in here), and I start going. Connor uses a stall.

I'm finished. Toilet flushed, pants pulled up, hands washed, and Connor says, "Hey, come in here, man."

"No." *That's gross. He wants me to go in there right after he's done his business? Why would I want to do that?*

"I want to show you something."

I hesitate. Common sense and friendship fight within me. Friend-ship wins.

"Okay."

In my slow, weaving gait, I move over to the stall and step inside. I use the side of the stall to brace myself.

The stall. Adults would say its blue door is tiny, but the door isn't tiny to *us*. It's one of the tallest things I've ever seen. The flimsy lock slides into place from right to left.

Connor locks the door. He is stronger than me, and suddenly he's shoving me. Up against the side of the stall opposite the door. I crumple to the dirty floor.

"We're going to have some fun now."

Fun?

He's on top of me. Crushing me. Knives of pain shoot through my legs and into my back. This is worse than *anything* Shannon Selby has ever done to me.

"Stop! I don't want to do this! Get off of me!" I scream.

He's pulling my pants down. "You'll like it."

It feels like forever that he's on top of me. But, when it's all over, it couldn't have been more than three minutes. Seconds refusing to tick by, frozen as my locked-into-place body. Looking down at the dirty tiled floor. Wishing Dad were here. He'd kick Connor's ass into next week, and he might even let me help.

When Connor tires of his "game" (that's what he calls it), he rolls off of me and, seeing me crying so hard it's making my whole body shake, he laughs loud. A laugh that gives me chills and echoes through the empty room. Then he pulls his pants back up, buckles his belt. Unlocks the stall door and is gone. I don't move until I hear the bathroom's big door close behind him.

Only then do I head to the sink, where I check my reflection in the mirror. My face is a deep red, and my eyes are dry and stinging. I wash my face as best I can (not very well at all), running cold water over it, and try to smooth out my ruffled shirt. When I get back to the daycare's portable, I'm sobbing.

If I hadn't walked into that stall… it was my fault.

I tell the teacher, "Something bad happened in the bathroom." I'm too angry to say much more, so all she can do is keep me and Connor separated for the rest of the day, with the same stern warning to us both. We ought to do unto others as we would have done to us.

At around six P.M., after work and a smoky tavern, my dad comes to take me home, and I want to tell him about what happened with Connor in the stall. I don't know what to say, so I blurt out the first thing that pops into my mind.

"Connor… touched me in a bad place!"

"What do you mean?"

I tell him everything I can about what I mean. I do a pretty good job of getting the story out.

His answer is: "Well, you're not really hurt, so… what do you want me to do? You have to learn to handle issues with other kids on your own."

I can't believe Dad is dismissing what I went through.

"Let's get some dinner. What do ya say?" he suggests.

"Dad, I can't. I want to go home."

"Why?"

"My legs hurt. They're killing me. I want to go to bed."

"Well, sorry to hear that."

No, he's not.

"We'll get home soon enough. Your bed isn't going anywhere. Give me a half an hour, okay?" He lights a cigarette as the chilled night air confronts us. "I'm hungry. Feel like I could eat a horse." We reach our car as the specifics of his dinner plans come together. "You want some Chinese, Terry?"

"What about Mom? She'll be upset if we're—"

He cuts me off. "What about her? You wanta get some chow or not, kiddo?" He puts his hand to his forehead, exhales heavily. Smoke mingles with his breath-vapor. "I need a drink."

All of me, every part, every cell, wishes I could go back in time, back to the innocence of Sunday. My chief worry Sunday was how big our log cabin might end up being. It was simple. Bearable. Full of rustic resplendence.

NIGHTMARISH ONES

Some dreams in protective hope we encase;
Wondrous fantasies on which we base
The future.
"I'll be a lawyer,
Whose powers of persuasion
Will convince juries
To let innocent men
Go free.
Or a doctor,
Whose ability to suture
Will arrest fears,
Elicit innumerable flurries—
Some from
Worried hearts gone hard—
Of joyful tears,
And the occasional Christmas card.

And then there are those dreams
We do not wish to perceive.
But once they come,
They come again,
Refuse to leave.
And these are dreams—
Nightmarish ones—
There's no way to outrun.

8

RELIVING A NIGHTMARE

THE REVIEW

"Okay, so it's clear to me Dad didn't know how to handle that whole thing. Not a shock. Anyone would have a tough time. But how could *You* let it happen?" I demand. "How could You let him do that to me?"

God is Charlie again. I don't think He's quite sure whose identity He should assume for this particular section of the review, so He's gone back to what He considers a safe choice. "You and Connor? I didn't let it happen."

"You didn't what?" My face reddens. *You didn't care.* I'm so irate I don't even bother to note in what locale we converse, except for one fleeting glance up to a chalkboard. The bathroom, where my innocence was lost, the last place I prayed to an unhearing God for a long while—Dad and I didn't pray that night when we finally got home, shelving our ritual; I wouldn't pray again until I had Megan to worry about, and then only sporadically—the bathroom is just down the hall. But this is my favorite elementary classroom, where I first learned to make words matter. My body is contorted into one of the tiny desks. He's at the front of the room. As if to underscore our roles. I am the student, and He, the teacher.

"I didn't let it happen," He repeats, defensive.

"How's that? You are God, aren't You?"

"An imperfect God." His head lowers.

"And one full of excuses, apparently. If I have to hear anything more about Your imperfections—"

He interrupts, ignoring my minor outburst. "It's not like I had a choice in what happened between you and Connor, or a chance to intervene, and I vindictively declined. It is My practice to allow free will to dictate what a person will or won't do in their life. Judgment, based on those choices, comes later."

"He hurt me. Scarred me. Made me into someone I hated."

"Yeah, well, you did your fair share of hurting and scarring, too, Terry. The person you hurt most was yourself. Not uncommon."

"What do You mean?" I rise from my chair, ready for a confrontation. Charlie's visage is surely out of place now, and He knows it. It's my father who climbs from His chair behind the teacher's desk to over six feet and stands with me. All that remains of my desire to fight—gone as suddenly as it came—is confusion. "You're gonna need to fill me in. I'm not sure what you're talking about."

"It'll come back to you. More often than not, when humans cross into this world, their memories are lost or compromised. But they do return. It's like amnesia. Something will shake you out of it. A memory. A melody. A scent. And, when it does, you'll be fine."

"How long do I have to wait for that something?"

"That's hard to say up here, and it varies with each person, but I don't think it'll be long." He takes an extended pull from the beer bottle He clutches in His huge right hand. Plops back down behind the desk. "Terrence, take a seat, Son. Want anything to eat? You and I never did get to have that first beer together. What do you say we go ahead and do that?"

"I can't have that beer with You. You're not him. You're not my father. Just like you weren't Charlie before him. You're You, the Almighty, the Great and Powerful, the Whatever-You're-Calling-Yourself these days. Were you trying to trick me into that drink?" I guess. The elementary classroom is gone. We're in the log cabin we never built.

"I wasn't trying to trick you. I just thought a visit with your father might help to jog your memory."

I shrug. "Maybe. If it were the real McCoy visiting. I have reason to believe he's in Heaven, with my mom."

"She told you?" He looks crestfallen.

I nod.

"She wasn't supposed to tell you."

"Well, she did. Plus, I mean, come on, we've already discussed how you're not human. Did You think I would think You and Dad switched places while I wasn't looking? Like some kind of Heaven's-waiting-room game of musical chairs?"

"No. Alright. Plan B."

"Which is?"

"I'm not sure."

I smile. God is at a loss. Whoever made the observation that a picture was worth a thousand words doesn't know how right that proverb is.

I have an immediate, unshakable, sinking feeling that I've overstepped my bounds. That God isn't upset, but He is disappointed. I organize my thoughts into a quick apology, the sentiment silent but heartfelt. Thinking, *Why choose this scenario in which to be cocky, Terrence? You have no leverage.* But the remorse is not enough to change His mind.

.   .   .

My smile is gone. I find the atmosphere instantly charged with an energy, an electricity, that makes my breath catch in my throat. The picture has changed. The unwritten words painting it are different. Accessible but vulgar.

Pain from those dreadful, murderous nights is with me still—it never fully ebbed, did it?—and it washes over me in a malevolent wave. Brutal. Roaring. Suffocating. God intends for me to recall the fervor with which I took to my nightly missions. The unchecked, unrelenting fervor. I do.

"I remember now. I don't need to see anymore."

"I disagree," He says.

So this is Plan B.

Shit. Not again. Anything but this.

.   .   .

His children. Two perfect angels, a boy and a girl, skipping out of a supermarket, sticks of gum in hand. Their brown hair is transformed, shimmers almost red in the late-afternoon sunlight. And there *he* is, bringing up the rear, carrying two bags of groceries as they head home for dinner, and the weekend.

"Connor?"

He turns.

I must have a crazed look in my eyes, or perhaps he always feared my appearance, often glancing over his shoulder just to make sure I wasn't in the vicinity, because he lurches back. Drops one of his bags.

"Yes?"

"Do you know who I am, Connor?"

He does, but he lies and says: "I'm afraid not."

That's all I need to hear. I no longer see his children with their brown hair transformed, their sticks of gum. I don't hear him say his last words:

"Listen, I'm here with my kids." Nervous. His fight or flight reflex kicking in. Walking backwards. Quickening with every stride. "We're just about to... my wife is waiting for us to—"

"I don't care."

I cut him off. Then I cut him down. One bullet. To the side of his head. He falls in a blood-soaked heap "No more games, you fucking bastard. The games are over. No more!"

Because of the silencer I use, and the fact that their attention was not on us but on making each other laugh—and nothing else—his children never have the misfortune to see me, or what I've done. I am glad for this bit of luck. It benefits me, obviously, to remain unidentified, but it also benefits them, as under no circumstances should they have to suffer for their father's sins, and seeing him shot dead would certainly constitute suffering. I suppose living without him is also payment of a kind well beyond anything they should have to surrender. I half-expect to be picked up a few blocks away by a waiting convoy of police cruisers, but they never show.

The kids make it all the way to the car before realizing something must be amiss ("Where's Dad?" "He was with us. He had all the groceries." "Where did he go?" "Well, he wasn't putting away our cart, because we didn't have one."), and then they go for help inside the store. The fatal shot fired, I am now strictly an observer. I am watching everything—my own actions included—unfold through someone else's eyes high above it all. By the time the authorities are contacted, I've tossed the gun in a dumpster, peeled off and discarded a pair of black gloves, and entered my home.

.　　　.　　　.

I wake in front of the television and a cops-and-bad-guys drama from a sleep full of nightmares. Typical.

It becomes routine for me to watch Connor die a thousand times a night. To feel the trigger under my finger. The kickback of the gun.

ORIGINS

The origin of things
Will always be debated,
Until we arrive in the one place
Where our curiosity can be sufficiently sated.
But, sometimes more pressing:
The origin of the individual.

If one never hears the truth of this phase,
Two parents blithely confessing,
If the issue is never properly raised,
One cannot help
But sigh and hunger for it,
Can't help guessing.
Not who am I
So much as why?
Throughout all their days.

9

CLASS IS IN SESSION

LISA BROWER IS 26. THE YEAR IS 1989.

The bookstore is deserted. Only me, in an overstuffed green chair, reading *The Great Gatsby*, and a bookstore employee who looks about as happy behind his counter as I would be writing a term paper. The little bell attached to the store's front door rings. I look up and see an older man—salt-and-pepper hair—wearing a tweed jacket, patches at its elbows. Five minutes later, a bundle of books in hand, he makes his way over to the little nook where I'm seated and begins paging through his loot in the chair next to mine.

"Why so many books?" I ask. I put down Gatsby, spread open where I've left off.

He glances over. "I'm running a book club in here," he says. "No one's here yet. Doesn't start for another hour. We have to decide which book among this bunch we want to read, and I just thought I should be prepared."

"Good idea."

We both get quiet and return to our respective reading. In a little while (maybe ten minutes, maybe fifteen), he looks up from making notes about his books. "I see you've got Gatsby there. One of my favorites."

"Mine, too."

He puts down his pen and paper. "Why don't you come to the book club meeting?" he suggests.

"Oh, no, book clubs aren't for me."

"How do you know? Have you ever attended one?"

"Well, no, but I—"

He gets out of his chair, offers his hand. "My name's Carl McDonald," he says, "and I promise you I run an absolutely painless book club. Parts of it are fun, too. I love the debates we get into. We could even end up reading Gatsby for the next month. It's decided by a vote. Would you care to join us? If you vote for Gatsby, it might save us from another Jane Austen."

I take his hand. "Well… since I was gonna be here anyway, why not?"

Our choice wins out by a count of twenty votes to nineteen. The swing vote belongs to me. As the group's advisor, Carl is not allowed to cast a ballot. In celebration of the victory, "And to thank you," he says, approaching me at the end of the meeting, "for saving me from yet another discussion of Elizabeth Bennet, what would you say to fettuccini Alfredo at my place?"

Now I know we've just met, and this sounds a tad impulsive, but being a sucker for any man who can cook, I accept.

⋅   ⋅   ⋅

"I certainly hope I'm nothing like Gatsby," Carl tells me over our meal.

"In what respect?"

"After serving his country, a commendable endeavor, he worked to impress and attain one woman his entire life. A woman who was impossible to impress and unattainable."

"Well, and he was a *criminal*," I point out.

Carl kinda chuckles. "And there's that, too," he says. "I'm a law-abiding citizen."

We're just two people discussing a beloved classic. This discussion lasts a long time and draws me closer to Carl.

"How did you end up overseeing the book club?" I ask him a little later.

"I'm a professor of American Literature. I've been running that club for ten years now. Geez, has it really been that long?" He looks to his bookshelves. There must be six or seven, each of them full. "Up there," he points, "is my collection of Hemingways. All of Robert Frost's poetry over there. Emily Dickenson there. And Faulkner below her.

"Don't get the wrong idea, though. I'm not just into the oldies. I like to stay up-to-date and in step with what's being read today, too."

I admire his intelligence. "I think men who appreciate books tend to be more in touch with their emotions," I offer.

"You do?"

"That has been my limited experience, yes." I slide the hand not holding my fork across the table, resting it upon his.

. . .

It isn't just his views on literature that I respect. I like to hear his perspective on the world, too.

"We're only in the middle east for the oil. We need to wean ourselves off of foreign oil, and I mean now, maybe look for alternative sources of energy, or else we're gonna find ourselves in trouble."

"What kind of trouble?"

"Carter may have been out of his depth in the presidency, but he was right to make his big speech on energy. Sure, people referred to it *afterwards* as the malaise speech. But that's only because they didn't understand it, and if you tell the American people something they can't get their heads around immediately, they back away from it."

It makes me think.

He makes me think.

This first date ends with Carl driving me home. Once we arrive, he asks to see me again. I want to see him again, too, but I don't want to seem desperate, so I decide to play hard to get. Tease him a little.

"You'll see me again at the book club."

"Yes, I know. I meant as a... for another date."

"Was this a date?" I mock-challenge.

"Well... not if you don't want it to have been. I just thought—"

He is flustered. A man who has his life as together as he does, and *I've* flustered him. I find it adorable that he's so vulnerable.

"How about next Friday?" I suggest.

"Works for me."

"Okay." As I hop out of the car, I thank him for a wonderful dinner.

"You're welcome. See you soon."

"Good night," I say, starting up the path to my first-floor apartment door.

·   ·   ·

Our second date is the true beginning of what becomes a whirlwind romance. First, there are the flowers, which you might expect. White roses. Then, on the fourth date, it's as though we have started our own book club. It is private, and we are the only members.

I was never a straight-A student. I worked my ass off in hopes of getting there one day, but it never panned out. Over time, and through tears, I accepted this failure. When I left high school, I swore I'd never set foot in another classroom. And I didn't.

But in *this* setting, I am brilliant. Maybe because there are no classrooms or term papers here, and a real teacher is doing his best to pass on his knowledge and understanding one morsel at a time.

If ever I begin to doubt my belonging in the same space with Poe's raven or Frost's explorer, who took the road less traveled by, Carl will stop the proceedings altogether.

"Sure, they're profound words, Lisa," he'll say. "But, in the end, they are just words. You have as much of a right to enjoy or form an opinion about them as does someone with a doctorate."

"Like you."

"Like me. To tell you the truth, I'd rather hear what you have to say than some of those stuffy suits from work."

"Why?"

"Your views aren't contaminated by years of frustrated attempts at writing a pretentious, thousand-page masterwork, or the vicious literary criticism that tries to tear one down. We crossed paths in that bookstore because you love words. You weren't forced to be there, like so many of my students have been. The words drew you in. Your reflections remind me of the wonderful surprises great literature can hold."

I could cry when he talks like this. Before I can get the water-works moving, he'll say, "Now let's see what you have to say about Mockingbird." Sometimes he'll be thinking out loud: "Where is Papa Hemingway's fish story?" And we'll consider Scout Finch and her unyielding curiosity or the grizzled, sunburnt Santiago and his marlin quest.

Being with Carl is like taking the college course I never took, free of charge. And it's far more involved than those classes would have been because of its one-on-one dynamic. The professor is focused on me. Though sometimes his focus drifts to my breasts or my legs or the perfume I wear. This pattern starts on date number nine, and we have to stop our studying or our spirited debates to make love, overtaken by the impulse.

We don't believe anything will come out of these lovemaking sessions. Thinking through the consequences isn't something that occurs to us. Odd, considering we think about so many other things. But in all our The Sun Also Rises banter, about bullfights, Robert Cohen, and doomed love affairs hindered by impotence, we never consider the possibility of becoming parents.

.   .   .

When I visit the doctor on a too-warm-for-Seattle June afternoon, I am complaining about a persistent bug I just can't seem to get over.

"I am so tired of feeling sick to my stomach all the time, Doc. When is this going to clear up?" I ask the old man when he returns with my test results.

"Oh, no more than another few months," he says, his blue eyes sparkling. "Ms. Brower, you don't have a bug. You are, however, pregnant."

"What?"

"Were you planning to get pregnant?"

"Uhh," I stammer, hardly able to speak. "No, not at all."

"Would you like to talk about it?"

I don't want to talk about my sex life with this guy. He looks like my grandpa, and he used to see Grandpa Gary as a patient on a regular basis. That's how we first came to know each other. "Umm… not now, thanks," I tell him.

"You might want to let the father know."

"I will. He's sitting in the waiting room."

I shake the age-spotted hand. "Thank you, Dr. Gordon." *What am I thanking him for again?*

"Good luck to you, Ms. Brower. Speak to the receptionist, and she'll schedule your next appointment."

Carl and I gather our things to leave. "Well, I don't have the flu," I announce.

"A clean bill of health, then. Good to hear," says my chauffeur.

"The bill's not exactly *clean*."

"It isn't?" He sets down the bag he's just shouldered. We make eye contact for the first time since I came out of the doctor's office.

"Carl, I'm pregnant."

"Are you sure?"

We'll get through it, we decide. Carl will do the honorable thing and marry me.

We wed on a Monday morning, in a ceremony officiated by a glasses-wearing justice of the peace. My mother is the only witness. Carl's parents died when he was young, and he doesn't have anyone he feels could rise to the duties incumbent upon a best man. For that matter, besides my mother, there isn't anyone in my life worthy of the maid-of-honor designation.

.   .   .

Now a much older Lisa is at her story's helm. Her voice waivers with age.

You might get the idea that I am an awful mother never suited for the vocation. In fact, I *love* being Terry's mother. I just have to do it from a distance. Any inadequacies he sees in me were gleaned from his father, whose view of me transformed over the years, from the woman with whom he debated books and ate fettuccini to the woman he and the alcohol tolerated. Or they came from my inability to deal with Terry's palsy.

It's an inability I will always regret.

.   .   .

On the day of his birth, a month and a half early, he is this tiny blue thing that comes out struggling to get his breath. He stays in an incubator for ten days. During that time, I can never once either hold or breastfeed my infant son.

He speaks in full sentences early, but he doesn't walk when the other children his age walk. His movements are stiff, his reflexes slow. That's when we know something's wrong with our "perfect" boy. When he's two years old, the palsy diagnosis comes down. Clean. Clinical. "This is what he has." There is no "Here's how to deal with it."

There is a doctor, his pediatrician, who likes to tell him as he grows, "Give those legs a rest when you can, young man. You ask a lot of them." Terry listens and is close to fanatical in his obedience.

The diagnosis sends Carl down into a spiral. A *What-the-fuck-do-we-do-now? This-isn't-what-we-signed-up-for!* spiral. It is a turning point on both our journeys.

I realize the magic nourished over *Gatsby*, *The Old Man And The Sea*, overcooked pasta, and a gaunt lust mistaken for love has faded and that there is no guidebook for parenting, palsy or no palsy. Without the mythic book, I'm lost, more a liability than the partner in the process I should be.

Overwhelmed, I spend a week at a time sleeping off a migraine; I snap at four-year-old Terrence, and he doesn't know why. I miss a shameful number of his birthdays entirely, shut up in the darkness. Carl complains that he might as well be on his own if this is the piss-poor effort I'm going to put forward, goddamn it.

Carl is no longer the carefree and exciting antidote to the real world outside of books and the apartment door. The antidote I once craved. He can't be Hemingway with a pen, so he mirrors the man the only way he can; drenches his life in rum and whiskey.

When I finally leave, after seven and a half years, I do so because I'm sick of dealing with Carl's unbridled alcoholism and think maybe the responsibilities of single-parenthood will force him out of the bottle. I do so because, one night as I go through Terry's backpack, I find at its bottom a paper he's scrawled out (He can't write without help. One of his little friends must have written it out for him.). It is titled "Words That Describe My Mother."

Loving
Kind
Caring
Baker
Weak
An alcoholic
A drug addict

A pain in the ass

A whore

The last three were favorites of Carl when he was drunk off his ass, which he often was.

I know. They aren't noble reasons to leave. Are there such things? They aren't well thought-out reasons, either. They're bullshit, really. But they are my reasons.

Leaving doesn't mean I stop thinking about Terry. In truth, he's *all* I think about. I wonder if he likes baseball, like I do. If he cheers for the Seahawks during football season. Sometimes, I entertain the notion of calling him and trying to learn his thoughts about me. Maybe they've changed over the years, evolved. Maybe his father's dogma has lost its hold, and he's developed his own perspective.

I never call. I can't. What would I say?

"Hi, it's me, your mother, the woman who left you with your bastard of a father all those years ago because she was too much of a coward to handle the fact that you're different."

This won't work at all. Reality's brutal honesty would crush my I'm-a-good-mother illusion to a wicked white powder.

THE REVIEW

"I never heard that story," I tell Lisa-God. We're back in my childhood bedroom, seated on my twin-sized bed. Appropriate. "The story of how my parents met, I mean."

"Of course you never heard it, Terrence. By the time you were conscious of life, your parents had begun to despise each other. That's why it was so important for us that we include the story of their happy meeting in your review."

GOOD STORIES

Good stories can be
About loves and cheers,
Frights and fears.
They might improve,
Get reworked and embellished
Through the decades,
Aging well with
Each set of ears that hears
The escapades within.

But what is sure to remain the same,
Besides the principle characters' names,
Are the tales' hues.
Time only deepening their shades.

Then there are those stories we rarely hear.
As to tell them might throw the bard into a rage.
The lessons in them so raw and severe
We fret over turning every page.

10

HOW I SEE THINGS: LISA

CARL MCDONALD IS 49. THE YEAR IS 1996.

Where did my good looks come from? I'm not sure.

Neither of my parents were known for their striking appearances. Yet my looks seemed to attract women without my having to lift a finger, aside from the occasional whipping up of a pasta dish, the opening and subsequent recitation from a treasured tome. And so it was with Lisa.

In the beginning, she is beautiful and easy to get along with. We're two lovers of the written word, and I am able to convince Lisa she is not unintelligent, her head bobbing just above society's waters; an image of herself she's clung to forever. She was brought up on stories of her mother's impoverished childhood and not much else. She likes hearing me talk about words. Their impact. How fewer words can sometimes hit harder when chosen by a deft craftsman.

Our union is destined to be a shooting star that burns bright and ends with a crash, violent and fiery. I know from the start it will fail, but I take the chance, anyway.

The crash comes late one night when she says, "Carl, I can't do this anymore."

"Do what?" My face is crimson, but it's not clear to me whether the color's source is anger or, perhaps, tequila.

"I'm not equipped to be Terrence's mother."

"So you're just gonna leave? And what am I supposed to tell the kid? 'Son, your mother wishes she could still be here with us, but she discovered a deep well of cowardice within her being and thought it would be unfair to you, so she left while you were sleeping?'"

"You make it sound like I'm an awful person," Lisa says. She's tearing up.

"Are you?"

"You're no saint, either," she reminds me.

"Maybe not. But I'm not the one who's leaving, dear heart."

"It's not just his palsy, you know?"

"It's not?"

"No."

"So what else is there?"

"I've tried for years to get you to stop drinking. Ever since I swore off alcohol and stopped drugging. I've begged, I've pleaded, but you and your buddies, especially Mel down at that goddamn bar you love so much, won't listen to reason. Do you know how many nights I've spent lying awake wondering if you were face-down in a ditch somewhere, sleeping off a bender? How many nights I feared the worst?"

Hold everything. Back up.

The instant I think it, I stop cold.

That's right. I forgot. How could I forget? Maybe I wanted to. Lisa swore off alcohol. She beat a monumental drug habit infamous for its tenacity.

· · ·

Seven years or so before the crash, a pregnant Lisa tries waking me in the middle of the night. I am groggy and hung over. *Whatever it is she's going on about can wait until later.* I try to push her away with a half-hearted, one-arm flail. But she's crying and screaming at me.

"Carl, get up! You have to get up!"

"What the hell do you want? Leave me alone."

She shakes me until I'm ready to slap her, until her face comes into focus for me, and I realize it is drawn with pain.

"What is it? What's going on?"

"The baby's coming, and it's too early. Oh God, it's too early."

I manage to get a robe around her and get her into the car. On the way to the hospital, she has her hands together, her fingers interlocked. She rocks back and forth and cries. I try not to look at her.

"Don't punish my baby for the mistakes I've made," she says. "Please, God, be merciful. Let him live. Let him be healthy. Punish me later."

"Will you please shut up? I'm trying to fucking drive," I fume, keeping my eyes on the road, still averted from her. "And if God *has* decided to punish you, bitching to Him now won't help much, will it?"

Lisa stops rocking. We've reached a stoplight that's just gone red and, cursing their invention, I slam on the brakes. Lisa lurches forward a few inches, coils back against her seat belt, and groans in pain.

"Carl, listen to me," she says. "I'm scared. Fuck scared, I'm terrified. And I need you to be something other than the drunk professor with the high IQ tonight. I need you to be here for me. I need you to focus. And I need you to not freak out. Or, if you do freak out, at least don't do it in front of me. Not tonight."

I nod, no words.

When we get to the hospital, I park at the emergency entrance, and Lisa is unloaded from our car and put in a wheelchair.

I say, "She's in labor, and she's only 32 weeks."

They wheel her into an exam room. I run alongside them. A nurse in the room takes fifteen seconds to determine her water has broken and says, "This baby's on its way." *We knew that.*

But Lisa's labor continues on through the next evening, until she is exhausted, racked with wave upon wave of contractions that don't seem to do any good. I can't handle seeing my wife in pain. I tell her, "I'm going out for a few cigarettes, if that's okay?"

"Fine. But you better be back in time for the birth. If you're not back, I'll—"

"I will. I'll be back in fifteen minutes."

Fifteen minutes and a few cigarettes turns into an hour and a half, *two packs* of cancer sticks, and a trip to the nearest bar. I drown myself, and our troubles, in too many shots of whiskey too quickly taken. I don't enjoy the drinks, but that's not why I choke them down, and they do their job. *I wanta forget today. All of it, and the consequences it portends. Fatherhood, for one. I'm not ready to be responsible for another being. For a family.*

With the alcohol gone, and the barmaid refusing to serve me any more, I reluctantly return to the hospital. But I quickly realize I should never have left the bar, its constant smoke-haze, its jukebox and the ever-present tunes, its relative safety. My son's birth turns out to be the most frightening. chaotic, and cacophonous experience of my life. It doesn't help that I am still good and hammered.

To begin with, the ancient doctor wrenches my boy out of his mother with a pair of forceps. Then, next in the harrowing process comes a terrifying wail. It does not come from the ironically named Dr. Goode or one of the composed, heroic nurses in the room. As Terry is being lifted into the world, I hear: "He's blue, Carl!" Lisa's almost primal scream still careens through my brain whenever I let it loose, and that's only at my psychiatrist's office, one hour per week. Otherwise, it stays behind lock and key.

"He's fucking blue!"

He is blue, his skin the consistency of tissue paper in the wind (blow on it, and it ripples), and the old bastard has nearly detached my son's right ear with those forceps. The nurses work feverishly to keep their young charge clinging to a tenuous new life. Once he's breathing, they continue working to reattach his ear. One of them tells me, after Terry's incubator is rolled away to the NICU, that he has a fifty-fifty chance of surviving his first night. Do I want to stay by his incubator?

I answer with a shock-stricken "No." I fear my boy is doomed, and I don't want to fall in love with him overnight when I might lose him in the morning.

The nurses' efforts to save his ear, and his life, thankfully succeed. He is a fighter, and the only people who will know of the near-catastrophic mishap are those who were present in the room and Terrence himself. The story of the ear will go in the very object it depicts countless times.

.   .   .

Yes, Lisa beat the alcohol and all other temptations that might have steered us wrong during the pregnancy. Even so, no explanation of Terry's condition will satisfy her. She'll be inconsolable after the diagnosis is finally relayed, two years later.

Lisa's headaches are the nefarious force keeping her locked away from our family and life beginning around this time. The headaches are to blame, and not a close kinship with the now-banished cocaine, or a love for vodka.

Unless the latter is my own.

Lisa wasn't as bad as I made her out to be. This is a revelation I never foresaw myself coming by.

She left, and that can't be overlooked. Yet somehow, I let the fact that she put the bottle down and cut out the coke in favor of her child's well-being fall by the wayside. I substituted venomous words and an egotistical I'm-better-than-the-bitch-who-isn't-here-anymore attitude. It was an attitude my young son held, too.

For a while.

A SPECIAL HARMONY

To see the struggle of another
Laid out so true, so bare,
Is to witness the battles of our own lives
Through others' eyes,
And to realize why those others care.

Life is a brilliant and musical classroom.
Every student humming their own unique tune.
But if we can correctly surmise
The reasons for the abundant ties
Among humanity,
Ties that pull—and keep—us together,
A special harmony will arise.

11

A TAVERN

THE REVIEW

White-coated Doctor-God and I move to a Pondering Park bench. There, we discuss my father.

"He always loved you, Terrence."

I find this hard to believe. My mouth hangs agape. "He had a funny way of showing it. As do You."

God does not give any sign He's offended. He replies, unfazed:

"There are things about your father you don't know."

"Like?"

At my request for clarification, the park disappears, and we stand on a dreary street corner in a light mist-rain looking at the non-descript building in its stead.

A tavern.

"Come on, Terrence. I want you to see something."

"Okay." I start towards the squat edifice, but I'm stopped mid-step.

"Before you go in, though, know this. In the scenario about to be enacted, you are no longer Terrence McDonald."

"I'm not?"

He shakes His head no.

"Who am I then?"

"You are your father's best friend, Melvin Broadbent."

Uncle Mel. I don't know much about him. He liked to drink, smoke, and play poker, and he and Lisa were pretty much mortal enemies. Chloe tolerated him for the short time she knew him. A year or so after she and Dad began dating, he was gone, and she didn't have to put up with him any longer. Liver cancer did Uncle Mel in.

"Why are we doing this?" I ask.

"Because I'm hoping this little exercise gives you a greater appreciation for who your father was and is."

Unhappy but resigned to the experience, I shrug. "Lead the way."

"Oh, no, this you're doing on your own. I don't drink. When you're done in there, I'll be waiting out here."

·   ·   ·

Through the thick haze of his own smoke, I spot my father at the end of a long line of stools. They are somewhere between dark red and light brown in color, but it's hard to know their exact shade because the lighting in here's terrible.

"Hey, Carl," I say, Mel's usual greeting. "How are ya?" I sit, Mel's usual stool. But for us, and the tired barkeep wiping down his domain—Dad would know his name; I don't—the tavern is empty.

"Sometimes, Mel… sometimes God's a son of a bitch."

"What?"

"You remember how I told you we thought there might be something wrong with Terry?"

Just go with it. "Yeah."

"Turns out we were right. He's got something called cerebral palsy. Whatever the hell that is. The doctor tried to explain it to us, but I sorta just shut down."

I ask the bartender, in a whisper aided by hand signals, for Mel's usual tonic. Dad hardly notices. He knows someone's listening, so he feels free to lay his troubled soul bare.

"When I heard him say those words," he continues, "*cerebral palsy*, you wanta know what it sounded like to me, Mel? It sounded like a god-damn death sentence, that's what. What are we supposed to do? *I thought, Lisa and I… we can barely take care of ourselves.* She was the one who wanted the baby. 'We'll be great parents, sweetie,' she said. Isn't that what everyone thinks? She had me convinced. We thought it would make our relationship stronger. Instead, look what we got. God's a fucking son of a bitch."

•   •   •

In an instant, everything's different. Everything except my location. I am still at the same bar stool in the same tavern, but it's years later. Dad has not aged well; his hair is grayer, his wrinkles deeper, and his gut protrudes thanks to beer and wine, and what I'm guessing was an unhealthy dose of self-loathing. I'll have to ask God if I'm right or wrong there, but the guess is educated. Mel has taken those years even worse. His skin is a frightening shade of yellow, his eyes and neck sunken ships receding together into his body's cancerous ocean.

"I don't know what to do, Mel. I'm at my wit's end!" Dad drowns his sorrows in tequila, straight shots.

"What's the matter?" *Is Mel's voice slurring?*

"Lisa wants to leave me. Says I drink too much, and she refuses to stand by and take it any longer. Can you believe that sanctimonious bullshit? She used to drink like a goddamn fish! Hell, aside from books, alcohol's how we bonded. We were both drunk and high off our asses most of the time."

Another draw of booze burns its way down his throat. I throw one back myself. *I'm playing the part of a drunk, so I best be convincing in the role.*

"If she leaves… if she leaves, how will I take care of Terrence?"

This is your cue, Terry. Take it.

"I'm sure everything'll work out fine."

"You think?"

"You're a good man, Carl." *An inebriated man at present, but—when you're not plastered—a good one.* "You'll find someone who'll be more than capable, not to mention more than willing, to help you raise the kid."

Her name is Chloe.

•   •   •

I leave the tavern my father and Mel never left. I leave with a new-found respect for my father. Or, more accurately, a rediscovered respect I had lost somewhere along the path to adulthood.

God is radiant as I push through the door. He is my mom, Chloe. For the first time, I can see why He *is* God. He glows with... what is that? Is it love? He knows all, so He knows I aged close to six years in thirty seconds in there. (Yet, if I hadn't known any better, I might have thought it was twenty-five years, as I was commandeering the body of an ill man). Feeling every creak, every bone-break, every tremor and shake. I am worn out.

LIFE'S EXPEDITIONS

We are never meant
To immediately understand
Why we've been sent
On life's expeditions.
So you may not comprehend a trip's grand purpose
Until it abruptly ends.
Only then will you contend,
"That mission must have been aided by God's steady hand."

Trial and error is the way of the world.
Be it in love affairs with beautiful girls
Or in the seemingly simple, life-long chore
Of parenting;
Like guiding a sailing ship
Deprived of its vital instruments
Safely ashore.

12

THREE MINUTES THAT CHANGE MY WORLD RELIVED

THE REVIEW

The image of Mom out here waiting for me brings to mind the memory of a time well before she ever arrived. As I think of it, the memory plays, a huge hologram just above a deserted city street. We stand and watch.

TERRENCE MCDONALD IS 7. THE YEAR IS 1997.

It takes a while for me to fall asleep. Once I get there, I become a superhero. "*The treachery I face in the real world will not stand,*" I say in my best booming superhero voice. I imagine I am riding atop a trusty steed, a shiny sword on my hip. The sword protects me.

Unfortunately, it doesn't come with me into the nightmare where I'd like to use it most.

.   .   .

Connor locks the door. He is stronger than me, and suddenly he's shoving me. Up against the side of the stall opposite the door.

"Not again!" I scream.

"What do you mean?" he says, leering. "You'll like it."

I'm crumpling to the ground under his weight. "Somebody help me! Somebody!"

"They can't hear you, stupid."

"I'm not stupid!"

You're the one who's doing something wrong, not me.

If I add that sentence, he might kill me. I don't know what he's capable of. I don't know his full strength. He may be holding back, going easy on me. We're supposed to be friends. I didn't think he was capable of what he's doing now. Once more.

"Whatever," he says. "Let's play a game."

"I don't want to!"

"Play along, or you won't wake up. Got it?"

I play along.

Where the hell is adult supervision when you need it?

I can't believe what Connor is doing to me. No one should have to feel this powerless. I taste bile in my mouth that has risen from my stomach (I don't even know what bile *is* yet, but I can taste it), and I experience the horror of losing the ability to trust all over again in one gigantic Hiroshima to the senses.

I wake up, my stomach a whirling dervish, and vomit the previous night's spaghetti. Lisa cleans it up, though she doesn't show the slightest trace of compassion for my plight.

·   ·   ·

As Lisa liked to intone, "Someone needs to put a stop to it. Someone needs to put a stop to that boy's belligerent behavior, Carl."

Dad would say, "Maybe," and then he'd take another swig from his beer bottle.

"Someone should put a stop to the way he talks to us." She would wait for him to give a solid second to this similar yet different idea, but he wouldn't, which put her in even more of a huff.

I wasn't a bad kid. But with the palsy and my tendency to tell people—adults, or bullies my age—exactly what I thought, even if they hadn't asked, coupled with my habit of standing up for myself when someone at school challenged my intelligence with the all-too-often used "Why do you walk that way? Are you retarded or something?" I wasn't the easiest kid to parent, either. I didn't fight with my fists; I couldn't. I fought with my sharp tongue, and if I felt like Lisa was being a bully, which she was sometimes (like the time I attempted to make toast, and instead of letting me do it she ejected the bread when it was barely crisp at the edges and said, "You can't do that! Why would you even try? You'll burn the house down! Let me do it for you!"), I'd fight her, too.

I lost every time. She'd refuse to engage in the exercise. This left me sad and frustrated. Under her breath, as she walked away from red-faced little me, these words came from her more than once. "Why couldn't you have been a *normal* kid?"

I never fit Lisa's portrait of the perfect child; seen but not heard. A houseplant that fed on breakfast cereal, lasagna, and—when luck allowed—chocolate brownies.

PAYCHECK

It rests, unspent,
Yet already earmarked—one portion for food,
One for rent—
In an envelope whose seal is loose.
From which he'll remove it
And take in the paper truth.

What is the value
Of an hour on the clock?
What tiny deductions
Will add up to a big shock?
How little money will be yours today
As you tuck that very first paycheck away?

"I *know* that, in my mind, I was punishing Dad for not understanding me. For not accepting the palsy more readily. He never stood up to Lisa on my behalf. He never said, 'Give the kid a break. He's doing the best he can.'"

"And you wanted him to do that?"

"Very much so. If there are good things my father did for me, and there *must* be—selfless moments where he put my welfare before his own—I want to see those moments. I *need* to see them. Otherwise, I'll be haunted forever by—and able to think only of—his faults."

"We all make mistakes, Terrence. Even Me. But, in spite of his own tribulations, your dad did all he could for you."

Our aimless walk has ended. It wasn't aimless, after all. We're back in my childhood bedroom. We didn't *enter* the room. It filled in around us as we strode along, and we're back in God's recliners, too. The change so gradual I don't notice it until it's complete.

.   .   .

God is now the spitting image of my first boss, old Mr. Chambers, who—when I was sixteen—gave me a job because he'd been on Earth longer than most surviving soil samples from the Jurassic period and knew my father when he himself was a kid. Chambers was a newspaperman, a dying breed by the time I set foot in the office. The place smells like newsprint and stale coffee. While our chairs are unchanged, God and I are looking down on the paper, observing the long-ago production of an issue.

"Never thought I'd be back here again," I say. "If I'm not mistaken, this place was condemned pretty soon after the paper went under."

"You're right," God confirms. "It was."

"There was a fire, wasn't there? Most people figured it was arson, but it was never proven. But if anyone would know, You would. So was it arson, and if so, who did it?"

"You don't need to know that."

"What?"

"That's not why we're here. It's not important to *you*. Remember, this meeting concerns your soul's well-being. There isn't anything more

13

TERRY'S FIRST JOB

THE REVIEW

Ours is an aimless walk away from the tavern. And, even as God glows with love, He's giving me a chance to voice my grievances.

"I'm mad at You," I say.

"Most people are mad at Me, at one time or another. I'm used to it. But what has you upset, Terrence?" Chloe-God asks, and God's hand goes to my shoulder.

"You're God, Father of all things. Everywhere in the world, someone is praying to You right now. But instead of listening to those prayers, you're here with me."

"I *am* here with you, Terrence. I still hear all prayers, though."

"I guess I don't understand why You're here. It's hard to get my head around it, I mean. I'm not special. You said so Yourself."

"You need to stop wondering about the *why* of it all. Don't worry so much about the *big* picture; that's not why we're here, and it's My job to worry about that. Instead, think about the scenes you've just witnessed. What did you think after seeing them?"

"I think it's not just You I'm mad at," I reply. "I figure I'm well within my rights to be pissed off at myself as well."

"For?"

"For the way I treated Dad toward the end… refusing to see him his last two years until the *very* end—it was shameful."

"Why do you think you did that?"

important, Terrence. Do you remember the job I gave you at the beginning of this review?"

"To discern the overriding lesson of my life."

"And what happens if you can't do that?"

"I will… cease to exist, in any form." *Gulp.*

"That's right. So you have to make sure you stay focused. Do you remember the job you had at the paper?"

"Sure I do. I was Chambers' right-hand man. That's how Dad thought of it, anyway." I rise and begin an impersonation of my father, complete with accompanying hand gesticulations. *"It's the same job I had when I was your age. You'll be writing stories, editing stories, coming up with ad campaigns'."*

"At a paper like this one," God and I are speaking these words together. They were Mr. Chamber's mantra. "Everyone must do double-duty. Sometimes triple."

"I never knew exactly why Chambers gave me the job. Sure, he'd known my dad forever, but so what? Why would he take a chance on someone who'd never had a job before? Chambers was not the charitable type. But I got the sense I was a bit of a pity-hire." I have gone from gesticulating to pacing the room, now recognizable as the paper's upper floor, where Chambers held meetings in lieu of a conference room, and whose furniture was dated even when I was living there for three hours each day after school.

"Do you remember anything specific about this issue?" God asks.

I look down upon the scene. I can't find anything all that remarkable at first. There is the usual hustle and bustle surrounding an issue up against its deadline. And… yes, we have finished the work just in time. The entire office joins in a collective exhale, and then… Chambers hugs me. He was a hand-shake man all the way. He only hugged me once in two years.

"I'll miss you, Terry," he'd said, and says again. "You did good work."

Something specific about this issue.

It was the last before the paper shut down and all of us lost our jobs. A minor inconvenience for me, devastation for Chambers and the people who'd been here with him for decades.

"I gave him hell that day," I say. "After the hug."

"Why?"

"You know why. Because he hadn't fought. He knew for months the end was near, yet he didn't do anything about it. I've always thought, if you love something as much as he loved that paper, you should fight for it."

"Who told you that?"

"No one *told me that*. It's just... what you do."

"It's what your dad did for you when you were too little to fight for yourself. Did you ever think that your fight—your grit and determination—might have come from your dad?"

"My dad? No. I mean, he was there for me when I had my surgery. Because he *had* to be. Because he couldn't rightfully call himself a father if he hadn't been there. But, other than that, he was too busy getting drunk in that tavern of his to give a damn about me. If he cared about me, he would have come home from work on time, instead of spending so much of his time and money getting plastered, and I wouldn't have had to spend so much of my early childhood trying to convince Lisa I was worthy of her love."

We're inside a library now. Not the Hall Of Records or the comparatively tiny library found where Dad worked but the University of Washington library.

God points. "Recognize that guy?"

We're directly above Dad, who's there alone after work in the middle of a late night. He is sequestered in his own little cubicle, darkness streaming in through every window, a reading lamp his only light.

"What's he doing?" I ask.

"He's poring over what little research exists and the few articles written on an experimental surgery rumored to relieve spasticity in people with cerebral palsy."

"My surgery."

"You got it." God squeezes my arm. *I know this whole thing isn't easy for you, but just stick with me, Terry. It'll all make sense eventually.*

"Dear God," my father whispers. My dad, praying. Other than our night-time prayer, I didn't know he prayed. I watch in rapt silence. "I know we haven't always been on the best terms, but I hope You'll help me to make the right choice. Help me to do what's best for Terry. I believe this surgery will help him live a more normal life, which is all I've ever wanted for him. But it's experimental, insurance won't pay for it, and there are doctors—well-respected doctors, mind You—who seem to delight in playing devil's advocate. They're warning me against the operation. They're sure it will paralyze him. I can handle the expense, however much it ends up costing, but I don't want to hurt my boy. What should I do? I have to make this choice soon, before he can't walk anymore and ends up in a wheelchair for life. Show me the way."

"He looks tired," I say.

"He's positively exhausted," God confirms. "Ever since your palsy diagnosis, he's been looking for anything that might make life easier for you."

"How come I never knew he did all this work on my behalf? I thought he was just a selfish bastard, too smart for his own good." Below us, Dad's head is in his hands, and the reading glasses he's removed are crumpled in one of them. He's done for the night. He leaves—now for the drive home, maybe a quick stop off at the tavern first—and the scene fades.

"He didn't want you to worry, Terry. He figured he was doing enough worrying for both of you. He wanted you to have as normal a childhood as possible."

FIRST DATE

Small-talk isn't supposed to last long;
Its duration might fill a first phone call.
Or, for the unlucky,
The lack of it could confirm that confab—
Or the date that follows it—
A bomb,
Its couple a mismatched wrong.

But for those successes,
In no time at all,
They're conversing beyond
Their favorite TV shows,
Or stocks and bonds,
The surrounding environs' chilly temperatures:
"Feels like an early fall."
They've come to deeper thoughts,
A fuller shared song.

14

HOW WE SEE THINGS: CHLOE COOPER

CHLOE COOPER IS 39. THE YEAR IS 2000.

One afternoon in mid-September, with a chill in the air hinting at the change-of-seasons coming—the leaves in mid-turn and falling—I move through the open door of his on-campus office. Since his desk is around the corner, he pays no mind to me until I give the door three knocks. At the sound, he glances up.

"Yes?"

I am five-three, give or take an inch or two. Shoulder-length blonde hair. Glasses that make me look dignified—or so I've been told—yet I'm not convinced I can trust the opinion. It is my father's, long-held. This might be his way of trying to protect me.

"You're Carl McDonald, right?" I ask.

"Right," says the man whose office I've entered. He smells strongly of alcohol, and I immediately begin looking for the source of the stench. "And you are?" His words aren't slurred… yet. But I have a feeling they'll be there soon.

"I was told I should meet you."

"By whom?"

I come to stand behind one of his two chairs. They are the only furnishings in this room. "May I sit?"

"If you'd like." His tone says, *You plan to be here long? 'Cause I sure don't.*

"You teach American Literature here," I say.

"Among other courses," he replies, bored.

"Well, I've been hired to teach American *history*, among other courses, and everyone said I should come and see you, that if anyone knows this place it would be you."

"Everyone?" He gives me a skeptical head-tilt.

"Everyone I've spoken to, anyway."

"Jesus," he says under his breath. And then, a little louder: "You work somewhere long enough, you start to get a reputation, warranted or not."

I chuckle at this, not sure if he's joking, then I circle around to the front of the chair farthest left and sit. I still haven't found the quasi-illicit liquor he's hiding, but I know it's here someplace. *Those who suggested I meet with Carl couldn't have thought of someone a bit more... I don't know... sober?* "I was wondering... that is, if you're up for it... if we might work together in some capacity to integrate our classes? It would certainly allow me a softer landing in a new environment. What do you think?"

He gives me a categorical no, followed by an explanation. An "I'm sorry" whose tone proves one thing. He's not.

"Your assumption seems to be that everyone enrolled in your classes must also take mine. You are not the first in your position to hold this assumption, but it is simply not the case, Miss—"

"Chloe Cooper. You can call me Chloe."

"Ms. Cooper," he says. I shoot him a look. *I just told you. Not so formal, please.* "Chloe, I would very much like to help you. You seem like a fine young woman." I'm pushing forty. Still a *fine young woman* to a man of Carl McDonald's age. "The problem is, I write my syllabi for the Lit classes well in advance, and, at this point, nothing can be changed."

I nod, and I note how he keeps glancing at the wall-clock in the corner. We both want out of here—it's awkward—but I can't let him leave by himself, *can I*? No. Not in his current condition. He must have family or friends, maybe a child or two waiting for him to come home, who would be crushed if something nefarious happened to him. And if I have the ability to prevent something terrible... which, as long as he's in my presence, I do... I'm going to prevent it.

"I respect your position, Carl. May I call you Carl?"

"Of course."

"I respect your wishes, and I will not bring the idea up again—until next semester, maybe." I smile, hope it doesn't look too forced.

CARL MCDONALD IS 53. THE YEAR IS 2000.

She laughs at her own minor witticism, closed-mouthed, and her dimples show. One on either side. Symmetrical.

Damn, she's a cutie. *If I were just a few years younger, maybe she'd consider going out with… but I'm not. So forget it. Get that out of your head, old man.*

"I *would* like to pick your brain a little, though, if you wouldn't mind," she says. "How long have you taught here?"

"Twenty years next month."

"So you know the dos and don'ts of this place?"

"I would hope so," I reply.

"May I take you to lunch? If you haven't eaten yet, that is, and you could give me some pointers?"

"I haven't eaten." I have—a roast beef sandwich on sourdough washed down with a small, brown-paper-bag bottle of vodka hidden in a locked desk drawer, where it congregated with much bigger bottles of courage—but she doesn't need those dirty details. "Let's go."

.   .   .

Chloe drives. Probably a good thing. If I'm being honest with myself, it's not the easiest thing to do when my mind's this foggy. In the car, we talk about work, the politics of the place ("You'll need to attend all the stupid meetings you're asked to attend, but that doesn't mean you can't fall asleep in them," I tell her. "If you didn't fall asleep, *that* would be strange."). Once we arrive at the restaurant, we switch topics. She tells me of her recent employment "in America's heartland," and how, while she did enjoy the work ("and the barbecue; I was in Kansas City for a while"), her roots are firmly planted in Seattle.

"This is where I grew up," she says.

"Did you?" I inject a note she'll read as whimsy, if I play it right. Less a question than a license for our confab to continue over steaming cups of coffee as we close our menus, minds made up. *I'm having a burger. And a genuinely good time. Didn't expect that.* A moment later, we signal a waitress over and place two orders, each for a "gourmet" cheeseburger bathed in cheddar and its steak fries. Chloe opts for soup, and I go for a Caesar salad, both as preludes to our main courses. Our orders in, we go on talking.

"My dad still lives out here," Chloe says. "And I gotta say, while I was gone, I sure missed the sights, sounds, and smells of home. Pike Place Market. Walking around Green Lake on a sunny day. Spending Seafair Sunday out on the log boom during the hydroplane races. So, when the opportunity presented itself to move back five months ago, I was ecstatic."

"What made you want to teach history?"

"History is the foundation of now," Chloe returns. "If we don't pay attention to our history, we risk losing our understanding of the present. What made you want to teach American Literature?"

"My love for words started when I read Poe's The Raven at eleven. I tried to write myself, but after three failed attempts at a novel, it became clear the craft wasn't a gift of mine, so I settled into a teaching career. American Literature was the logical fit."

.   .   .

"Do you have any children, Carl?"

This girl doesn't mess around. An hour ago, I would never have thought I'd be sharing such a personal piece of who I am with her, but now...

"Yes, I do. Do you?"

Is she frowning? I can't tell for sure, but there definitely was a small reaction just then.

"No." She takes a bite of burger. "What're your children like? Do they love literature like you love it?"

"I've only got one. His name's Terrence. Terry. I'm not sure if he likes books as much as I do. I hope so. He's a great kid. It's just the two of us now, since his mother left."

"What do you mean she left?"

"She walked out when Terry was seven. Hasn't been back since."

"I'm sorry."

"So am I." I sip my coffee. *Trending toward cold now.* "Let's talk about something else," I suggest.

We continue to converse for another hour and a half, go back to is-sues at work, much less painful than the divorce for which I still haven't forgiven Lisa. Or myself.

CHLOE COOPER IS 40. THE YEAR IS 2001.

Our ninth encounter outside of work—yes, I am the kind of neurotic person who keeps count of such things—is our fifth legitimate *date* in about four months. We're spending the evening at a popular pizza parlor near campus. The employees are familiar kids looking to pay their tuition without involving Mommy or Daddy. It is here, over a pepperoni and sau-sage pie and carbonated beverages, that Carl decides to let his guard down and tell me about Terry and his palsy.

"Terrence will never be able to drive."

"Never?" I take in, for the first time, cerebral palsy's significance. The forced immobility and dependence it all but necessitates.

"That's the aspect of his life that bothers me most. He was prema-ture, and complications at birth brought on the palsy and compromised his vision." Carl shakes his head. "Oddly, the most troubling part of his condition isn't the palsy itself—or the difficulty he has walking. It's his terrible eyesight."

"How much can he see, compared to you and me?" I ask. "Does it bother him that his eyesight isn't the same as everyone else's?"

"It's impossible to answer those questions, because he doesn't know what perfect vision is. He only knows the kind he has. And, of all his obstacles, *he* brings up his vision least. I mean, barely a peep. He might mention it when we go to a movie. He'll ask to sit closer to the screen than I'd prefer, and if the movie is subtitled, he'll ask me to whisper the dialogue so he can follow along. Or when he and I are somewhere crowded and he loses sight of me for a moment, then I can see how frightened he is."

I'm working on my second piece of pizza when I ask, "Are you wor-ried about what will happen to him when he gets older? When he goes to college? When he starts dating?"

"Sure. I worry like any parent, maybe a little more than most."

Carl picks up one of the three pie slices on his plate and takes a bite. "For now," he says, "I take him everywhere he needs to go, and that's fine with me. But he has immense trouble with fine-motor skills. He's never learned how to tie his shoes and can't use a knife to cut the meat in front of him at lunch or dinner into bite-sized pieces.

"Terry's a bright boy," Carl continues. "He's incredibly smart, but I feel like he's getting left behind in school, and I don't know what to do. I became a teacher because, when it came to literature, I always knew how to handle those situations that confounded my peers. I took them on and relished them. I thought I could handle anything and everything."

"No one can handle *everything*," I say.

"Yeah. Well, when Lisa was no longer there to lend a hand, I found that out pretty quick. My shortcomings were amplified."

"Did she leave because of the palsy?"

"Yes." He takes a moment to think this over before adding, "I *think* so."

"So you've been a single parent for how long now?"

"About four years. A little less."

"Does your son get teased or bullied a lot?"

"I'm afraid he does. I'm not sure how to tackle the bully problem. I would tell him, 'Stand up to your bully like a man'. That's what my father told me. But I'm not sure he can. At least not physically."

Treading lightly, I phrase my next question with the utmost care. "If I were to look at Terrence, what would be the most obvious sign that something wasn't quite as it should be?"

"He walks with a pronounced limp. That's what you'll see first. He walks with a limp, but at least he *can* still walk. When he was four, he had spinal surgery. He might want to show you the scar someday. He shows it to everyone he trusts. I researched the operation exhaustively. I was told it would make him more mobile. Without it, he might have lost the ability to walk altogether. There's no way of knowing for sure, since the surgery was experimental. But his hips would swivel when he walked. To think of them failing him… of my boy in pain… I wouldn't allow it.

"Terry's had his share of obstacles, definitely, but he's a pretty resilient kid, even with his mother walking out on us. He doesn't let his C.P.—that's the shorthand for it—bother him. Or, if it does, he doesn't show it."

"I'm sure he doesn't. But it sounds awful."

"The palsy? Oh, no, I wouldn't say it's *awful*," Carl counters.

I rethink my reply. "I meant that his mother's reaction sounded awful. I've been trying to put myself in her shoes while you were talking, but I just don't get it. Walking away like she did. Why would a mother do that?"

Carl says, "There's no way to explain it."

"I would love to meet him sometime, Carl."

"You wanta meet Terry?"

He looks shocked. I can see him thinking, *After four months? She's moving a little fast.* But, instead of dwelling on this thought, he asks, "What's your schedule like next week?"

"I'm sure I can make room for two eligible bachelors," I say.

THE REVIEW

"I don't know why Dad thought I wasn't bothered by the palsy. Wishful thinking, maybe?" I guess. Then I observe, "Chloe didn't like him at first. I don't know why this surprises me. Sometimes I didn't like him all that much." Admitting this to a God who looks like Dad makes me nervous, uncomfortable in the passenger seat of His car.

We aren't going anywhere. We're just out for one of what Dad liked to call his "Thinking Drives." He claimed they were good for the brain, they were good for getting a man pondering, but all they were to me was boring.

"No, she didn't," God says. "She *grew* to like him, to *love* him, but the first impression he gave her was far from impressive."

"And she only had lunch with him that first time—"

"Because she was worried about you."

She was worried about me, I think. "Before she *ever* knew who I was."

STEPMOTHER

A step-mother
Is best
When there is no step
Betwixt her
And the rest
Of one's relations.

To her, you can confess
When a bad day's
Turned from *typically* bad
Into a monumental mess.

She'll keep your secrets.
She'll defend your name.
But, perhaps best of all,
She'll walk you through
Any math problem
That becomes your existence's bane.

15

HER NAME IS CHLOE

TERRENCE MCDONALD IS 11. THE YEAR IS 2001.

My biological mother, Lisa (I referred to her as Mom before I knew better), is long gone by the time my eleventh birthday rolls around. Chloe, on the other hand, wants to celebrate.

A fact about me that I don't like sharing with most people: I can't cut my own food. No, I'm not *helpless*. But it makes my hands hurt to try and work a knife through a good piece of meat, no matter how tender the cut, and I have been known to exhaust myself for half an hour just to free one small morsel. My nearly fruitless efforts concluded, I would be frustrated, my appetite gone. So my Dad always ends up slicing my meats—and any other food that needs slicing—for me. Today, Chloe offers, unprompted, to do the job, and Dad and I gratefully accept.

"This is a momentous occasion, Terrence," she says. She takes one bite of the steak she's cut, adding her two-word explanation of: "My fee," at which her eyes twinkle, before she slides the plate back to me. "Not only are you and I meeting for the first time ever, and I couldn't be happier about it, but I get to be a part of your birthday festivities this year."

"It's really no big deal, Chlo," my father tries telling her, an edge to his voice. "The kid has plenty of parties and stuff in his life as it is. You don't need to spoil him."

She pretends not to hear Dad, tunes him out to focus on me. Elbows on the table. *I didn't know adults did that.* Leaning across it towards me. "Have you ever seen a walrus?"

"Excuse me?"

"A walrus. Have you ever seen one?"

"No."

"Would you like to? The aquarium's open for another three or four hours yet." She turns to my father. "Which is why I insisted the three of us go out for lunch instead of dinner, Carl." Eyes on me once more. "So what do you say, Terrence? You up for some walrus-ogling? They look sort of like blubbery old men with mustaches who've gone out for a swim."

Her description makes me laugh. "Let's go check out some Walruses," *I like this lady,* I think.

. . .

And, best of all, unlike the *numerous* women I've met at my father's insistence since Lisa left, Dad seems to enjoy her company, too. She really is cool without trying to be. *So* many women *try* to be cool in my presence, hoping to impress Dad—with disastrous results. He never buys their tried-and-not-so-true routines, often asking them to leave before our evening is through. He likes to call them the "one-and-dones"—referring to the one and only time they will ever be in the same room with me. As in, "Well, Terr, that chickadee was a one-and-done. You won't have to deal with her again." Unspoken subtext: *Neither will I.* But I know each of these failures is personal to Dad, because if a woman was promising enough to meet me, they'd been on many dates, and Dad was excited—in his own stolid, academic way.

None of these women ever offered to cut my food for me, not that it's a requirement. None seemed comfortable at dinner, which is probably more important. It went beyond nerves. There was the woman who could barely look at me. We didn't even get to dinner. Dad ended things with her before we left the house, and the two of us ate frozen waffles that night. Another woman kept asking how I was doing in school; she must have asked me that one question seven or eight times. I told her I was doing fine, mostly A's and B's, always polite. She seemed perplexed and, the last time, asked if I took the same classes the other kids took. Dad had heard enough, and she was gone. At least we made it to the restaurant that time. I'd been on ten or so "one-and-dones" when a woman took my father aside halfway through her chicken Parmesan. She hadn't said a word to me all night, just sat there looking like she'd rather be in a dentist's chair with a drill reshaping her mouth. The restaurant was quiet, so overhearing her words wasn't tough for me.

"I thought I could handle this, but now I'm not so sure. Terry's a great kid. He's just…"

"Just what?" My dad was breathing fire.

"I'm not his mother. I didn't ask for this."

"And you think I did?" Dad fumed.

"Life's hard enough when you're normal. But when you're—"

"You don't think my boy's *normal*?"

"Let's finish dinner," she said. "We'll talk after."

"No, we won't," Dad replied. "Come with me. I'll walk you out."

Everyone thinks they can handle a kid with special needs until they're actually across from a kid with special needs. Some people can. Many more can't. But nothing hurts more than the thought that I might be abnormal, in someone else's eyes.

"You shouldn't care what other people think of you, Terry," Dad tells me often.

Easy for him to say. No one snickers when he walks down the hall. No one whispers, "Who's the kid walking funny?" thinking he can't hear them.

"That's Terry McDonald," says another hushed voice. "I think he might be retarded or somethin.'"

In Chloe's eyes, I'm not abnormal. I'm not defined by cerebral palsy. I'm just me. That feels good.

.   .   .

"I love baseball," says my mom. Who isn't my mom yet. She is still only Chloe, the woman who introduced me to the walruses.

She takes me out of school early today. When I ask why, all she will offer is: "It's a surprise. If I told you too early, that'd spoil everything." She tells me what the surprise is just as the stadium comes into view. That's when she says, "I love baseball."

We buy hot dogs outside the stadium, massive sausages whose origins are questionable at best. Along with the dogs, we get a big bag of honey-roasted peanuts, two soft pretzels, a couple sodas. Concessionaires call out to us like carnival barkers, but by then our money is spent. Sharing the sidewalk with them is another barker; a small, curly-haired man holding a bullhorn. He stands on the corner to be sure all who pass by will notice him. The preacher.

"If you do not accept Christ," he screams, above the din of passing cars and general excitement, "there is only one place you can go! That place, ladies and gentlemen, is The Eternal Fires of Hell, where you will be set ablaze and destroyed! So make the right choice today! Christ died for your sins! Accept your Lord and Savior, and *live* for Him!"

His words bother me. Once we've left his corner far behind—following a congregation into Safeco Field—I ask Chloe, "Why is it so important to that man that I believe in God?"

She answers, "It's important to him that you believe in *his* God."

"Why?"

"Because, if he can make you or me believe, it will be easier for *him* to believe. It'll reassure him."

"What if I'm not sure what I believe?"

"Then the best thing you can do," Chloe advises, "is not to pay any attention to him. If you make eye contact with him... they're like leeches, so it's a good thing you didn't. They latch on, and they won't let you go. They make you their mission. You become someone they can pull to safety, territory to be conquered.

"Terry, always remember this. You can believe anything you feel comfortable believing when it comes to God. *Anything.* No one should force you into any belief at all."

"Is he always here, Chloe?"

"That man? Always. Every time I've been here, anyway."

THE REVIEW

It is fitting that our seats are now one long wooden church pew. My ass is already beginning to ache. *That seems right, too. I wasn't a churchgoer, but whenever I sat in a pew (for funerals, weddings, and other occasions when a church acted as the venue), it wasn't long before my posterior would smart.* Technicolor religious paintings light the windows all around. I could not detail the significance of any of the pictures, *let alone* each and every one. But some people can, and take pride in this talent.

"I see you paused things," says God.

I did, without knowing I was doing it. Chloe stands suspended above us. She has just finished telling me how no one should force me into any belief at all.

"Was Chloe right?" I ask Him.

"That's sort of up to you," He answers. "When it comes to belief, the key is to believe what feels right to *you*. Does what she said feel right to you?"

"Yes. It did then, and it does now. It isn't like that was the only time an over-zealous evangelist tried to convert me. It did happen most often at that stadium. At least twenty times. To be told, 'Believe in Jesus, and you will be healed' is like hearing someone assert: You're not quite good enough yet, but accept Jesus and, with faith, you might just get there. I did undergo my surgery, and it made my life easier to live, You know that, but I was never going to be *healed*. That first day at the baseball game with Chloe is memorable for me because Chloe wasn't swayed in the way Lisa might have been. In the way I *would* have been before Chloe entered my life."

"Lisa wasn't religious," God points out.

"No. Not when I knew her. But she was *searching* for something. Something my dad and I couldn't give her. I can't be sure, because I didn't know her well later on, but I wouldn't be surprised if she found religion when she got older. I kind of *hope* she did."

"Why?" He's wearing a priest's black vestments. Why has He chosen such formal attire? I never had a close relationship with a priest. Nonetheless, He must think it appropriate in this setting. His priest is white-haired, kind-faced, bespectacled, and He's letting me talk.

"It might have made the end of her life easier," I tell Him, and then I admit: "For some people, there's an order to religion, and I get that. It works for them. It's just never been impressive to me. Too many rules. Plus it asked me to perform rituals, to confirm my belief in God, rather than letting my belief stand on its own and just *be*."

TERRENCE MCDONALD IS 11. THE YEAR IS 2001.

It takes us a few minutes to locate our seats. The crowd nearly envelops me (proof, as if I needed any, that I walk slow and am short for my age), and there are a couple times when the two of us are nearly separated walking the concourse. But once Chloe finds our section, a light goes on in her eyes. "This way!" Our seats are about halfway up the aisle, numbers nine and ten in their row. We sit there now, and I take in batting practice.

"It's part of the whole baseball experience," Chloe claims. I do not doubt her. "You can't say you've fully experienced baseball's greatness unless you've witnessed a batting-practice homer."

"I've never been to a *game*," I say.

Now I'm the one surprising her.

"This is your first ball game?"

"Mhmm."

"Ever?"

"Yep. I watch baseball and football all the time at home with my dad, but we've never been here."

"Why not? Have you ever told him you wanted to come to a game? If he doesn't know you're interested, it's hard for him to do anything about it."

"I have. A few times. And I think there's a part of him that's wanted to take me. But whenever I tell him how much I'd love to go, he gets this faraway look in his eyes, chokes up, and says, 'we'll see'. I know that's his way of saying no *without* saying no and, after the third or fourth time this happened, neither of us ever brought it up again."

"Why would he get choked-up? You're just telling him you want to spend time with him. A boy spending a day at the ballpark with his father. Heck, If *I* told my father—you'll meet him soon, I think—if I told him I wanted to do that, he'd do anything he could to make it happen."

"Dad's sad that I can't play sports, Chloe, more because of the *reason* I can't play than the *fact* that I can't play. And I'm sad for him, that he didn't get the son he wanted."

The look on her face rests somewhere between befuddlement and downright, abject sadness. "Do you really think that's true?" She pauses long enough to watch a long fly ball land in the seats a few rows to our right. One of the batting-practice homers she was telling me about. *Boy, whoever's up there really did crush that ball,* I think. Then she adds, "I should talk to Carl."

"No, please don't do that. If he knows we talked about it, he'll wonder why I didn't come to him first."

"*Alright*. I won't breathe a word of this conversation then. But *you* should mention it to him."

"I can't."

She shrugs. "Is there anything you'd like to know?"

"About what?"

"About the game? About baseball? I kind of assumed your dad had filled you in on the basics." I didn't know then how these basics had been the foundation for the bedtime stories her father told her.

"Nope, he never did," I say. My father, knowing early the impossible odds of his kid ever playing any sport competitively, made athletics in general rare pieces of conversation around the house.

"Well, I'd love to fill you in, then. If you'll let me?"

I'm not going to turn down such a well-meaning proposition. Chloe begins by showing me how to keep score using the scorecard at the back of my program.

"Being able to score a game is a special skill, Terry. Say you missed yesterday's game. It was played during the day, and you had to go to work or school and couldn't catch it. Now you want to know what happened. Not a sports page's summary, which will tell you how your team fared, but the *truth* of the game. *Why* they fared that way. All nine—or more—innings, how each out was recorded, each run scored.

"All you'd have to do, in theory, is find a friend who used a scorecard to record every at-bat; and, if he's a good scorekeeper, reading over his work will generate a mosaic more informative than any columnist. Now, it's important to understand that every position on the field has its own corresponding number...."

THE REVIEW

"Terrence, do you still believe you weren't the son your father wanted?"

God is Chloe, and we're in the Safeco Field stands. The ballpark of my childhood. Down the right-field line, in fair territory, and surrounded by fans who aren't, strictly speaking, people. They are composites and representations of all those I sat with in what was the initial batch of my baseball-watching days. After that first game with Chloe, those days truly began, a life-long love ignited. We're all cheering a collection of the best and most exciting plays I witnessed here, performed on a loop, a precise and practiced ballet. I'd like to tell Him no, that I now believe I was exactly the son my father wanted, because I think that's what He wants to hear, but I can't say it.

"I do still believe that, yes," I reply instead. I lower my head.

. . .

Chloe's soft voice brings me gradually into consciousness. Better her than my father. His booming baritone routinely puts dreams into submission and startles me awake with a force bordering on violent.

"Terrence? Terrence, it's time to get up," she says. Soft but firm. "Come out to the living room please. Your dad and I need to speak with you."

"About what?"

I don't want to go anywhere if it means getting out of my warm bed. Chloe realizes this.

"I'm making breakfast," she informs me. That's why the whole house smells like bacon. She is trying a different tact to get me moving. And it's working.

"I'll be there in a few minutes. Scrambled eggs for me, please."

"I know. They're ready and waiting."

She leaves my room and shuts the door softly behind her. I roll over and look at the clock radio on my nightstand. It glows a blue 8:00 AM, and I think:

I should already be at school. I've missed the bus. Why the late start this morning? It's Tuesday, not Saturday.

Not that I'm going to complain. Chloe must have decided today was not a day to use her favorite motto. I've heard it non-stop for the past seven months or so. *Better to be early than late.*

Out in the front room, the TV is blaring. Dad's out there, in his chair, drinking a beer.

Wait. He's drinking a beer at eight in the morning? Even for Dad, that's jumping the gun.

"Goddamn bastards," I hear him say.

I seat myself in the kitchen, which doubles as our dining room—excepting those times when we invite guests over. (On those infrequent occasions, we'll make our way into the *formal* dining room.) I dive into my eggs and bacon. All the while, I'm in the dark as to what has Dad so riled up.

I'm about a third of the way through my meal when Chloe walks up behind me and says, "Two planes hit the World Trade Center."

"Hmmmm?" My mouth is full of egg. I stare at her with a what-does-that-have-to-do-with-me expression. *What is the World Trade Center?*

She gestures toward the TV, clearly visible from my position. She knows I can't see from this seat what someone with perfect vision could—it's all a little fuzzy to me, some details lost—but I can see *enough*. "Watch," she says.

As I look on, I see orange flames jutting out of two massive sky-scrapers. Accompanying the flames is a billowing black smoke. And… are those… are those people? Jumping? Falling? Out of the buildings? How horrible it must be in the midst of those infernos for them to leap to their deaths, flailing to earth like rag-doll bungee-jumpers whose cords have snapped. In a scene shown not much later, our transfixed stares see one of the two buildings implode in a cloud of dust and rubble and, still later, its twin comes down, too.

My dad takes another swig of beer. He has a bottle in his hand all morning long, and these bottles follow him into the strange, quiet after-noon and evening when—for the first time I can recall—I don't hear a single airplane fly above us. All planes have been grounded.

"Terrence," Dad says, "be sure you remember this day."

I know I will.

"This is the day God stopped caring about us. This is the day He gave up. I'd always thought He was a quitter. This makes it official."

THE REVIEW

"That was the day I lost my faith for good," I say. We're in Dad's kitchen, seated at the table, across from each other. I look into my father's eyes. His is *the only* image God could use in such a setting, considering the gravity of our dialogue. "Not that I had a whole lot of faith to begin with, mind You. But that day, I lost the small bit Lisa's leaving hadn't fin-ished off."

"You lost your faith, just as your father lost his."

"I guess I did," I concede.

"There's no guessing about it, Terrence. This is important. It's why we saw 9/11 at all in your review. Because it confirmed something for you at eleven—such a young age to be disillusioned."

"It confirmed for me that You'd given up. I had my suspicions prior—I figured if You hadn't given up, You'd certainly given up on *me*. And then those planes hit, those buildings crumbled, and faith wasn't important anymore."

"Why wasn't faith important?"

"Because... if You weren't there to receive it, if You were out of the office, as it were, then what good did faith do anyone?" My enquiry is an accusation, a cannonball shot at close range to lodge and to remain in the side of the battleship that is the afterlife's collective awareness.

"The fact that anyone would think I gave up... that hurts Me," God says. He gets up from the table, goes to the pantry, retrieves a box, and pours a bowl of cereal with milk at the kitchen's counter. *Who knew God liked Cheerios?*

"But You can see how some people come to that conclusion, can't You?" I ask.

"I suppose. Thinking I gave up is a comforting thought for some people." He brings the bowl back to the table, filled full.

"Comforting? How? It wasn't comforting for me."

"Are you sure, Terrence? That there wasn't a *tiny* part of you that felt... relieved, in a way? The whole world was devastated, but there was another prevalent thought that day, besides the devastation. If *I've* given up—Me, God, The Almighty and Most Powerful—that assumption takes all blame for anything evil that happens to or is perpetrated by humanity... out of humanity's hands. The truth is, it's in the aftermath of the worst days when I must work My hardest and yet be at My subtlest. People aren't looking for big things then. They're content with small signs of Me. So many are in danger of losing their faith at those times... it's My job to make sure anyone to whom faith means a great deal has a shot to keep theirs intact. I'm not gonna tell you I've got a perfect record. Some faithful do get lost—free will—and faith's composition may change over time, but if it's something an individual depends upon, and if they work on their end to maintain their faith as hard as I work on mine, I can't let it be broken."

"What does this have to do with *me?*"

"The composition of your faith has changed over time, too. But it *is* still alive within you. When you were a kid, your faith was hopeful and innocent. When you learned about your palsy—and how others would react to it—your faith became guarded. When Lisa left, it shrank back into a seldom-used room at the corner of your mind. And, when 9/11 happened, your frightened faith found the key to that room's door and locked itself away for protection. This scene is a reminder of how your faith never left you. It was merely waiting for the all-clear signal before it reappeared."

TERRENCE MCDONALD IS 12. THE YEAR IS 2002.

Today I'm meeting Grandpa Jack.

I tried to get Dad to come with me, with us, but he had to work. "Besides, I've already met the man," he said. "It's your turn. Chloe will take you."

The truth is, I don't want to meet anyone, least of all an old person I'm going to get attached to, and then I'll have no choice but to sit by and watch the poor guy waste away to nothing. But at twelve, I have no say in the matter, and I wouldn't make my true opinion known if I could. I will take this trip planned by Chloe, who loves baseball, the Mariners, Edgar Martinez, my father, and me.

·　　　·　　　·

We're using a sidewalk to climb the hill leading to the apartment complex where Chloe's father lives. Parking is hard to find around here, and we were forced to settle for a spot close to a mile away. The walk borders on too much for me. I'm breathing hard and sweating profusely, but I can make it.

"Chloe?" My hands shake. Sometimes the palsy makes them shake. But this isn't palsy. My knees are weak, but that isn't palsy, either, nor can it be blamed on our walk. My arm is in Chloe's arm, and she controls our pace.

"Yeah?"

"What if… what if your dad doesn't like me?"

"He will like you."

"How can you be so sure? Not everyone likes me, Chloe. The palsy, my eyes, and all the things I can't do. They can drive some people *(myself, for example; Lisa, for another,* I think*)* a little nuts."

Chloe puts her hand on my shoulder. *Calm down,* the gesture says. "My dad will love you."

"Why?" *Why should he? My own mother didn't love me. If she had, she wouldn't have walked away from her family.*

"You like to talk, and so does he." She stops walking. "You know the best thing about my dad, Terrence?"

I look directly at her. Into her rosy-cheeked face. *Tell me,* I think.

"The best thing about him is how he doesn't judge people. Look around. That's pretty rare these days, isn't it? Everyone's judging everyone else. But not my dad. He doesn't get involved in that stuff. He'd rather talk to you—about baseball, football, and he loves lively discussions on movies and TV—he'd rather talk about any of that stuff as opposed to judging you."

I grimace. Our walk is underway again, and I might have tweaked my back. It's yelling at me. My whole body is often out of alignment; one wrong move when I'm on a friendly jaunt up a hill, and I regret it for weeks.

"There's something else I should tell you, Terry."

We stop again. *I wish we'd keep moving, but whatever it is Chloe has to tell me compelled her to stop.*

"I can't have children of my own."

"You can't?"

She shakes her head.

"That's sad," I say.

It is. A woman as wonderful as Chloe being—what's the word they used in that sex-ed class I had to take a month ago? Infertile. What a crock of shit that is. I could never and would never repeat this phrase aloud, but I can sure as hell think it.

"Terry?"

"Yeah?"

"Could you do something for me?"

"Shoot." For her, anything. Well, I wouldn't become a Yankee fan, but she wouldn't request such a betrayal. She's told me more than a few times the story of Edgar Martinez and "the double" in 1995, a fairy tale recited by all true Mariner fans to their offspring.

She clears her throat and turns to look at me straight-on. "Okay. First off, let me say I know this is a lot to ask. And I wouldn't ask it of you if I didn't *know* you could do it. Anyway, no more stalling. Since I'm my dad's only child," she explains, "and I can't have kids myself, that means he'll never have grandkids."

"I gotcha so far." Her math does appear correct on that score.

"Would you mind being his grandson? I can't begin to tell you what it would entail; no one except God can predict what life holds in store. The rest of us have to wait and see. But you have my word that he'd be an excellent grandfather. I can vouch for him."

I stand stalk-still, thinking the thing over, until my body can't handle my lack of movement anymore and screams at me to let it continue towards Jack's place or it'll fall hard.

"I'll do it," I declare, pulling her forward.

"You will?"

"Sure. He sounds like a great guy, if your description is accurate. And he helped raise you, didn't he?"

"He did." She smiles.

"Then he must be alright. Plus, if we don't get there soon, I'm gonna land in a heap on this concrete, and that wouldn't feel good."

I break our arm-in-arm connection, and I run up ahead of her to meet my newest grandparent. Chloe trades in her fresh-as-a-new-car smile—it's only been on her face ten seconds or so—and begins to cry. Any other time, I might stay behind, stay with her to make sure she's okay, but I sense I've performed my duty.

Chloe becomes one of my best friends today. I respect how she's opened up to me; most adults wouldn't, and I enjoy cookies with the hefty, hearty-laughing Grandpa Jack.

In the course of this cookie-enjoyment, he says:

"So… Chloe tells me you've just discovered baseball, young man."

"Yes, sir."

"Did she tell you I worked as an umpire for years?"

"No, sir."

Jack turns to his daughter. "What *did* you tell him about me, missy?"

"Not much, Dad. I thought you guys could learn about each other together."

He snaps his fingers, bites off a sizable cookie chunk, and—mouth full—declares:

"Sounds like a plan. I'm up for it if you are, Terrence."

There isn't anything to say besides: "Sure."

CHLOE COOPER McDONALD IS 64. THE YEAR IS 2025.

All the panelists, including Carl himself, were meeting with God prior to Terry's review when a Carl-shaped God turned to me and said, "Think of your favorite memory of Terrence and recount it for Me. It will be included in his review. We'll surround him in the sights, sounds, and smells of it."

Coming up with this memory was not difficult. It ranks as one of my most cherished. An unseasonably cool Sunday near the middle of May. Mother's Day. 2002. I call it *The* Mother's Day. It is Terrence's twelfth, and it will prove to be my first.

Terry and Carl whip up a stellar breakfast of scrambled eggs, bacon, and hash browns, deliver said breakfast, then leave me to enjoy it. I feast in bed. Thank God for TV trays. This is the one day all year when an in-bed feast is expected of me. Its authors would frown on anything less.

Terry pops his head through the bedroom door. "When you're ready, Chloe," he says, "I've got a little surprise for you. No rush, though."

"Okay." I bite into a slice of bacon. "Are you gonna give me any hints?"

"No. No hints. But you'll like it."

An hour later, I decide I'm ready. I shower and dress, then I head for the kitchen, where dishes are being washed, hazelnut lattes brewed.

"Good morning, you two. What a great breakfast you made."

Still facing the sink, his demeanor guarded, Terry begins with: "Glad you liked it," and then goes on to say, "Chloe, I wasn't sure what to get you gift-wise, but I thought I ought to get you *something*."

"You didn't need to get me anything. I hope you didn't overextend yourself."

"Well, here's the thing." He turns to face me. Puts down the plate he's been scrutinizing. "I racked my brain for the perfect gift, and still I came up empty. You've done so much for me, Chloe. You've made me feel… you've made me feel normal, and when you have palsy like I do, that's some feat. Just ask my dad. So what gift can I possibly give the woman who makes me feel like I matter, like I'm someone besides the professor's crippled kid?"

"You're not *crippled*." I *despise* the word. He knows I despise the word. He is employing it for emphasis.

Carl is standing next to his son and steps forward now. Away from his own dish-work. I can tell he's thinking, *Let's move this along, shall we? Time's a-wastin'*. "Terry has a question he'd like to ask you, Chlo."

"Go ahead."

I await the query. Outside our beautiful home—it's a palace, Terry says—a confab of neighborhood garbage cans are gathered together at the curb for tomorrow's pick-up, it's raining hard, and an angry crow reports his displeasure with the inclement weather.

"Chloe. May I call you Mom?"

I smile and cry small tears that leak out of the corners of my eyes. "Of course, Terry. I'd be honored if you'd call me Mom."

"Okay, Mom."

We hug, long and tight, and from outside the embrace Carl suggests bowls of ice cream; mint chocolate chip. When the hug breaks, Terrence goes to the freezer, retrieves the ice cream, and sets it out to thaw. Once it's soft enough, he does the scooping—slow and imprecise; they're more tiny clumps than scoops, but it gets the job done—while Carl disappears, returning minutes later, holding the gift he's purchased.

A beautiful necklace. A thin golden chain leads to a silver, heart-shaped locket at its end. Once opened, two equal compartments—empty and waiting to be filled—make up the inner heart.

"There aren't any pictures in it yet," Carl says. "But it's got room for two great memories. We'll have to find them together. As a family."

"It's perfect."

.   .   .

There's an enlivening quality to the way Terry says it. *Mom*. A *conviction* that lets me know this is the day my maternal instinct has been waiting for all along. The day it awakens, leaves my imagination for more practical territory. This is the day it becomes *real*.

THE REVIEW

"I tried to give that Mom title to someone else," I say. "The person who was biologically entitled to it. But Lisa didn't want anything to do with it or, after a while, with me." God is Chloe, wearing the same jeans-and-a-Mariners-T-shirt outfit that she chose that day, standing in the same spot she stood when she accepted my invitation. "I was so afraid of rejection... so used to it," I say, "that I could sense it coming, even when it wasn't. That day, my nerves were as frayed as they'd ever been."

"You worried about rejection, even though Chloe had told you she wouldn't judge you?"

"Sure I did. It's one thing to *say* you won't judge others. It's another thing entirely to put this philosophy into practice. What if she didn't *want* to be my mom? What if she was perfectly fine being my *friend*, but that whole Mom-title business freaked her out? These were real concerns of mine. When she agreed to take on the role, I felt truly worthy of love for the first time. Dad and Lisa—they had made me, so they *had* to love me. Chloe was under no such constraints."

CARL McDONALD IS 55. THE YEAR IS 2002.

The proposal is no great production. That's not who I am, a magnificent showman who thrives on the attention of others and, for sport, stages spectacles that dazzle just to show that he can.

The weekend-morning warms early this late-spring day. Chloe and I sit out on the balcony of the home I share with Terrence and—as of recently—Chloe herself. Terrence still sleeps.

The ring I bought a week ago, a tiny diamond its centerpiece, is in my right pants pocket. Tucked down low so it won't fall out and be lost. Poised for its placement.

"Chloe?"

"Hmmm?" She sips from a sweating glass of lemonade and reads a baseball novel. *We are comfortable in silences,* I think. *Have I ever been comfortable in silences before?*

"I need to ask you something."

"Okay." Only now does she look up from her book. Take off her glasses.

"First, let me say how much Terry and I have enjoyed having you here with us."

"I've enjoyed being here. You've both made me feel so welcome."

Nerves gnaw their way through my confidence. Am I sweating? Yes. I wipe at my brow.

"I was wondering, Chlo... I was wondering if..." Out of my deck chair and onto one knee. Reaching for the ring. I can't find it at first, but then... there it is, hiding in a fold of pocket-fabric. "Chloe Cooper, will you marry me?"

She doesn't look surprised, the emotion I'd been going for. To me, she looks pleased. Just as good, I figure.

"Yes, Carl, of course I will." We kiss, then she draws away and adds a condition. "As long as it's alright with Terry...?"

"Are you kidding? He's the one who told me I should marry you. I took his advice and went right out and bought the ring."

.   .   .

My fiancée and I are in my office, going over seating charts, possible dinner entrées, what we want the minister to say, what might be better left unsaid. And we're arguing. Don't worry. It's not one of those arguments you look back on down the road and think, *Yep. That was the beginning of the end.* I had plenty of those types of disagreements with Lisa. No, this is the kind of argument content couples appreciate and, down the road, it becomes an inside joke. *Remember when we squabbled over who should act as my best man?*

"I would let Mel do it," I say, "but he's too sick. I'm not even sure he'll make it to the ceremony."

Chloe wears disgust. She tries to hide it, but plainly it says, *I just drank an unexpected mouthful of sour milk.* "Mel?"

"Yeah. What's wrong with Mel?"

"Oh, nothing, I suppose. I like him, and I'm sorry he isn't well. But it would seem to me your best candidate for best man is staring you dead in the face, and you don't see him."

"Who is it?"

"What about Terry?"

"Terry wouldn't want to do it."

"How do you know? You barely talk to him."

"And you do?"

"Sure. He calls me at work every day after he gets home from school. To check in and to let me know how his day went. If you want my honest opinion, I think honoring him as your best man would go a long way towards healing your relationship."

"Our relationship doesn't need healing," I huff.

"I'm sorry to say this, Carl, because I love you and, in the time we've been together, you've made great strides towards becoming a better you. I do think you *like* yourself a lot more than you used to as well. It's been a bit of a project, but then whose life isn't a project, a work-in-progress? I'm proud to be working with you on both of ours…"

She's proud to be working with me? I expect to bristle at this comment.

First of all, I can't stand incorrect grammar. A lot? God, I hate that phrase. It's not a phrase. It's a place where you park cars or build a house. And, second of all… second of all, how dare she say such things? I've always liked myself just fine, thank you! If she doesn't think this "project" of a man is coming along fast enough for her liking… well, then, missy, you are always free to leave.

My short fuse frustrates me, and can get me into trouble, but it has gotten a tad longer, and there's no bristling. I don't let go a syllable's-worth of these knee-jerk-reaction thoughts. I let Chloe finish.

"…But there is one thing in your life still in need of healing, and that, my love, is the connection between you and your son."

THE REVIEW

God and I are in Dad's office. God, as Dad, is eating a fun-size package of M&Ms from the vending machine right outside the door (Where is the fun in fun-size candy? *We're not going to give you enough candy to satisfy your sweet tooth,* they tease. *Instead, here's just enough candy to make you feel guilty for your purchase.*).

I say, "I always knew Chloe was the driving force behind me becoming my father's best man."

"If you already knew that, then why is it included here? What more could you learn from it?"

"There isn't anything more to *learn*. It's a reminder."

"A reminder of what?"

"Of how great that day was. Of the *respect* I felt. I truly was the best man. I calmed my Dad down when he freaked out just before the wedding. I used Chloe's own hand-on-the-shoulder, talking-softly technique. I got him down that aisle and waiting for his bride on time. And, when the time came, I made the traditional best-man's toast."

"I'm proud of you, Terry," says God. "This review stuff isn't always easy to grasp. People often ask why a particular scene is important—and, believe me, some can get a little testy about it—before they've had a chance to think things through. You are being methodical about the whole thing."

"I better be," I reply. "My afterlife depends on it."

God's chuckle is tempered by what He and I both know; I am speaking the truth.

We watch a much younger me deliver my best-man's toast. I can't help but feel nostalgic.

"To Dad and Chloe… I wish you the greatest and truest happiness any couple could ever have. I wish prosperity and joy for our family. Plenty of baseball games, outings to see the walruses, wonderful holidays, ordinary mornings spent eating breakfast and finding out together what went on overnight. Basically, here's to a good life together!"

"Hear, hear," my father seconds, and glasses clink all around.

PLAYING BALL

It's a beautiful,
Cloudless,
Sun-drenched day.
In the month of June,
Or maybe it's May.

Regardless,
A boy stands in the middle
Of a diamond of sod and dirt.
Wearing his uniform,
A grass-stained shirt.

16

REINCARNATION

THE REVIEW

God is my little-league baseball coach. A man I respected immensely in my youth, and whom I respect even now, for his seemingly boundless knowledge of a game with which I was still becoming familiar. My mom introduced us. He was a good friend she'd known since high school. I call him my coach despite two inarguable facts: He never coached a team sport a day in his life, and I never participated in the little-league program or an athletic pursuit of any kind a day in mine. But calling him Coach Ray made me feel *connected* to the sport I was learning to love. I didn't care if he'd never give me a sign from the dugout, or that I'd never smack a solid single up the middle, steal second, or blast a home-run to left and trot around the diamond. Yet we could pretend, couldn't we?

What hair survives on his head, the last of a dwindling crop, is caramel-colored and embroiled in the comb-over of all comb-overs. He wears a replica Mariners jersey with his own last name—Rowly—on the back.

Baseball-savvy comb-over God clears His throat.

"What's your feeling regarding reincarnation, Terrence?"

I sense this is a topic He deems vital.

"My feeling on it?"

"That's right. I want to know if you believe—as baseball season begins anew when spring comes around again each year—if life, too, has the ability to reset?"

I think over the possibility. "On one hand, it makes sense that humans would continue coming to Earth until they were steeped in each and every lesson set forth in humanity's curriculum. Until their souls were fulfilled."

"And on the other?"

"On the other… well, there are some religions that abhor reincarnation as outright blasphemy, aren't there?"

"True. Somehow, we have to marry these two viewpoints, wouldn't you say?"

"I suppose. But what does this have to do with me and my review?"

"Here's how to do it." God either didn't hear my question—unlikely—or has chosen to ignore it. His goal set out, He states, in a matter-of-fact tone: "Reincarnation *is* real. It happens. But only for those who believe in it. I am not in the business of breaking spirits by disproving long-held and cherished paradigms."

"Why are you telling me this?"

This is the first I notice we're standing on a baseball field. Not a full-fledged ballpark, it resembles a sandlot. Crude but playable, the diamond is a five-minute walk from The Palace. I'm at my position, the one my coach prescribed for me. "You're a shortstop," he'd said one day. I'm not sure how he came to this conclusion. Palsy made me slow of foot and kept my arm strength short of what was necessary for a shortstop. Plus I couldn't catch a batted ball. Maybe he'd just wanted me to feel empowered. I had. When he was coaching me—for the twenty minutes we'd spend talking baseball on the field, and then for the half an hour afterwards out at an ice cream parlor—I felt invincible. No bully could hurt or ridicule me then. *Let them try.*

"We're taking a quick detour, Terry. Your review is ongoing. I just needed to work this in. I wanted you to know, before it was announced at your hearing," God says, "that your mom, Chloe, intends to be reincarnated as your great-grandson."

I glance over toward second base, where God is stationed. He's decked out in an old-time wool uniform.

"She still feels she has more to learn?" I ask. "She wants to go back?"

"Yes, on both counts," He replies. "She's excited about it. But she wanted to make sure you were okay with it before she signed her contract and began building her chart. Made it official and all."

"And if I say no?"

"I assume she'll remain here in the afterlife, living with your father. Begin looking for another life to live. She wants *this* life because she loves your daughter and her husband, and because… she told Me not to tell you this, Terrence, but she thought it a good way to honor you."

My eyes moisten. "Did You really have to add that last part? I was gonna say yes, anyway."

"So that's a yes? Good. I'll let Chloe know."

I hear the crack of a bat not far off.

"Get your glove down, Terrence," says God's Coach Ray. "Here comes a grounder with some mustard on it."

I field the baseball cleanly—for the first time ever, my hands do not betray me—and fling it toward first with all my might. Clip the runner by a step. The first-baseman's stretch is long, low into the dirt, and graceful. It saves me an error.

"You're out!" the ump bellows.

That umpire isn't Jack, is it?

DRESSED

He pulls on his socks,
He puts on his pants.
The phrase most prevalent
In his thinking
Is: "I can't."
A constant reminder
That his body
Is far from strong.

But this morning,
He proves this phrase wrong.

He still has much to learn;
This is yet step one.
"Dress yourself without assistance."
His father's assignment weighs a metric ton.
He makes no fashion statements,
But his sweat pants and t-shirt confirm:
I can!
And…
He emerges from the bedroom…
Sweat pouring,
Job done.

17

GETTING DRESSED

TERRENCE MCDONALD IS 10. THE YEAR IS 2000.

This weekday morning is just like every other since I started school; unwelcome. But this morning is worse than most. It's the *first day* of fifth grade. Dad comes into my room around six-thirty, and he's my personal alarm. *So early. The long weekend called summer—it's long but never long enough—is over.*

"It's time to get up, chief," Dad says, turning on the light and yanking me out of a dream. "The summer has ended, and an exceptional public education awaits you!"

"Ugh." I slide from my pillow and cover my face with the blankets. *I don't like school. And I don't feel like being another teacher's show-and-tell today, either. Why go to school when I've got a perfectly good bed I could stay in? Why go when I know exactly what's going to happen?*

My new teacher'll meet me at the classroom door, watch me walk a second, get a sad look on their face, then brighten quickly. Maybe I didn't see the sadness, they'll hope. They'll call me to the front of the room as the school bell chimes and all of the new students are in their seats for the first time.

"We have a *special* student in class with us this year, boys and girls. His name is Terrence. Terrence has a disease called… maybe you should tell them yourself, Terrence." What teachers say to me when they're uncomfortable. "Do you want to tell everyone what you have?"

No. But I will. Most of them have been in school with me long enough that they know by now, anyway. "It's not a *disease*," I'll correct. I don't want the handful of kids who don't know me yet thinking *they could get it just by hanging out with me.* "And I'm not *special.* What I have is called cerebral palsy, and it means I walk a little different, a little slower. There are some other things I deal with, too, but I don't want to—"

"I'm sure everyone would like to know what those *other things* are. Right, boys and girls?"

"Right," my classmates will reply in an already bored unison. All of them are sick of me before we've met, and I'm sick of being the kind of broken that gives teachers impromptu lesson plans.

But that's the way the first day goes.

.   .   .

"I'll tell you what, Terry," says Dad. "You've got five more minutes. I'll get the shower started for you."

I say a muffled, "Thanks." After I hear him start the water flowing, I throw the covers off and move toward the bathroom. He helps me into the tub with a sure hand that's done this before. The water's a degree or two hotter than I'd like, but I don't say anything.

"Sit down," he reminds me. I do. Because neither of us wants me to fall in here. A fall would ruin the day too early. "If the day's gonna get ruined," he likes to quip over his toast, "it can wait until you've had breakfast."

Dad leaves me to a "private soak." I'm in a ball, because I can't stretch out in our tub. But the water warms and wakes me. Soon, my hair is wet, and my eyes are closed against the shampoo running out of it, and my thoughts are drifting. I think of what Dad says when I ask him why I can't stand up in the shower like he does.

"I know you're uncomfortable sitting like that, Terry. But if you were standing, and you slipped and fell… that would hurt a heck of a lot more than it does to spend fifteen uncomfortable minutes getting yourself clean."

I return to my room wrapped in a fluffy white towel (this is *not* one Dad uses). Dad waits there. He kneels in front of my bed. *Time to get dressed.* I let the towel drop, and I plop down on my unmade bed. I have never made my bed (no one's ever shown me how to do it), nor have I ever dressed myself—I'm not flexible enough to do that. It's always been Dad's job.

"Alright, bud. Give me your legs," he says.

I hold them out stiffly, because there's no other way for me *to* hold them out. He slips them into my underwear. I stand and pull them up. Then I sit back down. My sweatpants are next. I hold out my legs again. Right, then left. Into the leg-holes they go. Sweatpants are my favorite kind of pants—way better than the jeans everyone else wears—because I can pull them up and down on my own, and there are no annoying snaps or buttons to get in my way. So I can go to the bathroom at school on my own. I don't need to ask for help.

"All I need you to do is button my pants for me when I'm done."

Even the kindest teachers blush. "I'm sorry," they'll say. "You need me to do *what*?"

"You know, bud, I've been thinking," says Dad.

"Uh-huh…"

He slips a green t-shirt over my head, and I put my arms through the sleeves. "That maybe it might be best if you learned how to dress yourself."

A shot of fear dampens my forehead. *Dress myself? Is he kidding? He knows I can't do tha-*

"Do you want a girlfriend someday, Terry?"

I *have* just begun noticing "the majesty of girls" (that's my dad's phrase. I would never say something so… Dad-like). Not long ago, I'd do anything to stay clear of them, which wasn't hard because they were content to spend their time elsewhere. Now I *want* to be in their orbit.

Did I want a girlfriend someday? "Well, sure. Someday." *Hopefully someday soon.*

"Then know this: No girl is gonna want to dress you. You're gonna have to do that yourself."

THE REVIEW

"What do you remember about this day, Terrence?"

God is my fifth-grade teacher, Mr. Brumfield, who tried unsuccessfully to convince me I could be good at math, and that logic puzzles *were* fun. *If Gordon has three pieces of pizza and Jane has two, how many pieces does that leave for their friend, Bob?*

My answer: *Who cares? Tell Bob to eat something healthier. He'll live longer.*

"That particular day... I don't remember much," I tell Him. "It was the day Dad first suggested I dress myself, and it scared the crap out of me, but he was right. No girl wants to dress their guy, although they don't mind giving input as to what he *should* wear. But back then dressing myself was such a faraway goal, I didn't take him—or the goal itself—seriously."

"When did you *start* taking it seriously, then?"

"I think it was... yeah, it had to be the day I put a pair of socks on for the first time with no help whatsoever. I was twelve. It would have been no big deal for other kids my age, who did this every day. They took it for granted. But I cried, and Dad took me out for a steak dinner to celebrate that night. We had a lot more work to do, but I'd taken the first step, he said. As the years went on, putting on my clothes got easier and easier, with the fine-motor skills requiring less of a chore each time. So that, later on, I didn't even have to think about the effort it took to get dressed, and I could take it for granted like my peers always had. Although I would never be able to snap or button a shirt, a pair of pants, or a coat, without assistance. But that first time I put that pair of socks on, I used muscles I didn't know I had, and I asked them to do things *they* doubted could be done."

"Why do you think you're being reminded of that day here?"

"I'm not sure."

Brumfield-God rises and steps out from behind his desk. He goes to the chalkboard. *If I can't get the right answer, He'll write it in big, mocking letters on that board. He doesn't mean to mock me, but it is my perception that the letters are up on the board looking down on me. If I can get it right, He'll beam.*

"It could be another lesson in patience," I venture.

"Why would you need another lesson in patience?"

"Doesn't everyone, now and then? We both know I'm not the most patient person. It used to be—until I was finally living on my own—that, if I tried something once and failed at it, my default response was to never try it again. When I learned how to dress myself, I failed multiple times. But I gave myself permission to fail—I had patience with myself—*until* I succeeded."

Here comes that smile. *Good. I hate being wrong.*

REPRIEVES

Reprieves are impermanent but wonderful stays.
They avert one execution;
A few eyebrows raise.
But life will have all of us done in
As sure as the Earth on its wobbly axis
Continues a perpetual spin.
It's not a question of how.
Only of when.

18

THE REPRIEVE

TERRENCE MCDONALD IS 16. THE YEAR IS 2006.

Another new school year. Every kid dreads the thought of it, unless you possess a good amount of popularity you can either cling to or hide behind. I'm not popular, so I'm one of the dreaders.

Every kid also has a story. The story other kids know them by, fair or not. *There goes Paula Gordon. Her dad works at Microsoft, and she's the typical rich kid who thinks she's better than everyone else. Colin Hayworth is the quarterback. He's dating Shannon Selby, the head cheerleader, not to mention the biggest bitch in school.* I'm not usually that harsh. I don't judge people; really, I can't afford to judge *anyone*. But, considering her ever-present hatred for me, I'm okay judging Shannon and hating her back.

· · ·

"What's your dream?" she asked me once, about a year and a half ago.

"As if I'd ever tell you," I shot back, defensive.

"No," she said, her face for once soft. "I really want to know."

We were standing in the student store. I was in line to buy a pack of highlighters. She was behind me, waiting to buy a notebook.

I chose to see the goodness in her then, to trust and confide. *Maybe she's changed,* I thought. "I've got two dreams."

"What are they?"

"I want to be a father. I want to raise a child who will know how much they were wanted, and that the label of "*normal*" means little. Differences should be celebrated."

"That's beautiful," she said. "And dream number two?"

"I've wanted to be a writer since I was six years old. I love creating worlds where my characters can play. I love the feeling I get when my stories can make people think."

Shannon was still a moment before she revealed her true self and said, "Those… are the stupidest dreams I have ever heard."

I was caught off guard. "What? I thought you said you thought my dream was beau—"

"I was lying." She chortled. "You want the truth? Here's the truth. Who's gonna want to read your stories? Who reads books anymore, anyway? And… you raising a child? Come on! You really think a girl would *choose* you? You think she'd pick you over a normal guy?"

"I don't know. I thought maybe…"

"Truth is, there's no way that would happen. No way in hell. You're defective, Terry. And you'll always be defective."

I got to the front of the line, paid for my highlighters, and heard Shannon—in her friendly-cheerleader voice—say hi to the girl at the register. As if she hadn't just taken an anvil to my wishes. I walked out of the store slower than my usual slowness, my head down, wondering if the world was cruel enough to permit Shannon's assessment to be correct.

THE REVIEW

God is Shannon Selby. We're in that student store line, and I've got my highlighters in hand. God has Shannon's notebook in His grasp.

"That day shook me," I admit.

"You thought Shannon could be right."

"I didn't want *her* to be right. But I thought it was likely."

TERRENCE MCDONALD IS 16. THE YEAR IS 2006.

The scene resumes, and I am brought back to the thoughts running through my sixteen-year-old mind. How Shannon Selby is a bitch. How I can't play football like Colin Hayworth can (But, boy, would I love to! If only I could have an hour in the body of an athlete, just to know what it feels like not to feel like me). And how, as part of her "Constantly-Giving-Terry-Crap" initiative, the latest scheme in her ceaseless attempts to make me feel small, physically and emotionally, Shannon Selby has taken it upon herself to remind me on a regular basis how she doesn't think I belong here.

"Terrence, are you riding the short bus again this year?" She elongates the word *short,* along with the last two words. She either thinks I'm deaf or stupid, maybe both, and she has given me crap since kindergarten.

She's taller than me by five inches. She stands too close to me so as to accentuate this advantage. Intimidated, I answer with a simple, "No." The bus—*the regular bus*—comes to my house and picks me up every morning. As it comes for everyone else. It just so happens that my bus stop is at the end of my driveway.

I must look like a deer caught in headlights. The look makes Shannon Selby smile a tiny, not-so-nice smile.

"Hey, babe! Let's get outa here!"

Shannon turns, and there's Colin Hayworth at her right shoulder. She flashes him a bigger smile, one with a different meaning. This one says, *I love it when you call me babe, babe.*

"Aren't we going off-campus to get a pizza, Shan?" he asks. "I already called in our order, and I told the guys it was a pizza day!"

"Oh, right." She turns from me without glancing back, and they are gone.

I've been saved further embarrassment by a hungry jock. Colin does write the occasional football-based story for the school newspaper. He has to have seen me in there. I'm the features editor. Maybe he suspects his girlfriend isn't all that nice to people who aren't him, and he wanted to cut me a break.

No. I'm betting he's just hungry for pizza. Far more likely.

I eat my lunch at a sparsely populated table sprinkled with the kids who haven't hooked on with any clique and probably won't, and so they eat by themselves. I glance to my right fifteen minutes in and see Colin Hayworth and Shannon Selby at the "popular" table. They're sharing a pizza (the one they brought back onto campus, a clear rules violation, but no one will cite Colin Hayworth) with Colin's teammates, his offensive line. *Those guys can eat!*

I've got math with Mr. Ryan coming up next. What does that mean to me? It means I'll sit here at this empty table as long as I can before I get up, toss my garbage, and slowly meander down to his room. Not only do I hate math, but this is geometry. It's not even really math. It's shapes.

When the bell rings—the one signaling five minutes until the next class—Colin and his buddies toss the box that used to contain the pie they destroyed, and I do *finally* leave the cafeteria. I take my time traveling through the halls. Kids like to stop and talk to their friends about nothing, and they won't move aside for anyone. The fact is, though, no teacher will ever mark me tardy. The halls are empty by the time I reach Mr. Ryan's door.

Stepping through it, I am greeted by little more than the sound of chalk on blackboard. Ryan's up there, talking parabolas and parallelograms. He probably figures I had a tough time getting here. He has no idea I took the opportunity to be extra late on purpose.

I can't write by hand. Nothing but my first name. As far as schoolwork during the actual school day goes, I have peer assistants in every class. These are students who sit with me, who write for me, and who are graded on the level of help they provide.

My peer assistant in Mr. Ryan's class is Becky.

Becky Holton is the captain of our school's debate team. Everyone who knows her is convinced she'll be a lawyer one day. She is also beautiful. The fact that I get to be in the same room with her for an hour takes this fake shapey math from terrible to close enough to tolerable that I'm willing to suffer through it.

"So what are you doing tonight?" I ask Becky, in a lull when we're supposed to be working, but both of us are putting it off for a few minutes. I like making conversation with Becky. It makes me feel… is relevant the right word?

"I'll be here after school," she answers, "practicing for the Lincoln-Douglas debate on Wednesday. Then I've got a ton of homework."

Five weeks in, the amount of homework *is* beginning to build. And almost all the classes Becky takes are A.P. classes. This period with me is her only break.

"What about you?" she asks. "What are you up to?"

"My dad and my mom went out of town this morning, Dad for work, and my mom went with him as a kind of mini-vacation, so my Grandpa Jack is staying with us for the week."

"That must be fun."

"It is. Grandpa cooks dinner every night and breakfast every morning. My dad would never have the time to do that."

"I think you told me about your Grandpa. Is he the person who had cancer?"

She remembers! I missed a day of school to be at the hospital for his surgery, and she remembers.

"Yes."

"He's okay now, I hope?"

"He's fine. Thanks for asking." I smile. She returns it.

Nearby, I hear a sudden throat-clearing. Ryan's way of telling Becky and me to get on with the task at hand.

My head is swimming in cosigns and tangents and who-gives-a-damns when we finish. I can't get out of there fast enough at the end of the period. But getting out of there also means saying good-bye to Becky, and I don't really want to do that.

"Have a good time with your grandpa," she says as we're parting ways in the hall.

"I will. Good luck in your debate." I'll see her before the debate, but a person can never have too much luck.

"Thanks." She waves, and I watch her walk away until she's swallowed up in a crowd of our peers.

.   .   .

As I push through the front door that afternoon, the house smells different. Different than it would if it were just Chloe, my father, and me. It smells more inviting; an aroma that makes you grateful for the day at its end, even if the day was a grind.

Moving down the hall toward the kitchen, I can see him. He stands at our stove, stirring something in a pot.

"Hey, Jack."

"Hey, kid. How was school? Did you learn anything?" He doesn't look up from the stove.

"Not really."

"Meet any cute girls?" Now he looks up. Winks.

I shake my head. "Not really."

There's Becky, but telling him about her would only bring more questions, for which I could not provide good enough answers.

"What are they sending you to school for, if you didn't learn anything and you can't find a good girl to pass the time with?"

"To keep me out of your hair," I joke.

He chuckles.

"What did you do today?" I ask.

"I had a doctor's appointment." He has so many of those these days. "Then Judith and I went shopping at Value Village."

Jack often talks about Judith nowadays, but she isn't the woman to whom he was married for over twenty-five years, with whom he had Chloe. Judith is a friend he passes the time with now, and she's always been nice to me on the few occasions we've seen each other.

Let's be clear. As for their trip to the second-hand store, Judith went shopping. He sat in the car doing his crossword puzzle and waited for her.

"So what did the doctors say?" If he mentioned her, Judith must be in the house somewhere. That's just the way Jack operates. And that means she's here doing Jack a bit of a favor. *No wonder I can hear a vacuum cleaner—its motor muffled but distinct—somewhere downstairs.* If Judith made any monumental purchases, I'm sure she'll tell me about them as soon as she's finished giving the bottom floor of the house a good cleaning. Maybe she'll wait until dinner. Jack's appointment, and any news that might have come out of it, is what matters to me at this moment.

"He said, considering the surgery was only a month ago, he thinks I'm doing 'remarkably well.'" To emphasize the last two words having been exactly as the doctor spoke them, Jack's index fingers act as stand-in quotation marks.

·   ·   ·

A month ago, school was only a week old, and yet here I was taking the day off. I wasn't sick, and I didn't want to miss the day. I had a Spanish II quiz whose incompletion was gnawing at me throughout school hours, even though I'd discussed and cleared it with my teacher.

"Let's go, hon," Dad said as he woke me early that morning. "Today's Jack's big day." Later, as he drove Chloe and me to the hospital, he added, "Jack has been there for us, whenever we've needed him, ever since we've known each other. Now it's our turn to be there for him." Turning to me, he asked, "Did you remember to bring a book? We might be waiting a while. The surgery's supposed to take four hours or so."

I nodded. A Hemingway novel—*For Whom The Bell Tolls*, an ominous title, if you asked me—sat at the bottom of my otherwise empty backpack. Textbooks and other school supplies had been left at home.

Would the surgery to remove Jack's cancerous lung end in success? All of us waiting to hear news hoped so, and we tried to remain upbeat, but it was difficult.

Over those three silent hours when nobody working at the hospital would—or probably could—tell us anything, Jack and his doctors remained behind closed doors. As the day's tension encroached on my personal space (now inflated into a bubble of uncertainty) and on my thoughts, on everything that made me who I was, I found myself unable to focus on reading anymore. I put my book down and sat staring at nothing. Conversations, if they happened at all, were terse.

· · ·

"I'm gonna go to the bathroom real quick," Dad told me. "You want me to bring you back a soda?"

"Sure."

"Hey, Mom?" I said.

She looked up.

"What did the hospital do with Jack's teeth?"

"I've got them with me," she answered. That's when I realized she had to have seen her father after our arrival at the hospital but before the procedure began. *It must have been a quick meeting.* "I don't want them to get lost like last time." Last time was ten years ago. Mom has told me the story of that day, when he was hospitalized for what turned out to be a severe case of pneumonia, and the hospital managed to "lose" his "chompers."

I had thought the topic of his teeth might lighten the mood a little. Bring a smile to her face. I mean, come on; lost dentures are funny, in retrospect. They were eventually found, after all. But her pained expression remained.

I need to get some fresh air. This place isn't meant for the relatively healthy.

But how could I get some fresh air when the simple act of walking ten feet in either direction in an unfamiliar place like this raises my blood pressure? It raises my blood pressure because I could get lost, and if I do I might not be able to find my way back; especially if the stroll involves any kind of twisting, turning, or otherwise disorienting movements, as it invariably will.

"Do you need to take a walk?" This was one of Chloe's cousins. She's *my* cousin, too. That's the way our family sees it.

I hadn't seen her in five years, at least. She'd come with her husband and their four kids. One per year, almost. "If you need to get out of here for a bit, I'll come with you. I need a break, too."

Good, I thought. *If she comes with me, then navigation won't be my responsibility.*

I said nothing in reply. My only response was to take her outstretched hand. She helped me to my feet. I'd been sitting for so long that my legs were unsteady, and a sharp bolt of pain shot down my right side.

There was a Starbucks across the street. (There's *always* a Starbucks across the street.) We found a table, and she settled in across from me, drinking her venté soy who's-a-what's-it. I tried some kind of caramel-infused apple-cidery concoction that made my body think it was Christmas. It was good. All I needed to complete the simulation: a whip-creamed slice of apple pie.

"How are you feeling?" asked my cousin.

I looked up into her eyes, to try and determine if she wanted an answer that was something real or something that would make us both feel momentarily better about things. I decided she was looking for real. "I'm scared."

"So am I," she admitted.

"And I don't feel like I have the *right* to be scared. I can't believe I've only known Jack five years. Forget the right to be scared. Do I even have a right to be *here?* Everyone else, besides my dad, has known him so much longer."

"Of course you have a right to be here. Jack would be *crushed* if you weren't here."

"He would?"

"Sure he would."

"It's just, he's been such a big part of my life… our lives, and…"

"I know."

"…Losing him would be…"

"I know," my cousin said. "Well, we're not gonna lose him. We can't think like that."

"Gotta stay positive," I agreed.

Day was inching into night as we returned. Just in time to see a relieved doctor approach our little encampment. With his left hand, he wiped away a thin band of sweat lingering on his forehead, and with his right he shook our hands. Chloe's first. She looked like she might keel over from the stress of the day. Then my dad, trying to be strong because, sometime long ago, that's what his own father told him to do in times like these. Then my cousin with all the kids. She gave a glance my way, winked. Then me. Was the doctor trying to shake our hands in chronological order based on when he guessed we'd joined Jack's extended family? If so, he had guessed wrong, but for someone who didn't know us… it was a good try. When he got to me, the doctor was offering the kind of worn-out smile that said, *By the skin of our teeth, kiddo. We made it out of there by the skin of our teeth.*

Aloud, he said nothing except: "We did it."

Reprieve granted.

Each of us went back to see Jack in his room. We took turns, so as not to overwhelm him. When Dad's turn came up, he took me with him.

"Hey, kid," Jack said, looking my way.

"Hey, Jack."

"I guess the Big Guy didn't want me yet, huh?"

"I guess not. I'm glad you get to stay here awhile."

"So am I, kid." There was none of his trademark sarcasm. Only truth.

·   ·   ·

That successful surgery is what allows him to be *here* now, cancer-free and asking me inane questions about girls. Questions to which I wouldn't normally respond. I'd get upset if anyone else asked them, because the answer, in some fashion, will always be the same. *I have palsy, don't I? And eyes that suck. Who's gonna want to deal with all that?* But he gets a free pass.

That surgery also led to the perfectly cooked pork chop on my plate tonight, and to hearing him sing in the kitchen as he pan-seared it, and being glad I was hearing him sing. "Someone's in the kitchen with Dinah. Someone's in the kitchen, I know-oh-oh-oh." *This is what I wanted. A beat of time in which the normal I once knew seems easily achieved again.*

.   .   .

That feeling of normal stays with me, attaches itself to a grateful host. A week after Jack's celebratory chop, I am led to ask Shannon Selby, with as much force as I can muster, what exactly her problem is. Jack's survival has brought something more than normalcy; it has revealed a measure of courage I hadn't known was mine to access.

"I'm a good person," I tell Shannon, after asking the question but before she can respond. "No one's perfect, but I think, if you got to know me, you'd like me. You've never even given me a *chance.* I just don't understand."

We stand near our school's flagpole at the open of a Monday. I made sure Shannon was alone before approaching her. No Colin Hayworth in sight. This doesn't concern him, even if he's her boyfriend… for now. Everyone besides Shannon knows Colin *really* likes Katherine Haber, her second in command on the cheer squad, and he will eventually break her heart. (*He chose to do it five days before prom, if I'm remembering it right.*)

Shannon takes a long time before answering. "I'm so sorry for the way I've treated you," she says finally.

Wow. I hadn't expected that. Another instance of Jack working his magic in my life. What was his magic? Simple. The mere act of *being* in my life.

"My brother has palsy," Shannon explains. "Only his… his is a lot worse than yours." She's crying instant, silent tears. "He can't walk. He can't even talk. When I ask him a question, I have to wait for him to answer using this computer that's attached to his wheelchair. I've never heard his real voice. My mom says he has one, she heard it a long time ago, but he refuses to use it anymore.

"None of this is a good reason for the way I've acted toward you. And this isn't the time for excuses. I do hope you can forgive me, though. I'm a better person than you probably think I am."

"I forgive you." Her story makes perfect sense now.

"Are you sure?"

In lieu of saying yes, I ask her, "Shannon, what good would it do me to resent you? Now that I understand, the idea of resenting you is kind of pointless. I only wish you'd told me all of this years ago."

"I should have," she admits.

As I'm turning to head into school—first period English, to be exact—thinking our conversation over, Shannon puts her hand on my shoulder.

Another girl is coming toward us. A new girl I vaguely recognize. She's on the cheer squad with Shannon as of about a week ago. I saw her cheering in the school's most recent assembly with the rest of the team as well as walking the halls when we change classes. Her family relocated from somewhere back east.

"Hi, Shan," the girl calls.

Shannon waves her over, and when the girl is close enough, she introduces us. I hadn't expected the introduction, but I appreciate it. I'm not the kind of guy who readily approaches girls, as their first question is always along the lines of: *Why do you walk like that?* Words that hurt me whenever I hear them, no matter how many times I hear them. There's no getting used to that type of thing.

"Beth, this is my friend Terrence."

Her *friend*.

"Terrence McDonald, this is Beth Hawkins."

"Hi." Beth blushes. I was going to shake her hand, but Beth goes right for a hug. I accept it.

"Do you think you could walk Beth to class, Terrence? She's still pretty new here, and the layout of this place is kind of confusing."

I had to agree with Shannon. After two years, there were still areas of the school *I* had not yet ventured into (they may as well have been underground), and I'm sure this was true of many of my peers. Freshmen matriculated at the junior high down the street, so they weren't here to get lost. Sophomores stayed in the school's A wing, which was in its own small building. They had it easy. Juniors—Shannon, Beth, and me, to name three—were permanent inhabitants of the B wing, but to get there you needed to take a circuitous route through the southern end of the school's second building, the one that housed the B, C, *and* D wings. This meant you had no choice but to pass by the library, then the seniors (Colin Hayworth, etc.) in C, so eager for June they were barely trying anymore, and then the administrators in D. The Dreaded D Wing is where they spend their days dreaming up tests that will make the good kids throw up with nerves and will assist in expelling the bad ones. You must see all of this before reaching your destination. That might seem like a simple layout, but try finding the drama club among all that inner-school geography, or the tiny closet-classroom that housed "leadership", or the room that had the word "ART" written across a tiny piece of paper taped to its door. Basically, if you *haven't* gotten turned around and missed the first part of a teacher's lesson, you have yet to truly become part of the school.

I look to Beth as if to say, Do you really want me to walk you? I'm sure you could find your way without my help.

Her face—lit up with unspoken thanks—gives me all the confirmation I need.

She ends up walking *me* to class, if you want to get technical about it. We walk arm-in-arm, and I lean on her just a little, for better balance, which she says she doesn't mind, while she tells me what brought her family to the area.

"My dad lost his job, and he found a new one up here. We don't know anyone in Seattle besides my weird uncle Chet, my mom's brother, and we *wish* we didn't know him. But he's a relator, and he found us our house with very little notice. If I could have my way, I'd take the first flight I could get right back to Boston."

Somewhere back east. I was right.

When I told Jack what happened with Shannon, leaving out the Beth Hawkins situation for now—because who knows if that will end up being anything significant?—and how he had a hand in it, imparting to me the strength I'd used to stand up to Shannon, he said, "Glad I could help, kid."

I'm glad he could, too, and I thank God for reprieves like the one Jack was granted. For all the memories we'll make yet, memories he would have missed. Jack stands at my high school graduation and applauds. He gets to pass on his wisdom to another generation. We take a family vacation to Peru and walk the ruins at Machu Picchu. A trip he books as a birthday present for his daughter, the world traveler, who travels mostly in her dreams. (Chloe does take frequent jaunts into Canada, but considering where we live, that doesn't count, she says.)

The highlight of my eighteenth birthday party (calling it a party is a bit of an overstatement; let's term it a *gathering)* is the cake Jack bakes from scratch because that's the gift I ask him for. I thank God for allowing us to retain his magic a little while longer.

· · ·

Beth's the first girl ever to ask me if I want to meet her parents. I know the correct answer is *yes.* By now, it's been two months, we know we're dating, and everyone at school knows we're dating, even if some aren't quite sure why Beth would choose to date me. But her parents know nothing of our coupling.

"I'm nervous," I admit on the ride to dinner. We'll be eating in a steakhouse her father chose. "Your dad sounds like a hard-ass."

She's told me so much about the man. Maybe too much. He's a carpenter who gets work when he can, and he's finally found a somewhat stable job (he hopes). He values hard work and assesses such work by informally measuring the sweat and calluses it produces.

"He's got a tough exterior. But when you get down to it, he's a teddy bear. He'll love you, Terry."

He doesn't. He takes one look at me, registers my wobbly gait, and makes a decision. *Not this one. He's not for my Beth.*

Her mother likes me. She likes that I'm polite and courteous. I say please and thank you. I treat Beth with respect—something Grandpa Jack has always told me is crucial: "Listen to her opinions. Respect her thoughts, *especially* if they differ from yours. You might learn something. Spend time in the stores where she enjoys shopping. Find a girl who gets you, who can accept your interests and hobbies. And do everything you can to show her that her interests are important to you. That will all go a long way toward lasting happiness." But none of that matters. Her father doesn't subscribe to Jack's school of thought, and he has made his wordless decree.

Three months after the decree, her father calls me into his study—a small room made even smaller by its two towering bookshelves. There's barely enough room to walk between them.

He helps me navigate the narrow aisle, letting me lean on him much as I've leaned on his daughter walking the hallways at school. *That's nice of him.* Then we sit across from each other, looking one another square in the eye. His stare is unnerving, and I drop my gaze.

"Terrence, what are your future prospects?"

"Excuse me?"

"Your future prospects. Any idea what you'll do for money in the future, for example? My daughter seems quite taken with you, son, and I can't quite figure out why."

I'm a good person who cares about her. Did you ever consider that? Or is the palsy all you can see?

"Chances are Bethy won't know you in a year. But, just in case you *are* still around, I think it's fair of me to ask what you plan to do with your life."

I'm still in high school. None of my peers know what they'll do with their lives. If they were here, would they be getting grilled like this? At least I have a dream, and I'm willing to go after it.

"Sir, I'm not sure what I can tell you that will make you feel *good* about your daughter dating me." This is me, being bold. "All I can do is be honest. I plan to be a writer. Will that work out? I don't know. If it doesn't, then I'm not sure what I will do with my life. Hopefully something meaningful."

Looking thoroughly unimpressed, he says, "Should this relationship move forward" (which it won't, he doesn't bother to reiterate), "you would need to support my daughter. Do you feel you could do that?"

You may not believe in me, I think. *But—if it were my responsibility—yes, I believe I could do it.*

"Yes," I reply, a terse answer without any of the verbosity or bite of the comeback in my head.

THE REVIEW

"Neither of us had a clue then," I say, speaking to God now, in our chairs once again, this time in Beth's father's study, "that I'd get an opportunity to prove myself to Beth and her skeptical father."

"How do you think that opportunity went?"

"I think it was too short, and I always regretted the quick end Beth and I had."

Answer My question, please.

God has assumed the features of Beth's father, so the interruption is completely in character

"It didn't go well," I tell Him. "You—her father—wanted me out of her life, and while he couldn't quite achieve this, thanks to Megan, he got what he must have thought was the next best thing. I never forgave him for breaking up my family."

UNTRAINED

What was once frivolous fun,
Cavorting, care-free,
In summer's friendly sun,
Transforms
in a minute.
The minute you hear,
With a touch of
Deer-in-the-headlights fear—
The gravity of
Your new role,
Suddenly responsible
For an untrained soul.

19

BIRTH, PART I

Beth cries. Harder than I've ever seen her cry. Harder than I've ever seen *anyone* cry. We're on my porch, preparing to say, *Goodnight. Tonight was wonderful. I'll call you tomorrow.* All the typical end-of-date phrases content people say. But her tears mean the usual procedure will not be followed tonight.

I pull her close. "Beth, what is it? What's wrong?"

She pauses before answering, fights back another round of tears, then delivers the life-changer. "I'm pregnant."

My cheeks take on a flush, a sudden, burning redness. All of my extremities, in contrast, are frozen.

"Oh, shit. Your dad'll kill me." There will at least be a severe maiming. Maybe I'll lose my cock. Moored since its virgin voyage.

"I know."

I fold her into a hug, and she clings to me tight.

"I'm sorry," she says.

"It's not your fault. We both did our part."

. . .

I'm not present for Megan's birth. I am not *permitted* to be present. Beth's father makes this clear as soon as she goes into labor. I am welcome—expected may be a better word-—to take up a spot in the waiting room, where I can serve as a glorified cheerleader—unseen by those for whom I'll root in silence—but the birth will be "handled" with the help of Beth's immediate family and the doctors and nurses on call.

"But-" I attempt to throw in my two cents.

"You've done enough," her father says, scowling.

"I just want to be there for—"

"You've done *enough*! What if this child comes out like you, for Christ's sake?" *Like me?* "What if it has to walk with a limp its whole life… or deal with something much worse? What if it *can't* walk at all?"

I don't appreciate the fact that he's referring to *my* child as *it*. "That wouldn't happen," I say. "Cerebral palsy isn't hereedit—"

Before I can finish my explanation's final and most important word, he turns and enters the delivery room, preparing to welcome my daughter, his grandchild. Dejected and hurt, I wait where I've been told to wait. It is all I can do.

THE REVIEW

God is Beth's father again, and we're in that same waiting room. This time, I'm not the one who gave a silent PAUSE command, placing the review on hold. This time, it came from Him.

I'm slumped in my seat as God, towering over me, asks, "Why didn't you fight Beth's father?"

"Fight him? Why would I fight *anyone*? I'm not the type of guy who wins fights, so why invite them?"

"Not physical fights, no. You would never win a physical fight."

"Never, huh? Thanks for that."

"What I meant was—"

"I know what You meant. And I knew at an early age not to get into a fight like that. It wouldn't end well for me."

"But this is different," He argues. "You wouldn't have been engaging in a *physical* fight. This was a fight for something you deserved, something to which you were *entitled*; to witness the birth of your child, one of the greatest moments life can provide, and you just… you *gave* up on it. Why?"

"I… I guess I did. I didn't realize that's what I *was* doing at the time." I rise to stand at His height. It might be too late to stand up to Beth's father, but it's not too late to show God I do possess passion, *fight*. "I did have a tendency to give up on myself, didn't I? To either lose sight of or give up on my goals too soon. I didn't think I could reach them without help, and I hated the idea of asking for help. It was like admitting my deficits. Part of me was certain I'd turn out to be a deficient father, too. I think I believed what Beth's father said, as mad as it made me—that I'd done enough."

.　　　　　.　　　　　.

Hospitals frighten me. You're either venturing into a hospital for yourself, which can be eerie, breathtaking—and not in the way you *want* your breath taken—and more spine-chilling than any horror flick, or you're visiting at the behest of someone else. Someone you know and care about. Someone whose life force, slow but sure, is draining from their body, worn out and ravaged by age, malady, mind-loss. The latter is the case for the elderly African-American man seated next to me in the hospital's crowded cafeteria. Our two tables have been pushed together, likely the doing of a large family who left without separating them.

The old guy glances in my direction, tries to be subtle about it. I see this glance out of the corner of my eye, on the fringe of my lacking peripheral vision, but pay him little mind. The day's unspent anger has bubbled up and settled across my face.

He removes his glasses and inquires, "What brings you here, son? You look awful young for a place like this."

I'm young for lots of places. Like the bar down the street a few blocks, a fine destination, if not for their policy of constant carding and throwing you out on your ass when you don't turn out to be a forty-five-year-old Mexican man named Sergio. My fake-I.D.-making contacts are not reliable.

I decide to level with the old guy and turn my chair to face him more fully. "The birth of my daughter," I say.

He is taken aback for a moment but recovers quickly. *Admirable.*

"Ah, then this is a special day! I'm glad for you. I remember when my wife and I had our first. Boy, was I a nervous wreck that night. Back then, they wouldn't let the fathers into the room. I paced for hours until the doctor came out and told me not to worry." He pauses. "Hey, why aren't you in the delivery room? They let us guys in there these days, you know?"

I answer matter-of-factly. "Not me. It was her father's decision, and, to be honest, I don't blame him."

I'm not being honest. Of course I blame him.

The old man avoids mentioning my lie. Makes it into a secret between two souls headed on opposite paths in opposite directions who came together for this one day, a few minutes, really, a fleeting cosmic flash.

Any moment now, my unborn daughter will go from being an idea, a concept, a hypothetical, to a child whose life force is new and brilliant. She, like her grandmother, will be my salvation. I can't pinpoint how I know this, the salvation bit, but I do. I know it deep down in my soul.

I learn, through conversation that works to keep both our minds occupied, that the old man, whose name is Charlie, has a wife named Patty. She was his inspiration as they lived a meager existence on his sporadic income; he was often out of work, but not for a lack of job-hunting or skills. She bore two children, a daughter and a son, though neither could be with him to see their mother off, because they were already waiting to welcome her Home.

I want to ask the question anyone would want to ask, but I feel ill equipped to do so. Nonetheless, I give it a try.

"What happened to your children, Charlie?"

A long silence. In this space, I think better of my query, almost rescind it.

"You don't have to tell me if you don't want to. I realize it's none of my business." That's as close as I get.

He sits back in his chair and fingers the three-days' growth of stubble about his chin. You can almost see the wheels in his head turning. *Should I tell this kid what we've been through?*

"A fire," he says at last. "That's what happened. No one, not even the firemen I spoke with, knew exactly how it had started, but there was a fire. Patty and I were out at the theater that night. We had just deemed the children responsible enough to mind themselves while we were gone, and Patty wanted to see a play one of her playwright friends slaved over for years."

He wipes away a small stream of tears.

"We blamed ourselves. How could we not? If we hadn't been out, a tragedy that took two lives and defined two more would have been averted. Part of me still holds to this position. My hope is that, in passing, my Patty can find some peace."

.   .   .

A month has passed. My eyes ringed dark, lack of sleep my life's new normal, I try to stay awake long enough to chat with my new friend. Charlie smiles and sips his coffee. The stuff is black, a tad bitter, but in Charlie's words, "A cup a Joe is a cup a Joe."

"Patty and I, our first was named after her grandmother, Clara. We called our daughter Clare. Maybe because her namesake was the meanest old bitch I ever met, and the woman made a lasagna that was practically inedible, but Patty idolized her." He descends deep into thought, no doubt recalling times long past. "Hey, before I forget," he continues, "thanks for the coffee, son. And the invitation."

I invited him to join me this morning after running across a business card he'd given me—*Charlie Ewell, Entrepreneurial Spirit, Dreamer, & Willing Worker Bee*—and remembering our hospital visit.

"Since Patty's been gone, I haven't gotten out much. A job here or there, but that's about it. Economy's in the crapper."

"I understand. You're always welcome to join me. I either get a ride with whoever I'll be sharing a meal with or, as happened this morning, my Grandpa Jack will drop me off. Sometimes my parents will do it, when Jack's unavailable; and, on rare occasions, I might even take the bus. Either way, this place," I glance around the café in which we talk, "is my customary morning haunt."

"You a writer, son? You sound like one of them famous writer-types."

"I've written some stories. I'm not famous or anything, but I am a writer."

"I'd love to be a writer."

"Oh, yeah?"

"Yeah. To lose myself in words. Forget my troubles by creating, dreaming, scheming. And to see it all published in one of them hardcover deals sellin' for twenty or thirty bucks a pop in a fancy bookstore, with my big mug on the back and my name plastered across the front."

"I'd buy your book, Charlie," I say. I would.

"And I'll buy yours," he says.

THE REVIEW

"I didn't notice it back then," I say. God is Charlie yet again. For the third time? We're in our booth at the café. There's a full breakfast spread in front of us, but I'm not hungry.

"What didn't you notice?"

"How disheveled he looked. His hair wasn't combed. The suit he wore wasn't freshly pressed. I'm not sure he'd bothered to take a shower. I didn't know him well enough then to see just how out of character those things were. He never missed a subsequent breakfast meeting, and he always looked…. Immaculate. *That* was Charlie."

"Yes, it was."

"Should I have noticed his appearance? Did I do something *wrong?*"

"Oh, no, Terry. Noticing that stuff wasn't your job. You were a new father with too much to think about and not enough space in your head with which to do it. You didn't do anything wrong."

"So then why bring me back to our café?"

"That isn't *My* answer to give you," God replies. "All I can say is you need to remember this first breakfast meeting with Charlie. It's extremely important that you keep it in mind as we go on."

I sigh and roll my eyes at Him. *Why can't God just tell me what needs to be told? What's with the delegating? A symptom of an afterlife overrun by bureaucracy, perhaps?* "Okay," I say. "Fine," in a way that indicates His non-answer is *neither okay nor* fine. *What are You not telling me?* I wonder, half-hoping He'll answer with telepathy of His own.

He doesn't.

TERRENCE McDONALD IS 19. THE YEAR IS 2009.

A year and a half later, Charlie and I are enjoying the café's signature pancakes amid a communal signature all our own: conversation. These breakfasts have become a regular part of our lives over the past year.

"You mind if I tell you a little story?" asks the old man.

"Not at all."

He's got yarns aplenty to spin.

Therefore, I'm surprised when the subject of his oratory turns out to be none other than the war on terror. How… not like him. How… *unCharlie*. Charlie is a self-proclaimed pacifist, a man who subscribes to the non-violence and strength in numbers espoused by Dr. King. Why bring up the war on terror, the antithesis of his hero's mission? I interrupt just as his story's underway, to ask him why.

"Actually," he says, "I hate when people call it that. *The war on terror.* It's not a war on terror. Never was. Not even terrorists like terror. What they are trying to do is advance beliefs, misguided though they are. It is a war on—and of—ideals. And how can anyone know for sure when they've *won or lost* a *war* like that? How can they *know* when it's over?"

"I suppose they can't," I allow.

He helps me to cut up the new batch of pancakes that's just arrived at our table—our favorite waitress's appearance temporarily halting his tale—and then I syrup the cakes liberally and take up my first forkful. Charlie takes up his story again.

"A year or so before Patty passed, she and I saw that the house next door had been sold. We were getting new neighbors, and Patty, for one, was overjoyed. She baked cookies and made the acquaintance of the new owner, a middle-aged woman named Wendy."

I sip from a large black mug filled to the brim with orange juice. Sour and pulpy, it's delicious nonetheless, while Charlie goes on.

"Wendy had decided to sell her home in an effort to downsize after her son, Robert, who grew up there, was killed by a roadside bomb in Iraq. 'I just couldn't live there anymore,' she told us. 'In the same place where Bobby took his first steps, spoke his first words. In the same place where I cooked him breakfast every Saturday morning until he moved out at eighteen, and where I watched him get ready for his senior prom. The memories were just too painful.'"

Whereas I was, at first, skeptical of his tale's merit, now Charlie has my undivided attention.

"Over the year following our meeting and prior to Patty's leaving, Wendy—and her husband, Mark—became great friends of ours. So that, when Patty did take ill, they sent her a massive get-well card and made sure everyone in the neighborhood—mostly older folks who knew us well but were too frail themselves to leave home—signed it."

"Sounds like a wonderful lady," I put in.

"She is," Charlie agrees. "Anyway, I was going through Patty's papers—her will and a couple notes she'd left me, detailing where she'd stored certain heirlooms for safekeeping—when I came across this."

He lays down two pieces of white paper, one on top of the other.

"What are those?"

"It's a poem, Terrence. As near as I can tell, I think it's Patty's interpretation of Wendy's story. She took some license and liberties, obviously. In Patty's version, the alter-ego sharing Robert's identity lives, and Wendy's character eventually passes in old age. I think she let the boy live because… because, aside from being a *moderately* happier ending—she did cripple him somewhat—it was a symbolic outcome. Symbolic of the desire Patty felt to see her own children alive again. Our children, whom she could not bring back. She was also, however, vehemently opposed to the war in Iraq due to the damage she felt it had the potential to inflict upon the troops and those who loved them, and she made no secret of her position, made sure it came through. 'There is a fight to be had, Charles,' she said to me. 'One we've failed to fully undertake thus far. That fight is in Afghanistan. It's the only proper response to 9/11.' This is all a long-winded way of getting to a question, Terrence. I wondered if you'd have a look at what Patty wrote? After all, you are a writer."

"So are you," I remind him.

He takes in a gulp of air, exhales with a pained sigh. "Yes. And I've read it. But I'm afraid my opinion might be a tad bit biased. I love her, Terry. I will always love her. I can't give her work a fair judgment. Romance would impede it."

I give a small grin, respecting his admission. Then I inspect the text.

A FORGOTTEN VET

My countenance waivers when I glance up and see
A war-weary soldier,
Legs severed at his knees.
He wheels along,
In his new conveyance clumsy,
And chills wash over me like a winter breeze.

I stare as he nears, and
Shame meets with fears.
The sacrifice he's made
I could never forsake.
And his image I'll never be able to shake.

A broken man full of shattered hopes,
A sad day it will be
When he takes up his post
Not at a base or on a patrol
But in his own personal hell—
A neighborhood Y—
On a bedroll.

He'll meander through life,
A forgotten vet,
And die without an obit,
And always regret
The September evening he spent,
Awake 'till past ten,
Asking, "What the hell just happened?"
In the arms of a friend.

He hoped for an answer that shined with some sense.
Hope was a minor salve,
But nevertheless…
No answer came.

That night he was stone-faced,
Yet troubled,
Alarmed.
The greatest of nations was so blatantly harmed.

The soldier within him craved the right fight,
To be part of a necessary war,
Its combatants knowing
Precisely what they were on the battlefields for.
And he was.

But as he went on in unending tours,
The necessary war became wars.

Wars over oil and religious decrees,
Wars waged for clerics and a cowboy who'd seen
Too many pictures portraying war with a gleam.

One morning,
As he rode with the men—
Carver and Connor and the newest kid, Ben—
He became what he was when I saw him again;
A shell of the boy I'd sent away with "Just win.
"Win and they'll let you come back,
Psyche unmarred and intact."

He never again called me Mom, and
Lost all memory of his senior prom.
For his high-school sweetheart—
Who had agreed to spend her life as his wife—
He no longer longed.

The man she was to marry wasn't in there anymore.
I was worried for her safety,
Unforeseen horrors.
On my advice, she escaped his hazardous wrath.
There was for her another path,
And she travels it now.

When I died, he did not bare the pall.
He didn't know of my passing at all.
The decision not to inform him was a psychiatrist's call.

Impressed, I hand the pages back. "Your wife was quite talented."
Charlie doesn't reply but begins tearing up.
"What's wrong?" I probe.
"She was a gifted poet, you say?"
"Very much so, in my mind. Why are you bothered by that?"

"I never knew," he chokes out. "More than thirty-five years together, and I never knew."

.   .   .

The day is dreary. The kind of frigid capable of surprising an unsuspecting, coatless individual. Capable of making them wonder, *Is it gonna snow tonight?*

"A day like this... you almost *need* a good pancake and egg breakfast," says Charlie, patting his stomach as he pushes his empty plate away. "Warms a man right up."

"Yeah, I suppose." I can tell Charlie's headed into another one of his stories. Odd as this one's commencement sounds, I'm all ears.

"Did I ever tell you how Patty and I met, Terrence?"

"Nope." *Not 'til now,* I think.

"Well, she was a waitress. At a place sorta like this one. It was called Buck's Pancakes & Waffles, and it was run by an old man—he must have been about the age I am now—named Buck Hanson. He loved to cook, and he was very particular about his menu. Everything on it, he would whip up without complaint. But, if anyone ever asked for something different... Buck wouldn't hear of it. He'd send a waitress out to the offending patron. She would restate the menu in full... a menu that was always clearly visible. And then she would *re-take* the order."

I work on my breakfast of eggs, bacon, and a short stack of syruped blueberry pancakes, all the while listening intently.

"One morning," the tale continues, "on a day I didn't need a thermometer to let me know it was *freezing,* I came into Buck's, found a table—customers were expected to seat themselves—and took a look at the menu. Deciding I didn't want waffles or pancakes that morning, I settled on steak and eggs. While it was well within Buck's power to fix the meal, the exact combination I'd called for was not on the menu. So what do you think ol' Buck did?"

I take an educated stab.

"Did he send Patty over to re-take your order?"

"You got it. He surely did. And it was love at first sight. Well, maybe not for Patty, because I musta looked darned near disheveled. But me, I knew right then I would marry the beautiful girl with eyes the color of cocoa."

"How did you know, Charlie?" One relationship already washed aground in a sinking ship's wake, I am jaded. "How can you be sure you knew? It's easy to *claim* something like that *after* the fact, life having been lived, having turned out the way it did."

"It might have been in the way Patty winked at me when she made her way over to my table. Or in the way she read the menu—sarcastic, with a touch of how-stupid-is-this-arbitrary-rule-I-have-to-follow. Or in the way she smiled once we'd gotten to talking, and I told her I liked jazz, too. And the records coming out of Motown. Whatever it was, I left Buck's that day with her number scribbled on a napkin, and I never looked back."

SEARCHING THE HALL

I glance about
This room of plenty
To find
That needle-in-the-haystack century;
The 21st,
As the Christians count,
When we humans at last
Consume knowledge vast,
As though from an unending fount;
Without the freshest news,
We are not quite alive.
And anyone who has the drive
Can transform themselves
Into an author
In no time.

20
CHARLIE'S BOOK

TERRENCE MCDONALD IS 22. THE YEAR IS 2012.

On what's turned out to be an unseasonably cool morning, I'm at my laptop composing a short story, and I glance up from the work just as Charlie walks into the café. He's wearing a suit-coat, his shoulders back, head held high. A principled man who's come through on a promise to himself, he has hold of a book.

"Will you look at that!" he says, his eyes gleaming. He sets the book—his book—down in the middle of the table. "None of it would have happened if I hadn't met you, Terrence. Believe me, I know that."

This explains his dedicating the tome to me. Well, to me and, first and foremost, to his dearly departed Patty and "the kids."

Even so, I decide to act as though I am unaware of the role he believes I've played.

"Really?" I say.

"You inspired me, kid. Showed this old dog that, while he may not be in his prime anymore—he surely is not—he's still got some time left and a reason for being here. That reason turned out to be writing."

"I guess now I gotta make good on my promise to buy one." As he sits, I push forward the pastries I ordered for us. "Take your pick."

"You don't have to buy anything, Terry," Charlie assures me. "Are you kidding? I brought you a copy. Signed it, too."

I pick up the book. it *is* signed.

To my friend and writing buddy, Terrence McDonald. Father to Megan and friend to the under-appreciated.

From Charlie Ewell, Loving husband to Patty, father to Clare and Jessie, & first-time author.

I fixate on one particular portion of his note.

Friend to the under-appreciated.

Does he mean himself? Is that how life is going to be at his age? I'll feel under-appreciated, maybe even forgotten?

I don't mention the inscription. Take it in, accept it, move on. That's the way to handle it. Don't call attention to it, my dad would say, and that thought is with me now. *You might embarrass him.*

"What's it about?"

"I never told you?" He never did, but that's because-

"I never asked."

"It's about my childhood, it's about Patty, and it's about *our* meetings here." By now, we've met twice a week for going on two years. Breakfast Thursdays and brunch Sundays, the weekend get-togethers after his "church-going." And that's only counting morning visits, while not factoring in the few times we've met at night. They were rare, but when I needed a good meal, or a story, or an ear for *my* stories, or he needed the same from me, we were there for each other.

"Well, I'm honored to receive for free what I am certain will be a runaway best-seller." I pick up an apple fritter and take a bite.

"Don't get carried away now," Charlie cautions. "I self-published it. I'll be happy if the dang thing gets read at all."

THE REVIEW

"Why didn't I thank Charlie for dedicating his book to me?"

"I don't know," God says. But He *does* know. This is something He expects me to figure out on my own.

"I didn't want to embarrass Charlie," I say.

"That's your father talking, Terry. The question was why didn't *you* thank Charlie for the dedication? The answer has nothing to do with your dad."

God is Patty this time—*that's a change, but He must feel that she is the right person for this scene*—and we remain in the café. Yet suddenly I'm the kid who doesn't—can't—dress himself until he's twelve. Impotent in my bedroom. The boy who wears braces on my feet until he's a teenager and can finally convince his dad and the doctors alike he doesn't need them anymore. The guy who's never fixed himself a sandwich. My dad always says, "Just let me do it, Terrence. It'll be easier if I do it."

I'm so lucky to have met Chloe. Without her, I might never have learned to make a single meal. She taught me macaroni and cheese from a box, popcorn, both microwave and on the stove with a popper, the ever-elusive sandwich (hers was filled with pastrami and cheddar cheese), a few pasta dishes, including spaghetti. She taught me how to scramble an egg on a gray Saturday morning when I assured her I couldn't scramble an egg, no matter how long she spent trying to teach me. She was wasting her time. "Not true, Terrence. It's not hard to scramble an egg. I'll show you how to do it, then you can scramble one yourself. How does that sound?" It sounded okay. Chloe's egg got scrambled, as did mine, and then I gave my egg salt and pepper—as Chloe suggested—for added flavor.

Another thing I can't seem to do: I can't bring myself to talk to girls, lest they look down at my legs, glance back up at me—sadness their only currency—and tell me I'm really nice, but…

That day in the café with Charlie, my lessons with Chloe, my failed attempts to converse with the fairer sex: they seem unrelated. But, when I accept that they might be connected, I understand at once what the connection is.

"I didn't thank Charlie for the dedication… because I didn't think I deserved it."

OUR PATHS

Most warnings won't carry wrath.
Warnings,
If from a useful batch,
Are a balm.
Show us where our paths
Are diverging or
Going amiss.

The best warnings assist
In restoring calm.
Point out where our errors offer us lessons—
If we possess
A willingness to listen for them,
And, in their validity, trust
Will make worthy souls robust.

21
THE WARNING

"I wish Terry were here," I say.

With her expressive eyes, Chloe implores me to go on. *Why do you wish he were here?* I imagine she's thinking. *There's more to that wish than a need for good-bye. What is it you really want, Carl?*

"I didn't realize he harbored so much resentment towards me," I admit. "I do now, but what good does seeing it now do me? I certainly didn't notice it when being vigilant might have mattered." This long statement leaves me breathless. I cough, long and jagged, and a great chunk of phlegm is dislodged. I spit the gob into a cup on my bedside table. The sludge inside the cup is a murky brown; a day's accumulation of gunk.

"The resentment was because you didn't put him first. He felt like a nuisance, in your eyes."

"Didn't put him first? That's bullshit! I researched his surgery. Me, no one else! I made so many phone calls and met with so many doctors. I agonized every night for a year. Then I made the decision to have the surgery performed. He's walking today because of *my* decision. If that doesn't prove I love him, I don't know what—"

"He doesn't know that. *Any* of that. No one ever told him. By the time he was old enough to want to hear the story, *you* were so preoccupied with the demands of academia, you couldn't be bothered."

"How can you say…" Another shattering cough rocks my chest. Turn and spit.

"Until I came along," Chloe says, filling the lull, "your work and alcohol—getting tanked with Mel and the boys—those were your priorities. At the end of a tough workday, the *last* thing you wanted to do was face the past, and you had to do that anytime you spoke to Terry. Because the day he needed you most—"

"The day I picked him up after school and he said...."

"And he told you he'd been—"

The right word is eluding us both. "Touched?" I finally venture.

"Yes."

"What was I supposed to do? I mean, your child tells you *that,* and your first thought is, *I should have been here for him, and I wasn't.* Your body goes into overdrive and has nowhere to spend the extra energy. In lieu of spending it, you shut down. *I* shut down. I couldn't handle the guilt."

My wife of eight years nods, understands. "I think you should talk to him. One day as your best man does not equal full amends made."

"I'd love to talk to him, honey. But it's four-thirty in the morning. Terry's at home, asleep. If someone did let him know the shape I'm in, my guess is his first reaction would not be to come rushing over here. It would be to celebrate my demise."

"You're wrong, Carl. Someone *did* let him know, and he's here now. He's outside waiting to see you."

"You called him?" I don't know whether to be overjoyed or offended.

"I did."

"Why?"

"Because I love you both, and I despise the way you treat one another. I know you haven't spoken in a long time, and you're afraid he wouldn't listen if you tried to get in touch with him. But you can help him, Carl. You can still make a difference in his life."

"How?"

"By telling him why you did what you did. *Why* you 'shut down'. By telling him you're as sorry as I know you are. I'd hate to see a repeat of what happened between you two with him and little Megan. I'd hate to see a chasm like that open up between them. You can head that outcome off tonight."

TERRENCE MCDONALD IS 20. THE YEAR IS 2010.

It is four in the morning. I know this because, when the ringing phone wakes me, I look to the clock and make a note of the early hour. I'm angry to have been dragged out of a dream featuring Beth. I haven't seen her in a week and a half; yet, in the alternate universe of my dream, I could smell her perfume, hear her voice, touch her smooth skin. And I took the opportunity to run my hands lightly across her beautiful breasts, lingering on their perfectly shaped nipples. She'd never let me do *that* in real life anymore.

I roll out of bed, land on my feet. Groggy, I stand and test my legs and their muscles. Weak and tentative, as usual after waking. I am a tightrope walker on a gusty day, and my body waivers until I get my balance. When I can move forward, I go to the phone. Mom is calling. Less reluctant than I'd be if the call came from anyone else—and I do mean *anyone*—I answer it.

"What's up, Mom?" I ask. "It's really early." Then it dawns on me why one person might call another at four in the morning. "Is something wrong?"

She sounds shell-shocked when she replies. "Yes, Terry. It's your father. Please get here as quickly as you can."

I do as I am told, more for her than for him. Then I wait.

.   .   .

I wait in the foyer of my father's resplendent residence. Or, as I refer to it, "The palace." Purchased when I was three and a half to celebrate Dad's gaining tenure at work, one of my first memories was of our little family moving in.

I will never achieve the kind of success he's achieved, I am convinced, so I will never own a place like this for myself. Worse, and even more galling, the *success* he's attained was far from deserved. He may have gotten better under Mom's loving guidance, but he is still a drunken asshole at heart.

"Terry?" I jump at my mom's sudden appearance. Her eyes are no doubt red behind their sunglass shield.

"Yes?"

"Your father is asking for you."

"Okay. Thanks, Mom."

The old man's a pallid shell of himself. He lies on his back, his breathing labored. Later this night, it will stop altogether. His most faithful inanimate companion: a red plastic cup on his nightstand that my mother claims is up to its brim with disgusting phlegm earned by his illness. He calls it his milkshake. Mom calls this a sick joke, but I think she laughs at it when no one's looking.

I'm at the foot of his bed. "Why didn't you go to the hospital, Dad?" I demand. The hospital is where he belongs. I am sure of this after just the briefest glance.

"Why would I do that?"

"Because you're sick. That's what people do when they're sick."

"Sure I'm sick. But they're only gonna tell me what I already know. 'You're dying, old man. Too many unfiltered cigarettes. Too much beer and whiskey. Get your affairs in order'. I'd rather die at home, in familiar surroundings."

He's right, I decide. And besides, it's his choice, not mine.

"Have you gotten your affairs in order?"

"That's why you're here, Terry."

"Oh." I hope my tone will persuade him to continue. It does.

"Don't make the same mistakes I did, son."

What does he mean? Don't be a bastard towards my disabled son? *Well, I don't have one of those.* Don't blame alcohol for my poor choices and suspect parenting skills? Why not ask him?

"What do you mean?"

Hypocrite.

"The distance between us did not stem from your palsy."

"It didn't?"

"No. I wasn't unhappy to have a *disabled* son, Terry. I was elated to have a beautiful, differently-abled boy. You gave me a purpose beyond drinking and books, and publishing papers most people would never read."

"So what changed? Why did our relationship turn into *this*?" I challenge him.

"It was my fault. I had always been there to look out for you." He coughs violently. Spits a stream of brown saliva into his plastic cup. I cringe *for* him. He waits until he's regained control of his body before he speaks again. "I took a great deal of *pride* in always being there. Other fathers were absent, or they were present, but only nominally. Not me. I was *there*. Then the day came when I wasn't. The one day I should have been. The day that—"

"I know what day you're talking about, Dad."

"Yeah. Well, anyway, I wasn't there, and I couldn't put myself there retroactively, as much as I wanted to change what happened. I failed you, and a part of me sort of… gave up after that, I guess. I withdrew into my work and into myself. You might have thought this was because of you, or maybe just because I was a hard-hearted jerk."

"I thought you were an old man who loved his money, his books, and his drinks a hell of a lot more than you loved me. Your defective son, who would never be—*could never be*—what you wanted him to be. You even forgot about the log cabin promise."

"The what?"

"The log cabin! The one you said we'd build together, but we never did. You were always too busy."

"I don't remember saying that. A log cabin? Are you making that up?"

"No, Dad. I *promise* you I'm not making it up."

"Well, at any rate, I did my best to be there for you, Terry, but nothing I did could ever take away the blame I heaped on myself for my lapse that day. I wanted to tell you how sorry I am. I also wanted to warn you. I can only hope you'll hear me. Don't make the same mistake with Megan that I made with you. Megan is a wonderful little girl. She deserves a fully present father. Listen to her when she speaks. Take her seriously on your roughest day, because she could be having it worse, looking to you for help."

I am beside him now. Tears are streaking my face. I catch a glimpse of his cup, and Mom's right; it is nearly full, evidence of just how sick—how fragile—he is. *I want a hug from him. I want to hug him.* I go in for a one-handed embrace, for which he stays supine. I want to accept his apology, but the correct vocabulary is not at my disposal. In fact, where there should be words of thanks and forgiveness, there aren't any words at all.

CARL MCDONALD IS 63. THE YEAR IS 2010.

Chloe returns to my side and rests her head on Terrence's shoulder. I think I see her mouth, "Thanks for coming," but I can't be sure. He nods, then he leaves without another word. *Will he take my plea to heart?*

My final rumination among humankind.

At the end, Chloe takes my hand in that tender way of hers—my cold ghost-hand in her right limb; alive, pulsing faintly at its wrist as if to prove it, her left hand covering them both like a makeshift blanket. The warmth of her limbs, and the vigor coursing through them, impart a final good-bye and transmit one last time to their useless counterparts the truest love. A love at once unselfish, solid, and affirming.

Carrying her love with me, I leave this world.

PRAY!

Pray!
As morning dawns,
Pray like your prayers are all the day is for.
In darkness,
Pray like the night might never give o'er
To the sight of
A burning,
Brilliant,
Satisfying sun
That holds in its nourishing light
The promise of: "More."

22
MEGAN'S PRAYER

THE REVIEW

Beside me but not close enough for me to reach out and touch: a tall blue door. It's locked, and I'm on the ground, writhing in pain.

Overpowered.

Not again!

.   .   .

"Haven't we been over this already?" I ask.

"What you're seeing here, Terrence," God explains—I can't see Him, but I can hear Him; The Boss as Lisa—"isn't a memory per se."

"It's not? Because it sure looks like a memory. One I'd prefer to forget." *Why do we have to keep revisiting that one event? I'm over it, okay?*

"This is a nightmare of yours, I know—and I'm sorry for making you relive it. But it leads into a moment you shared with your daughter, one whose essence she treasures."

A moment with Megan. From when she was little, I presume? I'll endure any prologue if it means I can be a part of one of those gems again.

TERRENCE MCDONALD IS 25. THE YEAR IS 2015.

Tall blue door. Locked. Writhing in pain. Overpowered.

Not again!

What were those words Dad used that time (and probably so many other times, too) when he asked for a beer and the barmaid, who doubled as a waitress in that smoky restaurant where the two of us had dinner a couple of times—she was a good judge of people and their moods, in my opinion—refused to serve him and sent him home in a cab? He'd had enough for the night, she'd told him, and she stuck to this verdict. Unimpressed by the clumsy flirting he must have tried with her, unimpressed by his wedding ring. He came home angry. Steaming. I hid in my room, hoped the anger would run its course before running into me. It did.

Damn it. Damn her. What the fuck does she know? I was perfectly sober. Bitch.

Yeah, those were the words. And that's how I feel right now.

Damn it.

"Wanta play again?"

"No! No, I don't want to play again."

"Well, you came back. That *must* mean you want to play."

"I didn't come back, you idiot. This is a—"

Nightmare, I think, but he cuts me off before I can get it out.

"Don't call me that! I am not an idiot! You're going to play my game, or else you won't wake up!"

"Okay."

Leering.

Staring at the dirty tile floor while Connor plays the game. Removing myself from my body. I'm here, but I'm not. I'm here, and yet I'm *anywhere* else. *Think of someplace else, and you might wake yourself up.*

It's not working. He's hurting me.

Damn it. Damn him.

There's a sound at the door. Someone's trying to get in.

MEGAN MCDONALD IS 8. THE YEAR IS 2015.

I wake up in the middle of a Saturday night, my throat dry as a desert. My mission: get some water—and possibly a cookie, if it isn't too much trouble.

On my way to the kitchen-—about halfway there—I am stopped in my tracks.

Noises coming from Daddy's room. Is he screaming?

I step over to his door and lightly tap-knock.

He didn't hear you, Megs. Louder.

A bit more force, but still not too loud.

I try the doorknob. It turns, no resistance, and I push through. The room smells musty. Grown-up mixed with faded, day-old cologne.

"Daddy?"

With his face buried deep in his pillow, his voice sounds far away, and I can only pick out one phrase, repeated at least ten times. With each new revolution of this broken record, its intensity increases.

Finally, there is screaming. "No more!"

"Daddy!"

He jolts upright. "Megan?" Wipes his eyes, allows them to adjust to the darkness. "Megan, was that you?"

"You were yelling, Daddy."

"Was I?"

"Yes."

"Did it scare you?"

You're a big girl, remember? I remind myself. "No."

"Well, I'm sorry, anyway." He glances at the radio on his nightstand that tells time. "Hey, you want some ice cream, kiddo?"

Why tease me? He won't let me have any ice cream. He *shouldn't*. I woke up to get a cookie, but I knew it was wrong. Just like I know ice cream at this time of night is, as Mommy likes to say, "Out of the question!"

"But I'm not allowed to have anything after I brush my teeth."

"You can brush them again, gingersnap. Afterwards."

"Really?"

"Sure."

"Okay."

．　　　　　．　　　　　．

Daddy scoops a heaping bowl of mint chocolate chip, sets it in front of me, and sits down next to me at the dining nook table over his own bowl. He says, "So I was yelling, huh?"

"M-hmmm." Shoving a too-big spoonful into my mouth.

He looks sad. "What was I saying?"

I tell him. "You just kept saying it over and over."

"Don't tell your mother, okay? We wouldn't want her thinking your daddy's going batty."

"I won't." I smile at his almost-rhyme.

"Promise?"

"Promise. My lips are zipped."

But I'm worried about you.

.   .   .

Daddy's not like Grandpa.

When Grandpa got drunk, Daddy says, all hell would break loose. Screaming and name-calling and wall punching. "You'da thought the earth was gonna open up, Megs. I sure did. I thought it was gonna open up and swallow me whole, gingersnap. And, if it had… well…" This is where he shrugs. "If it had, at least then I'd have been free. Free from not just his pain and heartache but all of my own hurts, too."

I tell him not to talk this way. "But then you'd never have known me," I say, and he apologizes.

Sometimes, I forget which one of us is the parent. He's not like Grandpa, though. He's a happy drunk most of the time. But it still makes me cry, because there's nothing I can do to cheer him up when he's unhappy.

I don't even have any special talents, like playing a musical instrument or a sport. I can't dance, and won't, except in my bedroom with the door shut. At school yesterday, Mr. Difray, the principal—we call him Mr. Toupee behind his back—spoke at an assembly and asked us kids if we had any "exceptional skills" we wanted to share.

No, our blank stares said. And *if on the off chance we did have an exceptional skill, why would we waste it in front of the people most likely to make fun of us for it?*

.   .   .

It's Dad's weekend. I'm at Mom's this Friday night, waiting for him to pick me up after work, like he told Mom and me he would when we talked on the phone yesterday. I wonder if tonight might be a lucky night and he'll be sober so we can walk to the bus stop and, instead of going straight home, we'll go see the walruses or a movie or watch the people as they walk around Green Lake. He loves to people watch. So do I.

.   .   .

I don't know how I feel about God as I lie in bed at just past midnight. The supreme overseer. I learned both those words today from my teacher, Ms. Flynn, but we weren't talking about God. We've been studying a unit in history called "Slavery In America: An Introduction" for the last two weeks.

Dad and I pray every night, but we don't go to church. We say a prayer he learned from Grandpa Carl.

If God is so omnipotent, and gets to decide how we'll live our lives, couldn't He have kept my parents together?

Sometimes, doubting that He is out there, but hoping I'm wrong to doubt, I'll ask Him for things. Little things. Sometimes, when I know Daddy is alone while I'm here at Mommy's house and no one's with him to keep him company, to eat ice cream or cinnamon-sprinkled toast with him, to let him read bedtime stories to them—times like now—my prayers ask for bigger things.

"Dear God, my daddy is a good daddy. He's smart. I like to ask him about the world, because he always knows the answers. He roasts marshmallows with me, takes me to baseball games, movies, even Disneyland now and then. He's not mean, but he can get irritated if I'm not listening to him when he tells me to do something. And he tells me he loves me every night. He never forgets. Even when I'm not with him, he'll call and tell me on the phone. Like he did before I went to bed tonight. But he is sad.

"It makes me sad when he's sad. I know he still loves Mommy. He's never said so to me, but I can tell. She doesn't love him back anymore, though. She's told me that. 'I'm so glad your dad and I met, but we weren't meant to stay together, Megan'. "Please, If You really are out there, God, I need Your help. I need you to make my daddy happy again. Find him a girl who writes stories, like he does, like Uncle Charlie used to. Maybe she could like those old black-and-white movies he makes me watch that I tell him I like even though I don't, just to make him happy for a little while. And the aquarium. She has to like the aquarium so that she can go with Grandma Chloe and me to look at the walruses. Make sure she's beautiful and loves children. And baking. And Christmas. Please?"

FAVOR

To ask a favor
Is to heed an insecurity,
Announce a vulnerability,
A need,
And to say,
Either in somber quiet
Or with a plaintive shout,
"Can you please help me out?"

To take on a favor is to agree
To nullify an inadequacy
Via deed.
"I will do
Whatever I can for you,
That life might be made easier,
My friend,
Whether through a trivial
Or more complicated errand."

23
MATTIE'S VISIT

THE REVIEW

God and I didn't talk after the review of my father's passing—no big discussion. I am grateful for the chance He gave me to experience and learn from what I saw without comment. *We don't need to talk about everything,* He communicated.

As Megan's prayer fades to black—I'd never known she prayed for me like that, nor would I have guessed she was so specific in her praying; that she wished for someone who loved children, baking, and Christmas, or that God would think enough of this prayer to act on it—we're back where we started. In my childhood bedroom, and I ask Him, "How often do you answer prayers?"

"As often as possible. But there are certain parameters answerable prayers must meet."

"Like what?" I'm asking this question not just for me but for everyone who's ever looked to the skies with a wish on their tongue and hope buoying their heart.

"A prayer won't be answered unless it can be sensibly fit into a being's chart."

Bewildered (*A being's chart? What the hell is He talking about? Wait, didn't my panelists and my spirit guide, Patricia, mention something about a...*), I get my first glimpse, at His insistence, of *my* very own chart. It is a giant scroll that is not just filled with tiny writing—the tiniest I've ever seen—but every event it chronicles is also plainly visible, as though it were playing out right now. The events run in loops, so that when one finishes, it starts over again at the beginning. This scroll, *this living document,* governs my every moment on Earth.

Try as I might, however, and while I identify and reminisce with The Creator about all other crucial points ("Oh, that was when I…" or, "I didn't know how important my love of books would be until I met my wife and began writing for real"), the means of my death remains a mystery whose particulars have been blacked out, redacted.

By design?

I think so.

Whatever it was that happened to bring my consciousness to a full stop, I am not yet meant to be privy to it.

"No one who will be unaware of how they perished at their passing—so this does not include folks being treated for diseases, those who would know what did them in as a consequence of their suffering—is privy to that information. Until their panel has settled on a ruling, that is, except in specific cases."

"What kinds of cases?" I inquire. *Who gets to know the future? Besides true psychics and prophets, who have no choice?*

"Certain people of whom I request favors in life are given the *option* of knowing their futures."

"That can't be a long list of people. How many people have You appeared to? And I'm not talking about the image of Jesus burnt into a burrito here. I'm talking the real thing? And then you'd have to divide that small number by the even smaller number of those who are asked to do God a favor. And then remove from that the amount of people who say no outright, thinking they're going crazy."

"Actually, the number's much higher than you'd think. Not astronomical, by any means, but not miniscule, either. I've even requested favors from people you know."

"Really? Who?"

MATTIE MAILER IS 22. THE YEAR IS 2017.

I'm not sure if this is a dream. I'm asleep, but this is too vivid to be a nighttime diversion. This is *real*. As real as any traffic jam or argument or tight spot I've ever found my way into. At the same time, it's like nothing I know, another dimension altogether.

"Have you been here before?" the red-haired receptionist asks me.

"I… I don't know where here is exactly, so it's hard to say. I think I fell asleep."

"That's a no. Name, please?"

"Madeline Mailer."

The receptionist consults a ledger at her side. "Yep, you're on the visitors' list, Ms. Mailer."

"What does that mean?"

"Visiting means different things for different people. In your case, it means The Boss wants to see you. Go through that door." She points. "Then find the third door on your left."

When I first open the third door on my left, I believe the receptionist was mistaken. This place is empty. Is it an unused storage room? A remodel awaiting construction?

"Hello, Mattie," I hear a voice say.

"Hello?" I return, uncertain. A man stands before me. Tall and slender. It is too dark in here to see anything besides a profile, but I remember him from somewhere.

"Glad to see you're here. You made it."

"Yeah, well, I don't really—"

"Know where here is. That's okay. I brought you here for a reason."

My curiosity piqued, I wonder, *What reason is that, and who the heck are you?*

"I'm God, Mattie." He answers the question I never asked aloud.

God?

"No, you're not." I take a step back, expel a nervous laugh.

"Sometimes I *wish* I weren't, believe Me, but I am. And I have a favor to ask of you."

"A favor? What could I do for God? Wouldn't it be a safer bet to go to the Pope or the Dalai Lama and ask them to do whatever it is?"

"They're busy enough. Plus this isn't the type of assignment they're used to. And I'm not so sure you'll do Me the favor. Let Me be absolutely clear. I gave you free will, Mattie. You can do whatever you choose. But

I hope I can convince you. How would you like to be the answer to a prayer?"

. . .

The girl is strawberry blonde. She's sitting up in bed, and I can see she's praying, her fingers interlocked, head half-bowed.

"She'll be beautiful someday," I say. More a reflex than an observation.

"Yep. Soon. Too soon for her parents' liking. But then, isn't that the way things always go? The minute humanity gets used to one reality, another is upon them."

"Who is she?"

A pause. "That, Mattie, is your step-daughter."

"What? I don't have a step-daughter."

"You will."

Hearing this, I do my best to recover my composure. *I'm only twenty-two!* Leaving my seat, I walk toward the scene, stopping at its edge, right before I might tumble, headlong, into it.

I turn back to Him. "Well, since You know the future, who am I to doubt You?" I am not conceding defeat. Rather, I am trying to goad Him into an explanation.

"Megan is part of the favor I'm asking of you," He says, coming to my side. "A big part."

"Megan?" As I repeat her name, I train my ears on her soft voice. Her prayer. For her father's happiness, someone who likes the aquarium, black-and-white films, baking, Christmas. I am overcome with heartache. She is so earnest, so steadfast. "You've chosen me as the fulfillment of her prayer?" My tone conveys incredulity.

"That's right."

"Why me? Why not someone who's had a bit more experience with the whole mothering thing?"

"You'll grow into the role." A moment of silence between us ends when God transforms into Megan and continues speaking. "She has a mother, Mattie. What she needs—what she will find in you—is an ally to help her through the coming teen years. You'll grow into the role," He repeats. "Do not doubt yourself."

. . .

"Her father's name is Terrence," God tells me, "and he will have no qualms about allowing you to become that ally."

I learn so much about Terrence in what seems like the space between one breath and the next, and I'm annoyed.

"He's damaged. Is that what you're telling me? Were You trying to gloss over that fact, hoping I might not notice it?"

God is seated next to me, in the form of my favorite elementary school teacher, Mrs. Pryor, sixth grade, and she looks as I recollect her looking. Her hair the color of dandelions. You couldn't dye hair her shade of yellow if you worked at it for years. And I loved her skin. Wished it were mine. Smooth, and pale as buttermilk.

"And I'm supposed to not only date this guy but *marry* him, too?"

"Eventually. He's not damaged, though. He's not a broken man, Mattie."

"He's not? He certainly sounds broken, from what You've shown me."

"Terrence is not dissimilar from many of My creations, who give up on themselves too easily. But he *is not* broken. He simply needs assistance becoming the person he's meant to be. If you can't accept who he is, how will he ever reach that goal himself?"

"You're God. You could show him acceptance and love, and all the things You're supposed to be known for, which some would argue is Your *job*, and You wouldn't even need my help."

He says nothing in response. Remains stalk-still for close to half a minute.

I'm uncomfortable and break our loud silence. "So why haven't You?"

"Free will. Terrence possesses free will, as does every human being. The idea of his palsy pains him so deeply that he dreams of climbing trees only to fall from them, as a way of explaining his fate. I *could* change his self-image or his decision-making, but I won't. I usually don't. If I can't play by the rules I created, why should humanity? But I do send messengers from time to time to help out."

"How am I supposed to help?"

"You're a writer. He'll like that. You can start there. When you meet him, make sure you mention it."

"Okay, I will. I can tell him about all the stories I've got that are nearly finished, and that I'm on the lookout for an agent. But I'm not writing anything at the moment. What if he asks what I'm working on currently?"

"As of now," He says, "you're working on a novel about your mother. You've been toiling away at it for… four years, let's say. It's a ghost story."

"God wants me to lie?" I am taken aback.

"It's not lying."

"How do you figure that?"

"It's a truth in the making."

"But why?"

"Here's why."

All of a sudden, my favorite teacher holds in her grasp a scroll of sorts and gestures for me to examine it. "This," the explanation starts, "is your chart. It shows what has happened in your life and all that will happen. Think of it as your very own life-map, with the free will given to you at birth marking the important stops along the way. Your most important decisions in life."

"Okay."

Then I see it. The end of my chart—my life-story—written in bold font.

Cause of Death: Breast Cancer – Age 45

Surviving relatives: Husband & stepdaughter.

Accomplishments of note: Novelist, essayist, and popular author of short fiction. Hero to her family, memoirist and poet (posthumously, with husband Terrence McDonald, stepdaughter Megan McDonald Kolb, and granddaughter, Emma Kolb.)

"Your next project," God tells me, as I sit stunned and angry, "will be to begin writing a memoir about Terrence, his life before you, and your life with him. You will spend the rest of your days working on it, save for those times when you're preparing the odd novel or book of poetry.

"It will take another two years or so, but if you just keep at it you'll find an agent, and he'll find you a publisher. Your books will succeed. Not right away, but once you find your niche, the people who *need* what you do will love what you do. Don't misunderstand me. I'm not saying you'll be *rich*, by any means, but you'll have a modicum of fame and enough money to get by.

"As for the memoir, your sections, while they may seem out of order and incomplete to you as you write them, will lay the foundation. Then, when the time is right, Terrence and your loved ones will fill in the gaps they're each meant to bridge. Trust me, the story *will* have a proper beginning, middle, and end. And there is a *specific* reason for it.

"Don't worry. I know it all sounds like a lot to handle right now, Mattie, but the point of this visit was to get the ball rolling."

"Towards my *death*?" I say, behind clenched teeth.

"No. Towards the next phases of your life."

"What if I take on this favor and answer Megan's prayer, and put my best effort into it, but it proves to be too hard a task? Then what? Am I stuck living in a life I hate?"

"No," God says. "That isn't how free will works. Not on Earth, not in the afterlife, not *anywhere* that I created. I know you, Mattie. I know how stubborn you are, how committed you can be to seeing causes you're passionate about through to their ends. That is why I chose you for this favor. Will I be pleased if you say no, or if you say yes, then quit mid-favor? No, I won't. But, should you decide you've had enough, the option of quitting is always open to you, and I will not hold it against you."

"You won't?"

"Of course not. Souls living in the afterlife, for example, quit their jobs often. Not unlike their human brethren. Just as on Earth, fatigue can—and does—set in. If I stepped in and meddled in every instance I didn't agree with, how would humanity learn anything?"

"Alright, I'll do You this favor," I say, after digesting His words.

"Great."

"On one condition."

"What's that?"

Proposing conditions to God is a bold move, and I'm not sure what possessed me to do this until I answer Him. Then it's clear. I'd always been meant to propose this condition, even though I hadn't noticed it written in some of the finer print on my chart.

"I want a full tour of this hall. I'm gonna be writing that book, after all."

Writing that book means writing about The Hall Of Records. *How do I know this? Another fine-print fact?*

"I gotta start my research somewhere," I reason.

"I agree," He replies. "Take a walk with me."

.   .   .

"Everything you see in this first room—called The Great Room—has to do, in some fashion, with major works that saw not just publication but success beyond an author's dreams. You could find the work itself, in its finished form, waiting in these shelves. Or a discarded chapter, song, or frame of film left out of the finished product. Even the unpublished portions of these works are kept here. Makes it easier to trace them from origin to fruition. If you looked around, you'd find quite a few of your own writings, Mattie." He leads me down a hallway on one of the staircase landings and, to the left, another hallway close to endless and as wide as it is long. "Where we're going now, though... this is a room few souls will ever see. There's the hall curators—who might cull something out of here and bring it into The Great Room if asked by researching souls—myself, and then there's you."

"What makes me so special?" I have to admit I'm proud to be included in such select company.

"It isn't about you being special, Mattie. You are, because everyone I've had a part in creating is special to Me. But... why you're here with Me right now... it has to do with your book, in some ways, your life with Terrence in others, but that's all I'll say, because it's all you need to know. If I tell you any more, your ability to use life as a tool for learning could be compromised."

Stepping through a door whose only identifying mark is a sign that reads: PERSONNEL ENTRANCE: HALL WORKERS ONLY, PLEASE, we are in an even larger room.

"This," God announces, "is where all other works are kept. It could be a letter to your mother; a note you passed in class back in the third grade; a fight you had with your best friend when you were fourteen that you might want to review to see how that one moment affected the rest of your time on Earth; a grocery list; a half-formed thought. They're all here, all categorized and attainable."

.   .   .

I blink, and we're in the Hall of Records itself. Here to peruse its public archives.

Only now do I understand how impossible this place is. And yet I'm here. To call the building large would be like calling the Mormon Tabernacle Choir "a music group" or William Faulkner "a writer." Human language will always shortchange it.

It is a white-painted edifice whose size cannot be calculated, with any accuracy, standing on its outside. One *has* to find their way under-roof to understand its full grandeur. To do this, a patron ascends two equal flights of concrete stairs, thirty each, then steps through a pair of gold-handled double doors. After that rather unassuming entry, the enormity of the place—and all it encompasses—hits them. Just as it's hitting me.

Vaulted ceilings. Golden staircases spiraling high and away as far as the eye can see on all sides and up the center. Along every wall, on every shelf, on every table, there are books, records, magazines, films, compact discs.

The Almighty is now the kind, elderly gentleman—Bob, I think his name was—who lived next door to my parents and me, and acted as a quasi-grandparent between my birth and my eighth year.

"There is so much," I note, and He nods. "I'd hate to be the curator. All the hours and upkeep that job must require."

"Ah, we don't worry about time here."

"You don't?"

"We don't."

I glance about, and on all fronts I am assaulted by media, though I find the experience enjoyable. "So why did You bring me here? I mean, it's beautiful and all, and thank you for agreeing to give me a tour, but I sense there's a reason for our being here beyond the beauty."

"There is."

He goes over to a matronly woman wearing bifocals-—the stereotypical librarian. "Find Madeline Mailer's book please."

"Which one, sir?"

"The big one."

"Coming right up."

When He called it the big one, He wasn't kidding. It isn't so much in size or weight that the book claims supremacy. Rather, the sheer number of contributors—along with its scope—makes it "big."

"I write this book?" Hard to believe. *And I'm going to write books that will be sold in stores? Have my lifelong dream realized?*

"Yes," He answers. "This-" He places the volume in my hands, "is the work that will stand as your legacy."

"It's also the only work I won't finish."

"That is true. It will be published posthumously. While free will governs almost all actions, a few charted events are absolutely non-negotiable, death among them. At some point, every one of my creations must experience death.

"Do you have any more questions, Mattie?"

"Yeah, I've got tons."

"Any that need *immediate* answers?"

"No."

"Then your first date with Terrence will be on a Sunday," God informs me. "This coming Sunday, in fact."

"That soon? You think I'm ready? I don't—"

"You have everything you need. You'll be ready. Besides, I'll be with you every step of the way. Not that I can have you remembering anything specific about Terrence. So you'll need to forget the meat of everything I've shown you here. It will be all but gone when you wake up, and you will be left with only the vaguest recollection of this visit."

"Okay." My sigh is heavy and full of worry. *Can I really do this? A favor for God?*

"Good," God says. "The first thing you'll need to do—once you're conscious again, that is—you need to head for the grocery store."

"The grocery store? Why?"

"You're almost out of milk."

A MENTOR

A mentor lasts
Long after a body's ultimate gasp has passed
Through its lungs,
Marking the end.

So if you find it odd to pray to God,
It might be easier
To commune to a mentor,
As help they've proven
Willing to lend.

24

ONE MORE TALK WITH CHARLIE

TERRENCE MCDONALD IS 26. THE YEAR IS 2016.

As I do—and have done—every Thursday since his passing, I go to see Charlie. The ground beneath my feet is muddy and unstable from a morning deluge. I stand in front of his gravestone and just outside a massive puddle, speaking softly and weeping.

"Am I a good father?"

Yes.

"You really think so?"

Absolutely.

"You're probably just bullshitting me. Or you're saying what I want to hear. Or I'm *thinking* what I want to hear you say."

Terrence, come on now. What do you think is going to happen? What are you so damn afraid of? I mean, look at ya, kid. You look damn near paralyzed.

"That's just it. I *feel* paralyzed. I try to tell myself I fell from trees, from the big oak in our yard that was never there in the first place. But it wasn't a fall that put me in braces as a kid." The braces got smaller and less cumbersome as I grew older. They came off for good when I was around fifteen.

No, it wasn't.

"It was the palsy."

Yes.

"What if someone who doesn't understand it, who doesn't understand *me*, decides that, because of the palsy, I'm not fit to be a father?" I'm hyperventilating.

Calm down. You won't lose Megan.

"I won't?"

I won't let that happen, Charlie says, his voice turning jovial.

"But how can you be sure? You're not God."

No, I'm not.

For a moment, he's quiet, and I think, *There's going to be a punchline of sorts coming. There's got to be.*

Indeed there is.

I'm not God. But I'm a lot closer to Him than you are.

"Yes, you are."

I know things you couldn't know.

"So you'll put in a good word?"

You can count on it.

"Thanks."

Terrence?

"Hmm?"

Even though it might not feel like it, you've got people in your corner. People you can always turn to when the going gets rough.

"I suppose."

There's Chloe, Megan, Grandpa Jack. There will be others, too. I can't tell you who they are. That's against the rules up here. Besides, deep inside yourself, you already know who I'm talking about.

"I do?"

Sure. The thing is, that knowledge is buried for a reason. Because having it close at hand could compromise the life you'll live. Anyway, you'll run across another important person soon. As for me, I always loved you, ya know?

"You what?"

We never said it, but I hoped it was obvious. I saw a lot of myself in you. Different color skin, but who cares about that? The same heart, the same creative spirit. The same scared-shitless look on your face that I was wearing when Patty gave birth to our Clare.

"So that's why you started talking to me in the hospital?"

That's why. I never thought I'd see you after that. Figured you'd go on your way and have a warm memory tucked away somewhere of the nice old guy from the day Megan was born. But then you called me, asked if I wanted to go to breakfast with you, and I remember congratulating myself for having had those business cards of mine made up.

I smile. "I'll be by to see you next week, Charlie. Thanks for the talk, as always."

I'll be here waiting. And, just so you know, Terrence, I'm always with you.

FIGMENTS

The house shrinks away
And The Palace walls sway,
Both figments of the car's
Rear-view mirror.
As today,
For good,
I leave here,
My only childhood home.

I leave what is safe,
What is comfortable
And known.
To venture a fearsome step
Into a life lived alone.

25

MOVING OUT

TERRENCE MCDONALD IS 18. THE YEAR IS 2008.

Beth and I didn't last. The relationship crumbled. We were too young; starry-eyed high school sweethearts unprepared. This on top of the fact that her father's opinion of me began just north of abysmal and only worsened.

She had been taught obedience to her father from an early age. His was a "What-I-say-goes" household. He said multiple times that I wasn't worthy of her, that the care I would require in the future would put too much strain on our relationship, and she had been stupid to get pregnant in the first place. She disagreed with the former pronouncement, though never forcefully.

The last time I ever welcomed him into my home—the palace, where Beth and I were living, with Chloe and Dad there to help—was on Megan's first birthday. That day, I overheard him advising his daughter, "Get out while you can, Bethy. He's a loser."

"He's not a loser, Dad," she defended. "He loves me. And he adores Megan."

"He doesn't know what love *is*. Neither of you do. I am not questioning his fitness as a father. I am saying that, for the sake of your sanity, you should get the hell out of here. You can come and stay with your mother and me. The guest room's all ready for you."

The guest room was ready. *Big surprise. How long has he been plotting to get rid of me?*

Two weeks after my eavesdropping, Beth's gone, promising I'll see Megan on a regular basis. And I do, every other weekend from then on. A year later, Dad sits me down in the kitchen and says, "Terrence, you need to be more independent, son." Or, as I heard it, *It's time for you to go.*

Deep down, I know he's right, but it's easier to see him as my unfeeling landlord, my long-time chauffer giving his notice, than to admit he has a point. We both understand I'm scared of leaving.

"How will I get around, Dad? I need to be able to go places," I argue.

"The bus."

"I *hate* the bus." It doesn't matter what route they take or where a bus drops me. I am unsure where to go once the accordion doors open. With so little experience traveling the local roads, and no solo experience whatsoever (When I was a kid, and I'd ask Dad to show me how the bus—or pretty much anything else—worked, he'd say, "You don't need to worry about *that*, Terrence. I'll be with you. Anything you need to do, I can do for you. Anywhere you need to go, we can go together." As a kid, this seemed like a great deal.), I feel as though I don't know where *anything* is. The grocery store. The Post office. The mall. And, most important if you ask Mom, the stadiums where the Mariners and Seahawks play their games. I can't find any of them without a guide.

Dad sighs. "I know how you feel about the bus. And I understand how *the bus* represents everything I never taught you. That was my fault. I thought I was making life easier on you by doing everything for you. But now I see I was wrong."

His face is drawn. *This is a talk he dreads almost as much as I do.* He gets up and begins rooting around in the pantry for something to eat. Dad's a nervous eater. A trait I inherited.

"You want anything?" he asks me.

"No," I say.

"You could always call a taxi, or one of those ride-sharing deals; they'll take you wherever you want as long as you've got the money."

We're back to this. Great.

Dad settles on a large bag of peanuts meant for ballgames. He takes them down from the top shelf, finds a bowl in which to discard the shells, takes his seat again, and begins to nibble the legumes. "Speaking of money, I'm not a heartless bastard. I'll pay your expenses until you're on your feet."

I haven't had a steady job since the newspaper closed down. And that job wasn't *steady*. It was after school. If I spend too long thinking about my lack of work experience, and the lack of prospects out there, anger can become my mouthpiece. Dad will say that, if I really wanted to work, I could be working, that I'm not looking hard enough, and I'll storm off. I know how us McDonald men handle these things.

"You could ask Jack for help." Dad suggests, "and you know, if you're ever in the neighborhood, Chloe and I would be more than happy to drive you anywhere around here you want to go."

I want to put up more resistance. This is my home, and Dad's wrong to want me gone. I still need time to learn the basics; doing laundry, cooking, cleaning, all of which had been done for me as a child because it was quicker to cook or clean or to do laundry for me than it would have been to teach me how to do any of it for myself. How can he push me out before I have a solid grasp of those things? And, if I ever get lost on an unfamiliar street—something I see as a very real possibility—he would never forgive himself. I want to say all that, but I don't.

Instead, I go online, once I'd finally convinced myself it *was* the thing to do—this took two months—and find three acceptable-looking apartments. Chloe and Dad come with me to look at them in person.

The first one turns out to be a filthy dump. The carpet looks like it hasn't been updated in years, let alone cleaned in all that time, and the smell of cat urine mingles with the stench of long-dead cigarettes. When Mom lifts the window shade in the "living room", a galaxy of dust floats into the air, and the view out the window is nothing but an alley dumpster.

The second is adequate, nothing more, but I'm tired from a day of walking and standing and walking and standing some more, ready to make my home here. My credit history is non-existent, though, and that means I have to look elsewhere.

Thankfully, the third apartment's better than the other two, which is good, because if it hadn't worked out there might have been another month or two of searching in my future. The tiny apartment building—only ten units—is watched over by an altruistic elderly couple. Where their predecessors had balked, they choose to welcome me. The white-haired woman brings a batch of fresh-baked snicker doodle cookies by as a house-warming gift.

It is the evening of my first full day on my own in the new apartment; Dad and Mom moved me in yesterday. Just before I bed down—I'm in a too-long-to-wear-in-public nightshirt and boxer shorts—there is a knock at the door. It's a little late for a casual visit. *Maybe it's my landlady wanting her cookie plate back,* I speculate. *I need to remember to thank her. Those cookies were delicious. They were warm, but not too hot, and exact in their level of chewiness. I'd ask her for the recipe, if I were the kind of person who bakes.*

But the visit is neither casual, nor is it from my newest neighbor, the amateur baker. I open the door to find Mom on the other side. She looks purposeful, determined.

"What are you doing here?" I ask, but what I hope I'm communicating is: *I'm so glad to see you.*

"I'm here to help you," she says, stepping inside and throwing her coat over the only chair in my tiny living room.

"Help me with what?"

"I think your dad was being a tad unreasonable asking you to move out."

"That's what I tried to tell him! He wouldn't listen to me, though. Typical Dad! He's so—"

"Terry?" She places her hand on my shoulder.

"Uh-huh." I take a deep breath.

"I said he was being *a tad* unreasonable. And he was. But asking you to move out wasn't a crazy request."

"But I don't even know how to—"

She ticks off a list, tapping her right index finger against the palm of her left hand. "Cook. Clean. Shop for groceries. Or go pretty much any-place by yourself." Her tone is a seasoned reporter's; *and that's the way it is.*

"You're afraid you won't be able to do all of this on your own. You're mad at your dad because he's known you forever, and he should *know* what scares you."

I bow my head. *She knows me.* "Yeah," I say.

"Your dad understands you're scared. In fact, he was *so* worried about you he asked me if he was being too harsh, if he was doing the wrong thing, and he was up all night last night popping ant-acids."

I indicate Mom should sit in the chair over which her coat haphazardly hangs. A red pleather piece of crap I will replace the first chance I get. I land with a soft thud—a sound I'm used to after years of landings like that—on the floor beside her, crossing my legs uncomfortably in front of me.

"Your Dad doesn't know I'm here, by the way," she reveals. This surprises me, and I look up into her eyes, open-mouthed. "That's right. He has no idea. He thinks I'm out to dinner with my girlfriends."

I am suddenly aware of how dry my mouth has become, and I close it. Then I ask her, "I have so much to learn. Where do we even start?"

"Well, that depends. What is it about living on your own—something here in the apartment that you might think comes as second nature to other people—that scares you most?"

It takes me less than a millisecond to come up with the answer. "The oven," I say.

"The oven?"

"Yes, using the oven scares the hell out of me. Lisa never let me near hers. 'This is my oven, not yours,' she'd say, and she had me convinced that, if I *did* try to use it, I'd do something horribly wrong. What if I turn my oven on, in order to pre-heat it for a frozen pizza, for example, and I end up burning this place down? It would be confirmation that Terry McDonald, the palsied little boy, turned out as helpless as everyone thought he was."

"No one thought you were helpless."

"Lisa did, she was sure of it, and it pissed her off. It's why she left. She couldn't handle having a kid who needed *so much* attention."

"Okay. Well, you're *not* helpless, and I will teach you how to operate your oven. Let's head on in to the kitchen and get started."

.   .   .

"Your oven shouldn't scare you," Mom says, "but I can understand how it could *seem* scary if you've never used one before." She reaches high above the oven into one of the kitchen cabinets and pulls out a cookie sheet. "We're not *actually* going to cook anything, Terrence, so I don't want you worrying. I'm going to teach you how to pre-heat the oven. Come stand next to me."

I move into the kitchen with steps smaller than my usual cautious footfalls. I am a careful pedestrian by nature, but tonight I'm frozen from the knees up, and my blood pressure is rising.

She points to the oven's ON switch. "'Flick that switch, will you?"

"Are you sure?"

"I'm sure."

"Nothing's going to happen? I mean, I won't burn down the whole build—"

"Flick the switch!"

Mom says it'll be fine. I give her my absolute trust. *She is not Lisa, and you can do this, Terrence. You have to believe in yourself.* I flick the switch, which glows a dull red.

"Good. Now turn that dial there-" she taps it with a finger- "to bake, and that other one there to three-hundred and fifty degrees."

I roll the first dial into place. Bake. Then the second. *350. Got it!*

"Everyone I've ever met would laugh right in my face if they knew I'd never pre-heated an oven before."

"No, Terrence, they wouldn't. Anyone who knows you like I do would be overjoyed for you. Just like I am."

"But it's such a small thing. *Preheat an oven.* Am I supposed to see it as a victory? Yay, Terrence discovered how to do something tonight that most people his age have taken for granted for years."

You're a failure, Terry. I suddenly find myself lost in unhelpful thoughts. *Think about it. You and Beth: failed. You love to write. Since you were a kid, you've told anyone who would listen about how you were gonna write books for a living. And yet when have you ever written anything of significance? Never. Failed.*

"Terry, get out of your head. Stop seeing yourself as a goddamn victim because you aren't one. Plus no woman wants to be with a victim. Trust me. And yes, you *are* supposed to see this as a victory because it *is* a victory. You're gonna have to accept and rejoice in small victories for a while, because only with a succession of small victories will the big ones follow." She shoves the cookie sheet back in its cabinet. Slams the cabinet door shut. I sigh.

"And with that," she announces, triumphant, "you, Mr. Terrence McDonald, just pre-heated your oven. You will notice that no one was maimed in the performance of this task."

THE REVIEW

"This was the first of a group of meetings between us. They went on for two whole years. Sometimes, little Megan would lend a hand." As I describe each meeting, they recur below us. Learning to work the washer and dryer. Hanging clothes (Shirts were easy; slip the hanger through the head-hole, then hang the shirt and feel like I've accomplished something momentous. Pants were harder, since I can never seem to fold them exactly right, and I am easily distracted and upset: "This is so simple. Why can't I do it, Mom? What am I doing wrong?").

I see myself learn how to vacuum. "You'll need a lighter model than this one." Chloe holds up the monstrosity she brought from her own house. "But I *know* you can do this." She was right, I could, and after a while vacuuming became its own strangely relaxing kind of fun.

God is my Dad. Odd, since Dad never knew of these meetings. But God finds an asymmetrical symmetry in the juxtaposition. We aren't seated in any one spot. Rather, we float above the proceedings so we can view any lesson as they're happening, whether inside my apartment or, in the case of shopping for dinner one Friday night, at the neighborhood supermarket.

"The people here want to help you," Mom says. "It's their *job* to be helpful."

"I know that. But I hate asking for help. It's like announcing to the whole world that... that I..."

"Need help? That you've encountered a task you can't perform on your own? I know. How terrible. You'll get used to it... eventually. And soon you'll shop here so much you won't need help. It'll become second nature to you."

"Did it?" God, as my father, asks me. My conversation with Mom fades into the background as God's question takes precedence.

"It did. *Everything* Mom taught me became second nature, with practice. There isn't one moment I can point to where I can say, 'Right there. That's when I knew how to do everything I would need to know.'

"But one week, when I asked Mom what day the following week she'd be by for my next lesson, she said, 'Actually, if you don't mind, I think I'm gonna go out with my girlfriends next week. We're gonna play bingo!' I knew immediately what this meant. It was the end of our lessons."

TODAY'S NEWS

I got some news today
When I entered the shoppers' fray.
To the market I went,
The one where they bilk
You out of a bundle
No one's eager to pay
For a gallon of milk,
And there was much more than the milk—
With its exorbitant fee—
Awaiting thirsty, unsuspecting *me*.

26

OUR BLIND DATE-AND OTHER TALES OF COURTSHIP

TERRENCE MCDONALD IS 27. THE YEAR IS 2017.

I didn't even *entertain* the concept of dating until Megan turned ten. I told myself I was keeping my focus where it needed to be. On doing my part to raise Megan into a smart, caring, respectful young lady. I knew a part of me was scared of trying to forge new relationships. Afraid of rejection. But I could not admit this aloud. Finally, I got up the nerve to put myself out there.

My first few adventures back in the dating pool weren't adventurous at all. They were sad. I asked three women out in a span of four months, only to have every relationship fail before they got started and to be told by all three that they couldn't possibly go out with me.

"Why not?" I asked the first.

"You're a nice guy and everything," she told me. I've found this to be code for, *You kinda freak me out.*

"But?"

"But… but you're crippled."

There it was. Each of my dates gave a version of this excuse. Each woman thinking she was doing me a favor, letting me down easy. I was discouraged (How could I not be?), but something told me not to give up. *The person you're looking for is out there, Terry.*

THE REVIEW

"I took every bad date I ever went on so personally," I say. "And the reason the dates didn't go well, I thought: the women I dated didn't accept the palsy. That had to be it. What a terrible miscalculation on my part."

We're in my apartment, on the recreation of a night ended early; a bad first date over before dark. I spent many such nights muttering to myself: "If only she knew who I really was… but she *obviously* doesn't want to *know*. She gave up on me," my daughter by my side, eager to hear the tale of the night's unsuccessful encounter, to commiserate with me.

"So, if that *was* a miscalculation, if the palsy wasn't the reason your dates didn't go well, what do you think the *real* reason was?"

"Well, it makes sense that those women would "give up." True, one or two women did refer to me as "crippled", and that wasn't fair, and they weren't right for me, but how could I ever expect a woman to want to be with me when my habit, in any situation that presented a modicum of difficulty, was to so quickly give up on myself?"

.   .   .

I've come over to visit Jack, who called me, all frantic. At first, I couldn't understand a word he was saying.

"Jack, slow down!"

"You have to come over. I have some great news, but it's the kind of news that's too important to tell you over the phone. I need to see you. Would it be alright if I come and pick you up and take you back to my place?"

An hour later, I'm at Jack's kitchen table while he pours me a Coke over ice. "Okay, so what's this news of yours?"

"I was in line at the market for ten minutes, and I started talking to the girl behind me—"

"Ten minutes? Must have been a long line," I guess.

"It was. On top of that, I'm pretty sure the cashier was in training… slow as a knuckleball… but back to what really matters. I told this girl all about my brilliant grandson."

"You told her I was *brilliant*?"

Oh, great, I grouse to myself.

"You are. I wrote down her number for you." He hands me a slip of paper. "Then I told her you'd be in touch."

I ask, "Why do you want me to humiliate myself like that, Jack? I hate blind dates. The idea of them is just… they're glorified job interviews. And they're nerve-racking."

"Just call her. Go out to eat. Hell, the worst that can happen is you decide you're not a good match. But you'll never know if you don't take a shot. You should give this girl a chance, Terry. She's a winner, I'm telling you."

"And you know this thanks to a five-minute conversation in line at the grocery store?"

"You can doubt me all you want. But I'm a great judge of character. This girl has a kind heart. And, Terry, she loves baseball. We talked about the Mariners. And it wasn't five minutes. It was almost ten."

MADELINE MAILER IS 22. THE YEAR IS 2017.

I meet him at a semi-fancy restaurant. *What is his first impression of me? Does he like what he sees? Am I his type?* I'm a tiny, brown-eyed brunette. His countenance gives nothing away.

"My name is Madeline," I say. "But… please… call me Mattie; everyone else does."

When we discover we enjoy many of the same films (Anyone up for a Frank Capra double-feature? "Yes, please," the two of us agree.) and much of the same literature ("A book should make its reader *feel*. You should be able to picture the scenery as if it were under your window, hear the autumn leaves crackle underfoot as you step outside. Bathe in the fragrant air as the trees surrender their bounties," he says. I'm with him on that point, too. "The best at this kind of writing, in my opinion," he finishes, "was Steinbeck."), I'm relieved.

"I'm actually a writer," I inform him, and my pride reveals itself in an almost indiscernible smile. "Or I'm trying to be."

He's intrigued. *Somehow, I knew he would be.* "I dabble in storytelling myself. It isn't a full-time job. Yet. I'm still a paper-pushing office drone. But, if someone asks my occupation, I put forward the more exciting of the pair. It's a good conversation-starter at parties."

THE REVIEW

At that time, I'd been in the same blank cubicle—a picture of Megan was all I had to claim it as mine—in the same monotonous office, with its ugly maroon carpeting installed before I was born, since Dad died, and the paying of rent became my responsibility (guess I never quite got on my feet until I was forced to). I detested the waste of my time that my job was, and the work itself—annuities—bored me. But it kept me and Megan fed. I wrote when I could find time on the weekends. I was "trying to be a writer" also, but it was difficult to be honest with myself.

MADELINE MAILER IS 22. THE YEAR IS 2017.

"I would do the same thing," I tell him. "I have been working on the same manuscript for over four years and still haven't managed to finish it."

"Well, what's it about, if you don't mind my asking?"

Before I am able to answer, our waitress stops by our table. Passing out paper coasters, she asks, "What can I get you folks to drink this evening?"

With a quick swipe of my hand in his direction, I defer to Terrence and mouth, "You go."

"I'll have a Coke," he says.

(His fallback drink whenever he goes out to eat, *comments an older, wiser Mattie.* Old reliable. I'll learn this over time. Back then I only knew what Jack had volunteered.).

.   .   .

"Gotcha." The waitress writes this down. "And how about you, ma'am?"

"Can I have one of your strawberry margaritas?"

"Of course. Can I see some I.D.?"

I reach for my purse, whip out my wallet, and hand over my driver's license for the waitress's quick glance.

(Terry has identification, but it is merely a card picturing him above all of his pertinent facts; no license. He tells me he thinks women in general find an odd form of joy in the "I.D.-ask"; It makes them feel young. Or beautiful. Or both. I think he's onto something there.)

Satisfied that I'm of age, the waitress says the drinks will be out in no time, and she promises to return for our orders in a few minutes. We're alone again, and I answer his *what's-your-book-about* question.

"My book is about ghosts." As matter-of-fact an answer as I've ever given anyone. Yet both of us have loosened up, and I see real potential here.

"Is the story about people you knew, who have passed away, or just your garden-variety ghosts?" He winks.

I chuckle.

"It's about my mother."

"Oh. How long has she—"

"Been gone?"

He nods.

"Seven years now."

For a second, he's lost the grip on his vocabulary (what he wants to say is sorry; *everyone* is sorry), then he says, "I'm sure she'd be so proud to know you're writing a tribute to her." He pauses. "It is a tribute, I assume?"

"Yes, it is. But it's more than a tribute. She always wanted me to write something beautiful. That's the way she put it. 'Write something beautiful for me, little girl.' Before I could, she was gone. But an unspoken promise is still a promise, and I intend to fulfill it."

"A gorgeous sentiment," he says.

"What type of stories do you write, Terrence? And *why* do you write? Is it an escape for you, or something you feel compelled to do?"

THE REVIEW

I hadn't examined my motivation in forever. "Every writer must work on stories they'd read themselves. Otherwise, they'll be bored."

This was my father's favorite piece of advice, an empty chorus given in the spoken word annually at commencement. Mattie didn't push me to be more specific. She didn't say, "So what kinds of stories would you read?" Instead, we began to chat about which books inspired us.

MADELINE MAILER IS 22. THE YEAR IS 2017.

Towards the end of the night—the waitress is bringing our check—when it's clear the date has gone well, I can put it off no longer. I have to know. *Am I right?*

"Terrence, if you don't mind… I need to ask you something."

"This isn't Megan-related," he says with a knowing pitch.

"No," I confirm. We spent twenty minutes on his little angel. "But there is something I've been curious about all night. I wasn't quite sure how to bring it up, Or *if I should.*"

It started when he told me he needed to go to the bathroom a half an hour into things. He rose to his feet. Used the table to brace himself. Without it, I imagined the task would be exponentially harder. Then, confusion the only emotion I could read, he said, "Could you point me towards the restrooms?"

I did. "They're right over there."

Confusion was instantly relief. "Thanks."

And then he walked away from me towards the MEN's room. His gait shaky and deliberate. *I've seen that same walk before*, I thought. *But where?*

"I don't mean to sound insensitive, but I think I need to be blunt here."

"Go ahead."

"I don't know how to say this without sounding mean, but I'm going to try. So please know I'm not *trying* to be mean."

"Got it." His body stiffens. In preparation for my verbal assault.

"When I arrived tonight, you were already here. You had reserved our table."

"That's right."

"I didn't think anything of it other than, *How nice of him! Waiting for a table could have been awkward.* Then, when you went to the bathroom, I couldn't help but notice the way you walk… slow and meandering is how I'd describe it. Like your body is trying to go someplace, but your limbs and your muscles have a hard time working together to get you there. And then I noticed your hands shook a little bit when you were using your silverware." He ordered spaghetti and meatballs. His fork wasn't always steady in his hand, gave in to the occasional tremor. His knife remained untouched throughout the meal. "Is there… something… I don't want to say *wrong* with you, but… oh, geez, how do I say this? Why can't I think of the right words to—"

"I have cerebral palsy," he says, his declaration the clemency that allows me to stop rambling.

I feel the corners of my mouth turn up. "I *knew* it."

"If you don't want to see me again," he says, "I'll understand."

I can tell this isn't true, but it's an acceptable lie. Here's your out, it says. *Take it, or forever hold your peace.*

"You asked what kind of stories I write," he goes on. "Truth is, in all the books I've read, in all the years I've been submerged in literature, I have never found a character like me in any one of those stories. People in books are either too perfect—the athlete or the millionaire who gets to date the beautiful woman—or they're too damaged to do anything but depress the reader. I think there should be a middle-ground in there somewhere." Nerves have ahold of his vocal chords, a stammer surfacing. "So… so I decided… that… I should write… it's my dream to write… stories about p-people who d-d-deal with the same stuff I do. I want everyone to know what having c-ce-cerebral…"

"Terrence?"

"Yes?"

"Take a deep breath," I advise.

He does.

"You don't have to talk so fast. I'm not going anywhere. I haven't even had any dessert yet tonight. And I was counting on a big piece of chocolate cake." Where there had only been upturned corners of a mouth minutes ago, there is now a full grin. "When I was in elementary school, a friend of mine had palsy similar to yours," I tell him. "Not severe but noticeable. I figured that's what you had, but I wanted to know for sure."

"Are you okay with it?" he asks. Translation: Sometimes he's not okay with it himself.

"Everyone's got issues," I answer. "Your biggest one just happens to be on the surface. Is it ideal? No, it's not. I won't lie to you. But let's just see where we go from here. How's that?"

"Thank you for giving me a chance," he says, and he relaxes. For the first time tonight, he isn't waiting for a figurative axe to swing.

MATTIE MAILER IS 22. THE YEAR IS 2017.

The light that illuminates the jazz club this night is a soft shade of blue. Terrence is in his element here, head bobbing, fingers snapping in time with the live music (Okay, so they're not *really* snapping; he tells me he can't actually *snap* his fingers—"It's a palsy thing"—but he is making a very reminiscent motion. No one here cares that it doesn't produce a sound and isn't quite right.) Every now and then he glances over at me and winks, like he and I are sharing a closely guarded secret.

"This was one of Charlie's favorite places," Terrence says. "I think it's because his family moved up here from New Orleans—he was born there—and this hole-in-the-wall brought him as close as he could get to living the stories his parents told. Of the food. The music. The Dixieland spirit.

"When Charlie was two, his dad got a job at Boeing, as part of the war effort. His family joined a massive African-American migration west, and he missed the culture and the feel of the crescent city ever since. Money was always too tight for vacations, so his parents' myths and tall tales became his only connection to The Big Easy."

"Sounds like this Charlie was really special to you."

"He was."

"Tell me more about him."

He waits until there's a lull in the music—the band is taking their set break. "We'll be back in a little bit," the singer says. "You folks enjoy your dinner. And I'm supposed to tell you that Happy Hour pricing is in effect until we return."

In the relative quiet, Terrence says, "Charlie was a second father to me. While it was difficult for me to communicate with my own dad, Charlie always respected my opinion—from the moment I met him to the last moment we had together—even when he didn't always agree with it. And, most importantly, Charlie *always* had time for me. Our brunch meetings were where I learned my palsy could sometimes be an asset. He spent many hours trying to convince me of this. 'If you can show Megan you can do anything an able-bodied person can do, with some notable, unavoidable exceptions,' he contended, 'she will see being *different* does not equate to being worse. That is one of the greatest lessons you can teach her.'"

"Did you believe him?" I ask.

"I think the correct question is: Do I believe him? Charlie isn't here anymore, but I still ask myself that question every day. Do I believe him? The answer is: Sometimes I do, sometimes I don't."

"Well, *I* believe him. I know we're still getting to know each other, Terrence, but I hope you know I believe you can do anything you have the courage to attempt. Damn the palsy. What did I tell you the first night we met? The palsy is one of your issues. It doesn't define you, though. And you shouldn't let it."

"Thank you for saying that, Mattie. You have no idea what it means to me."

THE REVIEW

"What *did i*t mean to you?" asks Mattie-God. We're in the jazz club. *Where else?* I think.

"It meant love," I say. "I was pretty sure I was falling for her before that night. I'd been entranced by her since my first glimpse. To know she believed in me confirmed my suspicion. What I felt was real."

TERRENCE MCDONALD IS 27. THE YEAR IS 2017.

Our third date, a movie.

"I hope those actors got paid," I tell Mattie afterwards, as we eat a late dinner. "If they didn't, they might never see a dime."

"I can't believe some of the crap that gets made these days," Mattie agrees.

The reviewer in our local newspaper—raving over the brilliance, the unmatched acting, the shocking twist—convinced us to take time out of our lives and see this disappointment.

"Well, we did get to spend time together," Mattie reminds me. "The movie may not have been worth the price of admission, but you were."

"Really?" I smile, blush.

"M-hmmm."

"I just feel bad. I was the one who suggested we see that pile."

"No worries. Besides, I was looking at you the whole time, anyway."

She was?

"I'm sorry I didn't pay more attention to you."

"It's okay." She chuckles. "You're paying attention now. You were watching the onscreen train wreck, I get it."

"I couldn't take my eyes off of it," I share, embarrassed.

Changing the subject, Mattie asks, "So how do you think tonight went, the movie notwithstanding?"

"What do you mean?"

"Would you want to… see me again?" She is vulnerable, exposed. Her motives are transparent. She sees us going somewhere, being something. She *believes* in us. All she needs is my confirmation.

"I'm free next Tuesday night."

"So am I," she says, sounding almost giddy, and then she goes back to her meal, making a valiant effort to tuck away her pleasure for fear that it might have been put on exhibit too early.

THE STRONGEST MAN I KNOW

The looks we get
Out on the town,
The quick glances over shoulders
And the even quicker turn-arounds;
The leers;
The loud whispers and the phony
"We'll-pray-for-you" tears
That set my face and ears
To burn,
Or, at least, on the verge…

They are all from people
Who don't understand
The way a man walks
Doesn't define that man.
But they won't have to think about
The glimpse they got
If they can throw him in a deep, figurative hole
Locked in a small, figurative box.

27
ALL'S FAIR IN LOVE

Megan's always been an old soul. Kind. Empathetic. Trustworthy. Beautiful. Imaginative yet logical. Practical, yet a steadfast believer in magic. She knows her dad isn't normal in the way most people's parents are normal, and she does all she can to make the task of parenting easier on me.

So I'm astonished at how stubborn she's being tonight. *There has to be a reason.*

"I don't want to meet her."

There it is.

"Why not?"

"I don't want to meet her, and that's that."

"Why not?" I repeat.

"Because," Megan replies, petulant.

"Because? Come on, Megs, I need more than that."

"Just because. Because she's not Mom. Is that good enough for you?"

No matter how old her soul may be, she *is* just a kid. I can't forget this as I stand with her in the space my landlords call a living room. *Megan doesn't want the life she knows upset any further. Remember when you were her age, how painful the divorce was, how you cried every night for a family that was together, a family that loved each other?*

"You'll like Mattie." I soldier on. I am determined to win her over.

"I like *Mom*."

"Megan, please listen to me, sweetheart. I love you. I love you more than you can imagine, and every other weekend—four days a month—you are with me. I treasure both you and Mattie. Can't you do me a favor, just this once, and meet her?"

I'm only half-convinced as I'm speaking that my plea will work. But, when all is said and done, it does. Megan's granite exterior gives way. Her body slackens. Tiny tears come to her doe eyes.

"What if you end up loving her more than you love me, Daddy?"

Suddenly we've reached the crux of the problem. The worry holed-up inside Megan's subconscious.

"That will *never* happen, Megs." I take her face in my hands. "Do you hear me, little girl? That will never happen. You have my word."

"I'm not a little girl anymore, Daddy. I'm eleven now."

"Eleven?" I smile. "Coulda sworn you were twenty-five."

She laughs. "You're weird, Daddy."

"Sure I'm weird. Which explains a lot about you." I pause for a second. "So, do you think you'd be willing to meet Mattie?"

"Where would we be meeting her?"

"There's a restaurant she likes. It's just down the street. We're supposed to be there in half an hour."

"They have good food at this restaurant?" says my beautiful progeny.

"I don't know. I would guess so."

"Alright. I'll go. The food's probably better than what we have for dinner every night I'm here."

Eggos every night. What can I say? I'm not a professional chef, and I'm still learning to trust myself in the kitchen. It's a process. The store-bought waffles serve their purpose.

"Thank you?" I say, not sure I *should be* thanking her.

.   .   .

A moonless night. The air warm but not humid. If there are stars up there, our locale's man-made light drowns them, renders naked eyes blind to celestial brilliance.

The Puyallup Fair. A summer tradition. Renamed The Washington State Fair years ago, for reasons likely corporate and stupid, it will always be "The Puyallup" to loyal attendees. Mattie and I walk its midway.

"Thanks for inviting me," she says.

"Absolutely. I could think of no one better."

"Why didn't you invite Megan? I would have loved the chance to see her again."

"She's with her mother this weekend. Couldn't have brought her if I'd wanted to. Want me to win you a stuffed animal over there?" I point to a booth to our left, where a man is trying and failing to pop a not fully inflated balloon with a dart.

"Yeah. Let's see what you can do."

"No promises now."

"Trust me," Mattie says, "I'm not holding my breath." She elbows me playfully.

"Ah, we have a doubter in our midst, I see. I shall turn you, madam. By the end of this night, you will believe."

.   .   .

Part of my hyperbole comes to pass. By the end of the night, Mattie *does* believe in something. Not my ability to wrestle a stuffed elephant away from its carnie captors. Something better. More concrete.

She consoles me when I leave the fairgrounds empty-handed.

"At least we got some scones." She holds up the bagful of treats we're taking home. Those fair scones are famous.

"Did you have a good time, Mattie?"

"A wonderful time. This was a beautiful day."

"You're not just saying that, I hope?" We halt our slow amble towards the exit, moving off to the side to let a group of teen-agers behind us get by. "You don't have to coddle me," I tell her.

"I'm not just saying that, and I *am not* coddling you. I mean what I say."

"I was so sure I could win you an elephant, but I guess spending all day at the fair is not the ideal way to kill nine hours when you've got cerebral palsy to contend with. I *am* sorry I couldn't—"

My hands are shaking, and Mattie is trying to steady me as she interjects, "Terrence, I love you."

"You what?"

She what? Stay upright. Don't tip over.

"I love you."

She loves me.

Don't cry. Don't fucking cry.

"I thought that's what I heard," I say. "I love you, too. I've loved you ever since our first date."

BONDS

Bonds can be forged with
The simplest gesture.
A wave of the hand,
A bat of the eye.
Baking cookies
On a Monday night

When a sadness—
Allowed to fester—
Turns to a calorie-heavy treasure,
The first expression in a love new
And predicted by few
That, nonetheless,
Will be proven true.

28

COOKIES MAKE THE HEART GROW STRONGER

MEGAN MCDONALD IS 11 & ¾. THE YEAR IS 2019.

"Cut the turkey, Daddy!"

"Yes, ma'am."

On my command, he begins carving—his is the first ceremonial stab; Mattie does the rest—and they dole out the bird. In doing so, the magical spell of our Norman Rockwell moment is broken. He and Mattie at opposite ends of the table, and me—"the beautiful Ms. Meg," Mattie calls me—seated next to her.

"Would you like light meat or dark, Megs?" Daddy asks.

"I'll have some of both, thanks. I'm not picky."

"I'm glad we could have you here tonight, Megan," Mattie says, grinning ear-to-ear. She really is glad. I'm thankful that she makes Daddy happy. "When you're not here, your dad can't stop talking about you." She lowers her voice and whispers in my ear: "He loves you so much. So do I."

My eyes ask what my mouth cannot. Do you really? Don't bullshit a bullshitter. I'm eleven, almost twelve. I know how to play the game.

I know how to play the game, too, her face says. I'm telling you the truth.

This night, over turkey and all the trappings of a Thanksgiving feast, the relationship Mattie and I share is continuing to change. Deepening. She's no longer just "The girl who's with my dad." She is now "The woman who makes my dad and me part of a family again."

The bonding that made this possible took root not when my father thought it had; at the not-quite-large family-run restaurant, Lena's Café, where we met about six months ago. It is true we were both nice to each other on that evening, me in the best dress I could find on short notice, and Mattie looking great in her most flattering color; red. But nothing came out of it other than our meeting.

The day our bond truly started growing into something profound was two months after café night. It was a Monday afternoon, and I had just been dumped by my first-ever boyfriend, Jimmy Davis. Our storybook romance lasted a week. Devastated, I came home to my dad's split-level apartment, where I was staying while my mom was out of town on business, and I ran straight up to my room, hoping no one paid any attention to my tear-filled entrance.

Someone had.

Mattie, preparing to bake cookies, let stand a bowl full of dough and followed me up the stairs.

"Megan, are you alright?" she asked at the top.

"Yeah. I'm fine. I just want to be alone, if that's okay?"

"Sure."

"Thanks."

I thought I'd handled the situation okay. I'd only given a week of my life to Jimmy Davis, yet my heart was missing a chunk. I closed the bedroom door behind me, collapsed down onto the bed, and cried quiet sobs. A minute later, there was a knock.

"What?" I snapped.

"Sweetie, it's Mattie."

Who else could it be? Dad was still at work, and we were the only ones home.

"Can I come in?"

"Why?"

Mattie had never come into my room before without my father leading the way.

Silence outside the door.

She's trying to come up with something. She's probably been right where you are, Megs, and knows what you're going through. You have to respect her for reaching out. If anyone can help you right now, odds are it's her.

"If you want to come in, come in," I called.

The door opened a crack.

"Really?"

"Really."

Mattie swung the door wider, crossed the tiny room, and sat beside me on the edge of my bed. "Is there anything I can do for you, sweetheart?" she asked.

"I don't know. I don't think so."

"Tough day?"

"The worst."

Her eyes flashed with sudden understanding.

"What's his name?"

"Jimmy."

"How did he do it?"

"On the bus. In front of all our friends."

"Ouch."

Mattie slipped her arm over my shoulder.

"The same thing happened to me, you know?" she said.

"It did?"

"Yep."

"What did you do? How did you get over it? Over him?"

"It took time. I'm not going to lie to you. It wasn't easy, and it didn't happen overnight. But, after a while, he was just another boy."

Just another boy.

Mattie wiped a stray tear, slower than the rest in its resolute, downward march, from my cheek. I leaned into her. Her warmth calmed me, and a full-blown hug blossomed.

"You know what helped me get over it?"

"What?"

"My mother came into my room and asked if I wanted to bake cookies with her."

I threw her arm off my shoulder. "You think *that's* gonna make this better?"

"Well, no, I just—"

"You just what? You thought you could fix everything with cookies? Look, lady, I'm not five. That's not how this works. You think you've been where I am, but you haven't! Maybe baking cookies worked when *you* were my age. Maybe they worked on *you* because you got to bake them with your mom. *My* mom is out of town. She's not here right now. I don't need to bake cookies. I need to be left alone!"

"I get it. I'll leave you alone, then. I'm sorry. I've never had kids. I guess I don't really know how this works."

Just as she reached my door, I asked, "What kind of cookies are you making?"

She turned back around. "Chocolate chip."

Mattie held out her hand to me, I took it and rose to my feet. "You wanta bake cookies with me, Megan?"

"Not really. But I will." *At least it's something to do besides wasting my night crying in my room,* I thought.

.   .   .

"We're using my mom's recipe," Mattie said. "Extra vanilla. It cuts down on the richness of the chocolate, my mother said."

"Do you think that's true?" I asked.

"It was my mother, and if she said it, and it had to do with baking, I just accepted it as true. She could do no wrong in the kitchen. Other places, sure, but not the kitchen."

"Where is she now?"

Mattie's stirring in our yellow mixing bowl, but my question stops the motion. "She passed away when I was fifteen. She had an aneurism. One minute she was talking to me on the phone—she called me at my best friend's house to say I needed to come home for dinner—the next minute, I heard the phone hit the floor, and Dad was on, telling me to come home right away, something had happened. When I got home, our driveway was packed with cars. Everyone I'd ever known was there, everyone saying how sorry they were. I heard all of their *sorry*s and *be strong*s. All I wanted to hear was my mother's voice again."

I can't imagine losing my mom like that. "I'm sorry," I said.

"Not your fault."

"Do you remember when we first met?" I asked her.

"Sure."

"We had dinner at that place you suggested."

"Uh-huh. Leena's is still my favorite restaurant." She spent a moment remembering. Then she snapped back into our present. "Can you bring the butter over here?"

I went and got it, and she put a chunk in the bowl.

"I hated you back then, Mattie," I told her.

"I could tell. You wore a scowl all night, and you only perked up when it was time for dessert."

"I'll never forget that fudge brownie," I said, and we both laughed. "I told Daddy before we left the house that night how I was afraid he'd end up loving you more than he loved me."

She went back to her stirring. "We gotta work this butter in. Can I tell you something really important?"

"Sure."

"I love your dad very much and so, by extension, I love you, too. But you've got a mom, and I'm not trying to *replace* her. I just want us to get along, that's all."

"I want that, too."

"Can we both agree that, from now on, we'll try our best to get along with each other?"

"That's fair," I said, then I asked, "How much longer 'till we can put these cookies in the oven?"

THE PLACE WE CALL OUR OWN

The place we call our own
Is so much more than a home.
It's a sanctuary, ballast.
It may not be a palace,
But you'd be hard-pressed
To convince me of that
When I'm in my beautiful kitchen baking cookies,
Be they the kind known to
Pack on the pounds,
Or non-fat.
Defending the place we call our own,
I'd go to any mat.

29

A PLACE TO CALL OUR OWN

TERRENCE MCDONALD IS 29. THE YEAR IS 2019.

We've found *our* dream house.

Our palace.

Something I thought I'd *never* find. If my father was not entitled to such a luxury, in my mind, then how could I justify such a thing falling to me?

And I can afford it. Mattie and I can afford it together. She is eager to make the purchase. She told Megan and me, with happy tears at the corners of her eyes as we ate dinner—Megan's favorite; chicken strips, corn on the cob, and macaroni and cheese—that she was pregnant. *We* were pregnant. That was two months ago, and we're all so excited, Megan to be a big sister, me to be a father again, Mattie to be the mother she's wanted to be since girlhood.

"We'll get you moved out of that cramped apartment of yours," she says. We've been wanting to do this for a while, and now we have reason. "And we'll get to start our life together in earnest."

Mattie's looking around the property with longing. The house sits on a quarter of an acre, far enough outside the city limits that the deep night will not be contaminated with traffic, sirens, domestic disputes heard through open windows on hot summer evenings.

"This will be the perfect place for Megan and her little sister to grow up," she adds.

Megan. I have not floated to her the idea of our moving, that she might register her opinion. How could I forget to do this? Not that she's a huge fan of my apartment, but still.

"Should we make an offer?" Mattie prods me along.

We should.

"Yes. But I gotta make a phone call first. Can you wait just a minute?"

·   ·   ·

Megan answers her cell on the second ring. She's at her mom's. I can hear a TV droning on in the background.

"Hey, Dad. What's up?"

"I have a question for you, Megs. How would you feel if I moved out of my apartment and we got a new place?"

"Fine with me." That was less painful than I'd expected. The upcoming caveat might cause a stir, though.

"How would you feel if Mattie and I moved in together?" *Talk quickly. Don't let her comment until you're finished.* To that end, I keep my gums flapping. "We found a beautiful house we could share," I say. "You'll have your own room, and it'll be bigger than the one you've got at my place now."

There's a long space. Just before I start to wonder if she's gone mute, Megan says, "She's pregnant, Dad. It's time, don't you think?"

"That's what I figured."

"I should still ask you some cursory questions, though, just to make sure. Otherwise, I won't be doing my job."

My daughter knows how to elicit a chortle from me. "Okay."

"Okay, Dad. Here goes." She takes a moment to clear her throat, and I can almost see through the phone as she composes herself, working to think up her queries. "You've thought this through? You're sure this is what you want?"

"Of course."

"And you love her?"

"I do, Megs."

"And you love me?"

"Of course."

"And you'll both love my little sister?"

"We will. Without a doubt."

"Then it sounds like you'd better get ready to move. Do you need me to come over and help?"

I chuckle again. "I think we can handle it, but thanks for the support, kiddo."

"You're welcome. I love you, Dad. See you next weekend."

"Love you, too, gingersnap. I'll talk to you later."

.   .   .

Mattie and I go on an in-depth tour (our third stroll around the property) conducted by the middle-aged realtor. The place is resplendent. It doesn't have a foyer like Dad's castle, but it *does* contain two stories and an expansive kitchen with a brand-new stove. Mattie can't stop championing the amount of room she'll have to cook and bake and maneuver among all of our combined pots and pans.

We make our offer.

The day's house-hunting done, Mattie backs her car out of the driveway, and we head down the highway toward a glimmering destination in the distance—our life together.

.   .   .

Miscarriage is a dirty word.

It may not fit the four-letter criteria of most profanity, but when spoken by a white-coated doctor, it strikes Mattie and me with an impact reserved for only the most thoughtless phrases. Or a speeding semi-truck, whose driver runs me down and doesn't bother to stop, not even to memorialize the part of me he's just killed. Our worst fears are realized, and the reason for Mattie's pre-dawn abdominal pain, accompanied by heavy bleeding, is understood.

"I'm sorry to be the bearer of such awful news." An image of the young physician burns its way onto my life's kaleidoscope of images.

"Was it something we did, Doctor?" I ask.

"I don't think so. Sometimes these things just happen."

Okay, maybe so. But why? There has to be a reason why this thing, this life-altering, horrible thing, just happened. Without a reason, the one conclusion left for me to draw is that God is unfeeling, merciless, a real bastard.

"Terry?"

"Yes?" I look to Mattie, so beautiful in the muted light of the hospital room.

"Take me home. We'll try again soon. But, for now, I want to go home. Take me home."

I do as I am told. I phone Grandpa Jack, the relative closest to the hospital. His apartment is only a few blocks south, and Jack has offered up his assistance as "your personal driver" at any and all times we might need him.

In a few minutes, he comes to our aid. He re-parks Mattie's car—our original transport—in a space that can be legally occupied overnight. We'll make arrangements to have it retrieved. Then he drives us home in his truck.

"There's no reason to buy anything but a Ford," he is fond of saying, and then he'll pat the dashboard affectionately. This late afternoon, though, conversation is non-existent, save for one instance. Jack speaks in conjunction with the work of his misting tear ducts. "You're gonna be a great mother, Mattie. If you want my opinion, I think you already are. Megan adores you, missy."

"You think so?" Devastated, Mattie wants to believe him. *Needs* to believe her maternal instincts will still be put to good use even if her ovaries won't allow reproduction.

"I *know* so."

As the three of us pull up in the driveway, I recognize Beth's car parked off to the side and see that both she and Megan, twelve-and-a-half, wait by the front door.

Jack helps Mattie out of the truck. I clamber out the back. My exit is slow—some might call it plodding—but it *is* without assistance. I fall in behind the two of them, and we move together toward our visitors, the refuge of home. No one utters a word. Our faces betray our feelings. Just as we reach her, Megan bursts into tears.

"I love you, Mattie," she cries, throwing her arms around her emotionally beaten stepmother. Beth winces at the proclamation, but our daughter does not take notice.

It's a Friday night. I know why Beth is here. She's handing Megan off to me, fulfilling her duty as custodial parent.

"Do you still want her this weekend?" she asks, once Megan has taken Mattie's hand and led her into the house.

"Sure. It'll do Mattie good to see Megs. They've gotten pretty close this past year."

More wincing.

"Okay. I'll be back on Sunday, then. As usual."

"As usual," I parrot back in agreement.

Grandpa Jack gives me a heartfelt "I'm so sorry" and a hug good-bye, and then he's in his truck again and follows Beth back down the drive and out toward the main road leading to the interstate. Meanwhile, Mattie, Megan, and I sequester ourselves in the house after it empties. We watch old black-and-white movies, hold each other, and cry for the loss of someone we'll never know over buttered popcorn.

THE REVIEW

"So what was the reason for Mattie's miscarriage? I've waited all these years, and now that I'm up here with You... God, the all-knowing, I want to know why my wife and I had to endure such pain? Why couldn't we know our child?"

God is the doctor who first gave us the news. Diplomas plaster His office walls. That He would choose this guise does not surprise me. However, I cannot say the same of His reason for the miscarriage itself. I am stunned when He says:

"It had to happen."

"What? Why?"

"Terrence, that miscarriage cemented—more than Jimmy Davis or cookies baked together or Thanksgivings *spent together* ever could—the connection between your wife and daughter. Once that pivotal point passed, this connection could never be torn asunder by anyone or anything. It was a connection both would *need* in the years to come, when heartache and mortality made concurrent visits upon your family, as they must upon every family.

"You may not like *the reason, My reason.* I don't *expect y*ou to like it. *But there it is."*

"Will I ever get to see my child? I was sure she—I always assumed we were going to have a girl, though we never knew for sure, because Mattie didn't want to know—I assumed she would meet me in Heaven. I'm not all that religious, I know, but I convinced myself she'd be waiting for me."

God gives me the doctor's serious face. It is on the border of grim, and it worries me. "Should you be judged worthy of Heaven, Terrence, then yes, you will get to see her."

"If we'd had a girl, we were going to name her—"

"Chloe, after your mom," God interrupts.

Don't forget who you're talking to, I remind myself.

"Keep your mind on this review," God advises. "Learn from it."

That's right. The overriding lesson of my life? I have to decipher it.

God nods, as if to say, You got it, then says aloud, "If you can do that, you *will* meet your child in Heaven."

THE INEVITABLE

No matter how hard we fight it, and
Despite the agreements we make with time
To gently bide *it*,
All of us will come to a point
Where we can go no further,
When our every joint aches,
And we ask
A favor that takes
All our reserve strength.
For God to extract
Our souls from this painful place,
Up into the sky.

Why deny our mortality?
We should embrace the inevitable reality
That's never been hidden
And *make* something remarkable
Out of what we *are* given.

30

EMBRACING THE INEVITABLE

TERRENCE MCDONALD IS 35. THE YEAR IS 2025.

As I sit with Mom in the waiting room, I'm slumped in my chair, and I'm trying not to cry. Crying is just about the least manly thing I can think of. Maybe it's appropriate, considering the situation, but it's just not something I do. Ever.

"Mom?"

She looks at me—almost through me—with those eyes, piercing and yet still loving. Ice blue, they're perfectly paired with her white-blonde hair. "Terry?"

"Do you think…." I stop. I can't ask her *that*.

"Do I think…." She wants me to finish the thought, which means I have no choice but to finish it.

"Do you think Dad's in Heaven?"

She sits back in her chair and considers the possibility. "I do. You may not agree with me, and that is your prerogative—I know you two didn't always get along. And, from what I've heard, he was a different man before I met him."

"You definitely changed him for the better," I credit her.

"Thank you, Terrence. Since you're asking my opinion, I'll tell you that I choose to believe the man I love is in Heaven."

"Do you think he's waiting for you?"

"I do."

·   ·   ·

The doctors tell us the cancer will be quick in its progression. Any treatment undertaken would only delay the inevitable a short time. So they send Mom home where, it is reasoned, she will be more comfortable.

She is. Her remaining time is spent on the phone with friends sharing stories of the past, when she has the energy to talk. Consuming her favorite meals, when she has the appetite to eat. Otherwise, she watches TV, listens to music, reads. She lives life. If you didn't know of her illness, you wouldn't know she's being held captive by the end it portends.

CHLOE COOPER MCDONALD IS 64. THE YEAR IS 2025.

It's a cloud-ridden, frostbitten November morning. The light outside my bedroom window is snow-sky gray. As I wake to this light, breath is hard to come by. The wheezing pants I *can* muster are abbreviated and arduous. I reach for the telephone nearby, secure the receiver, and dial.

"911. What's your emergency?" the dispatcher asks.

"I need an ambulance."

.   .   .

Terrence, being next of kin, is apprised of my condition and calls a cab. My father, his Grandpa Jack, is not notified yet; the news that Jack's only child is dying could very well stop his heart.

Terry darts into my room. "I got here as fast as I could."

"Good," I say. "'Cause there's a big event about to happen here. Better to be early than late. I wouldn't want you to miss it."

He frowns. "Mom, that's fucking morbid."

"It's the truth. I'm glad you're here."

"So? Doesn't mean I want to hear it."

"You're gonna do fine, you know that?"

"I don't know shit."

"You're gonna do fine," I repeat. "You don't need me anymore."

He doesn't. He'll mourn my passing and move on, thinking of me whenever he sees a baseball game, whenever he takes little Megan—she's not so little anymore—to the aquarium, whenever another Mother's Day dawns. He'll think of me on sunny days and recall our family trips to the beach; on dreary afternoons, remembering how we reveled in the game of Dominos. The first time I brought it up from the basement on a rainy, darkening Saturday evening in November, he said to me, "What's so great about a bunch of tiles?" But he only said it once, grew to love the togetherness those tiles fostered. He'll think of me…

"I'll think of you always, Mom. I'll never forget you or the lessons you worked so hard to teach me. You can't tell me teaching those lessons was an easy chore."

"Jesus, Terry."

"What?"

"I'm dying, but I'll still be around," I say. "So don't you go all sentimental and sugar-sweet on me. I know it won't be as simple for you to see or hear me once I'm gone, but I won't have cancer anymore. It's worth the trade."

. . .

Five minutes elapse. Terry is still, keeping a vigil. Then, just when I suspect sleep will be the next visitor through my door, someone else appears.

Carl?

He is younger than I remember him by two decades and more. The crow's feet that were his constant companions, making pronounced showings during trying times, have yet to be birthed. Any tinge of gray is gone from his thick head of hair. But there is no mistaking his identity all the same.

You're here for me.

I am, he says.

I'm ready.

Turning to Terry, I see my son is staring off into space, his hands clasped together, fingers interlocked, eyes vacant.

What is he thinking?

I clear my throat to get his attention.

Trance broken, he glances up. "What is it, Mom?"

I point to the doorway. "I was right, Terr. Your father made it to Heaven."

These are my last words. After which my soul slips out from under the ravages set upon my body. Crossing the wispy veil between Heaven's outlying areas and Earth's aromatically stained hospital room invigorates me. It is as though I am born anew, charging into Carl's arms.

From a bench in Pondering Park, we watch a nurse check my vitals for a final confirmation. Switching off the machines, she tells Terry, "Take as long as you want. There's no rush. When you're done in here, just let me know. I'll be right outside."

LISA BROWER MCDONALD IS 62. THE YEAR IS 2025.

Terrence calls me.

His first word to me is:

"Lisa?"

I would have preferred *Mom*, but I don't tell him this. I don't dare say *anything* like that. This is our first phone call since my leaving. He might never call again.

"Yes?"

"My mom died today. I thought you should know."

His words slice at whatever bond remains between us, but they do not sever it.

"I'm sorry. How's your father taking it?"

"Dad? He's been gone for years."

"I didn't see anything in the obits," I say.

"It was only a few words. I'm not surprised you missed it."

He *is* surprised. There is silence between us. Now it's his turn to take a step back, to realize how far removed from each other's lives we've been.

"I wanted you to know also that you have a granddaughter. Her name is Megan. She's all but grown now, into the sweetest young woman I know. And Lisa?"

"Yes?"

"One last thing. I don't know why you left, or if you regret leaving. I don't know if Dad was right about you, and you were heavy into drugs that will remain nameless here, and that might have been the reason I turned out the way I did. Certainly it *might* have been the reason. Speculation is not truth, however, and it really doesn't matter, in the long-run. I am who I am.

"All I know for sure is I can't go on hating you just because he did. I can't blame you for something you chose to do thirty-odd years ago, at a time when you were unaware of your pregnancy. Dad felt like he was never good enough for you, could never do enough to keep you happy, and so that's how I felt, too. For a while."

I flash back to Carl's worry of turning into a man always chasing the unattainable.

"But I'm done feeling that way. I forgive you, Lisa, and I hope you can forgive yourself."

.   .   .

Three uneventful years pass. Then, one night in my sixty-fifth year, life ends. I'm asleep when my heart beats its final percussive note. I feel no pain.

Sleep ends.

A dream cut short. All is black, and I'm floating in space, but something tells me not to panic. A tunnel appears, and I move into it.

It's time, Lisa.

Is that Carl McDonald's voice I hear? I haven't heard his voice in years.

Time for what?

You're ready. Come Home.

What is this place, Carl? Is it Heaven?

It can be, if you want it to be, he answers. *It's the afterlife.*

I don't deserve to go to Heaven.

Why not?

I wasn't a good mother, or a good wife.

The Boss said you'd say that. He sent me to welcome you. See those two doors at the end of the hall?

Yeah, I see them.

Open the door on the right. I'm at the top of the stairs, waiting for you.

.   .   .

I make my way up the golden staircase and find Carl right where he said he'd be. He reaches for me, and we embrace.

God sent my ex-husband to welcome me into the afterlife? I say when we're apart again. *Why not my parents?*

I know. It seems weird, doesn't it? But He sent me for a reason. Remember when Terrence called you and forgave you for the things you did when he was a child?

Sure. That phone call is the clearest memory I have.

Well, The Boss was behind it. It was up to Terence to make the call, and he did so of his own free will. But it was something God wanted very much to see happen.

Why?

Put simply, Lisa, the afterlife is all about forgiveness. Without it, no one can ever fully understand the lessons life has taught them, and no one can attain true peace.

Carl drapes his arm around my shoulder. *We were no match made in Heaven,* he thinks in my direction, *but we were meant to come together for Terry. And I am meant to tell you that I forgive you all your faults, all your missteps.*

Your turn, Lisa, says a new voice. The Boss, I know without asking.

I forgive you yours, too, Carl. And thank you for raising our boy when I couldn't. He grew into quite the man.

THE REVIEW

God is Lisa. He has chosen an older, grandmotherly version of her, as opposed to the Lisa I knew, the Lisa who left. We're in what I can only assume is her house. (I've never been here). It's small—only two bedrooms, one of which goes unused—but warm with woodstove heat. God has stationed us in front of that stove.

"Has viewing these scenes affected your perception of Lisa any?" Lisa-God asks.

I search inside myself for the answer. *Don't give the response you think He wants to hear. Tell the truth. Your truth.* "It has," I reply.

"In what ways?"

"I never knew she regretted leaving me. I thought it was a choice she made, and I figured she'd remained content with it throughout her life. Because, if she did regret it, she would have made an effort to contact me."

Why are you so sure of this, Terrence? I challenge myself. *Can you honestly say you made an effort to make amends for every regret you had in your life? No, you can't, no one can, so don't even try to lie to yourself.*

BLIND DATE

This date was
The scariest kind.
No picture.
No description.
Other than his name,
It was totally blind.

She went in with apprehension,
And out with hope
She came.
She went in expecting
Dinner with a dud, a dweeb,
A dope.

But she found a man
With whom one conversation ran
Into a myriad of others.
His best quality, though
(Besides loving his mother):
Her new beau
Was himself,
Didn't put on a show
For her benefit.

31

THE NAME GAME

TERRENCE MCDONALD IS 37. THE YEAR IS 2027.

Nerves raw with worry, I wait up late this Friday night. Unable to sleep. I pray from the pillow that is not facilitating my sleep that I will soon hear my daughter's key sliding into the locked front door downstairs.

"She's fine," Mattie works to convince me. "Megan's fine. If there were a problem, which there isn't, Megan would either have called it a night early, and she'd already be home, or she would have found a way to contact us. She's got her cell on her, doesn't she? She's having a good time. Don't begrudge her that, Terry. You raised a responsible girl."

"You think so?"

"I *know* so."

Tonight, Megan is on a date. Like my first date with Mattie, this encounter, too, is blind.

.　　　　.　　　　.

"All I know is his name." She made this admission while putting on her makeup in the bathroom mirror. "A friend set us up."

I stood figurative guard in the doorframe of the bathroom. *No one shall mistreat my little girl.*

"And his name is?"

"I'm not gonna tell you."

"Why not?"

"Simple. When and if you do meet him, Dad, you'll grill him as it is. Telling you his name now would only give you more time to build up ammunition for the firing squad."

Acting like I would rake her latest boyfriend over smoldering coals, which I might very well do—*if* I found him unworthy—is a pastime for us. You might call it a ritual. Performed anew to coincide with any boy who enters Megan's life with the intent of remaining in it. It's Mattie's job, prior to their going out, to offer up his name, provided to her by Megan sometime earlier. It's Megan's job to pretend this name was shared in confidence.

"It's Tom," Mattie revealed. She was sauntering past the open door, mock mischief her co-conspirator.

"Mattie!" Megan feigned outrage.

"He would have learned it eventually."

"I know, but who said you had to tell him?" They smiled.

My daughter wore an apprehensive smile of her own—thinner than her usual grin—as she glided out the door, into the unknown of that evening's rendezvous.

THE FLAWED CREATOR OF MEN

To error is human,
But what if it is Godly, too?
If we accept this precept,
That God makes mistakes
Like me,
Like you?

Accidents wouldn't be accidents, then.
They'd merely be unscheduled meetings between
Shaken beings
In a land that began
At the behest of
The flawed creator of women and men.

32

THE ACCIDENT

Megan—in love and elated by its odorless elixir—brings Thomas by for dinner and a meet-and-greet with our family. She also admonished me prior to the get-together. I am not, under any circumstances, to scare him away.

"You scare *all* my boyfriends away, Dad," she proclaimed at the outset of what she called our "briefing." "You're so intense." That I can be. "Try and ratchet the intensity level down a touch this time, okay?" Mattie and I were on the couch in our front room the day before dinner with Tom. Megan across from us in our leather recliner.

"I'll keep him under control," Mattie promised, putting her arm around me and squeezing my shoulder in a way that communicated, in our silent short-hand: I love you, Terry, but Megan's got a point.

She does. Until they walk in the door, that is.

"Hi, Thomas," I say, holding out my right hand for the obligatory father-boyfriend handshake. "Glad to meet you. My name is Terrence."

When I look up into his eyes, I blanch. I swear I turn ghost-white. I *know* those eyes.

Intimately.

"You alright, Mr. McDonald, sir?"

Megan's throwing daggers. *You better be alright.*

"Yes. Yes, Tom. I'm… fine."

I'm not.

Stomach churning.

Grip tightening.

"Can I have my hand back, sir?"

Do not misdirect your anger. He has done nothing wrong.

Reluctantly relinquishing grip.

"Thank you."

"Tom, if you don't mind my asking, how old are you?" *He's got to be younger than Megs with that baby-face.*

Besides, I need an icebreaker. I can't come right out with, You look awful familiar. Why is that?

"I'm eighteen." Now *he's* getting Megan's dagger-eyes. This was not something she wanted revealed. "But I'll be nineteen here in a couple months," he corrects.

Let's get to what's really on my mind. "And what's… what's your father's name, Tom?"

"My father? His name is Connor. Connor Kolb. Do you know him?"

He senses I do. The specificity of my question must have tipped him off.

"Did you go to school with him or something?"

I want to vomit. "Or something."

"I'll tell him I talked to you." His voice radiates misplaced cheer.

"Yeah. Yeah, you do that."

The tornado in my stomach is no longer within my control.

"Dad, are you okay?"

"If you'll excuse me a moment," I manage.

I run for—and shut myself away in—the bathroom, lay my head against porcelain, and groan. I didn't really want to vomit, but my body has not given me a choice. It is going to happen.

My head against the side of the toilet, I hear Megan comment, in a loud whisper, to her guest, "I'm so sorry. That was *so* weird."

"I hope your dad's okay. He was white as a sheet," Tom replies. He is in full voice. *Does he know I can hear him? Probably.*

TERRENCE MCDONALD IS 39. THE YEAR IS 2029.

Connor Kolb did not attend his son's wedding. Nor was he present at the rehearsal dinner preceding it. That's not to suggest he hadn't *planned* on taking part in both events—because he had—but when you're in the hospital immediately following one of the biggest and most tragic accidents in Washington state's history, and any number of pain medications are being administered to you in drip form, the doctors are not going to be inclined to let you out for anything.

Furthermore, months spent mapping out everything from dinner's main course to the exact timing for the couple's first dance, down to the second—with a number of non-refundable deposits to be considered—meant the wedding could not be canceled. It would move forward as scheduled, but not quite as planned.

As for the details of the accident, Connor had been making his way across I-5, toward the rehearsal dinner, in as close to a blizzard as the Seattle weather wonks had ever witnessed. By the time seven o'clock rolled around that night and everyone, except Connor, was seated and ready to be served, a foot and a half of powder had fallen. An uneasy fear was setting in amongst the guests. Something was wrong.

The police report stated that Connor hit a patch of black ice at around 6:30 in the evening and lost control of his vehicle. There was no way for the poor souls behind him to avoid their fates. The pile-up didn't end until fifty cars were involved.

It was eventually determined—weeks later—that Connor, whose survival was nothing short of miraculous, would not be prosecuted.

"There was no wrongdoing here," said the district attorney, in a press-conference covered by all the local news outlets. "There was only an unfortunate circumstance resulting in a catastrophe."

When I was told Connor would not be present for the ceremony at which I would walk my daughter down the aisle, I spoke four words. "That's karma for you."

"What do you mean, Dad?" Megan asked, thinking my reaction callous.

I refused to elaborate.

THE REVIEW

My mind cannot contain the image of an evil, unthinking man so gleeful at the crumbling of another's existence without forcing me to comment on it. "It's official. I'm an awful person."

"Why would you say that?" God is Connor Kolb. Not the older Connor, but the best-friend version I once knew. Tiny plastic blocks, soldiers, a few of my G. I. Joes, and some construction-worker guys—who might also drive dump trucks from time to time, in this world my best friend and I created—are strewn across my bedroom floor. In the scene I've just entered, we're on that floor, and we've just finished an afternoon lost in Legos.

"Why *wouldn't* I say that? Connor was paralyzed. *Paralyzed.* He never walked again, and what was my response when I heard he'd been in an accident? I all but celebrated the news. What an asshole I was."

"You made a mistake."

"You're damn right I did. I spent my life complaining that people didn't understand me, contending that, if they only got to know me, they'd see what a good person I was. And yet I would judge people, too, and just as readily."

"Everyone makes mistakes. If you ask for forgiveness, Connor will more than likely give it to you."

"That's great." *Is it?* "But, the truth is, I couldn't imagine asking him for forgiveness."

"Why not?"

"How can I ask Connor for forgiveness when I can't imagine forgiving myself?"

"Try to imagine it, Terrence. Imagine that your own existence were at stake."

I can do that. Because it is.

"Can you tell yourself it's okay that you made mistakes; after all, you were human? Then allow yourself to be forgiven?"

"I can *try.*"

RECIPE

We live in a world
Hesitant to forgive.
Everyone can secure
A second chance,
But they have to be willing
To engage in
A specific dance.

Admit all shortcomings and
Expose all hurts.
Of your fragile state,
Do not equivocate.

Tame all worries,
Replace with mirth.

This recipe in use,
One can flirt
With a clean slate.

33

BIRTH, PART 2: EMMA JOINS OUR WORLD

MEGAN MCDONALD KOLB IS 22. THE YEAR IS 2029.

Feet in the stirrups, my labor is underway in earnest.

It's a wonder the human race continues. Women should put a moratorium on any action set to eventually cause *this* ungodly level of pain. No man, no matter how perfect his penis, is worth the torment.

"You're doing great, honey." Tom, my husband of thirteen months, tries to be supportive. His voice, his vote of support, is small, though; barely audible, not what either of us expected.

We planned our pregnancy. (Does anyone really *plan* a thing like this? You can *want* it, but can you *plan* it?) I refused to bring a child into a world that has not done all it can in preparation for them, hence the painstaking planning.

"Of course I'll be there for you, Megs," Tom said one Saturday morning as we laid in bed after one of my nightmares, trying his best to assuage a new fear I'd come across in the night.

"You say that, but what if… what if we get in over our heads? What if you decide you can't handle this? I mean… being a parent. That's a big deal. What if you decide it's too big, and it might be better if you weren't here? People do that, you know? They make snap decisions just like that. I don't know what I'd do if you left. I think I might lose it. I mean, I've got Mattie and Dad, but otherwise I'm kind of on my own here."

"Megan, stop. Just stop. You've got Mattie, your dad, and you've got me." He smiled. "We *want* this baby, don't we?"

I nodded. We did.

"You're freaking yourself out, and you don't need to. You know me. Haven't I always been here for you?"

I didn't answer. I just snuggled into his arms, and we kissed. The pregnant wife petrified of the unknown. Her doting husband, just as scared, but he won't show it.

"I'm not going anywhere, Meg. This will all be a team effort."

So easy to say before everything gets real. It's real now.

Is he going to faint on me? Sure looks like it. He better not, the bastard. If I have to be awake for this agony, so does he.

He faints. Did I predict that one or what? Smelling salts are brought in and restore his consciousness. My usual practice for such an infraction is to rib him good-naturedly, and I would. But I have more pressing matters to attend to.

Like, for example, a birth.

Emily "Emma" Madeline Kolb is born at 5:31 P.M., at Seattle's Swedish Hospital. Her arrival races the setting sun and crosses the finish line victorious. Ten minutes and a strawberry dusk to spare.

. . .

All our relatives gather expectantly around the big window looking into the hospital's nursery, and they beam.

"She's the one with the red bracelet," Dad notes, to anyone within earshot. "See? It says Kolb. That's our little gingersnap."

I smile when I hear him say it.

I don't *hear* him say it until I'm cleaned up and resting, long after the ordeal is through. Yet word has it he's used the term of endearment several times, including at the nursery window. Why not pass on the nickname to the next generation?

TERRENCE MCDONALD IS 39. THE YEAR IS 2029.

Seated in his wheelchair—a necessity as a result of the blizzard-influenced crash—Connor is not the personification of evil I empowered him to be for far too long. He is a weak, sad, and prematurely old man.

I come to stand next to his chair. I am ensconced in the stupor that often trails euphoria. I think we both are. We've become grandparents

tonight. Alone down a hospital corridor, I surmise we'll have a few minutes to ourselves before our loved ones start wondering what's become of
us, and they send out a ward-wide search party.

"Connor," I say.

He looks up into my face. "Terrence." He nods.

I want to tell him congratulations. On raising a sterling young man.
I want to celebrate our shared good fortune. But I don't do either. In celebrating's stead:

"I've never forgotten what happened between us. It's been with me…
always." My timbre is a low rumble.

"It's been with me, too." His is a high-pitched, old-man warble.

"I've always wanted to know why, Connor. Why did you do it? We
were friends. I trusted you. When everyone else treated me like an outcast
and a freak, you made me feel important. You made me feel like I mattered. And then—"

"And then I ruined all of that in three minutes." He finishes my
thought.

"Three minutes of terror. Why?"

A grimace. "I can't give you an answer," Connor replies. "I can't give
you a *why*. I know you want something tangible, something that makes
sense that you can hold onto. But I can't give you that."

"Why not? I deserve it, for Christ's sake."

"Yes, you do deserve it. I can't give it to you because I don't have it
to give. I haven't found it myself. In place of the why, there is guilt. It fills
my sleep with horrors. It wrenches me awake at night, and its volume is
louder than all of my other emotions combined. I try to ignore it, but that
only amplifies it even more."

I don't give a damn about your guilt, I silently seethe.

"I have guilt, too," I say.

You're not the only one. You're not as unique as you'd thought.

"That you let it happen?" my former friend guesses.

"That's right."

"I understand. When it happened to me the first time… that's when
Guilt and I met, and we haven't been apart since."

When it happened to him? My heart aches for a man I'm so used to hating. *I can't let him see that his words have affected me. I can't show weakness to him. I already did that once.*

"I have guilt about other things, too," I admit.

"What other things?"

I take a deep breath and hold onto the air, cold in my lungs. It wants to be released, but release will mean confronting an unpleasant truth about myself.

Let it go, my mom advises. I let it go.

"For many years, Connor, I wanted to kill you. I dreamt of shooting you dead more times than I could count."

His reaction is barely perceptible. I wonder why. If someone I knew—especially someone I'd *wronged*—confessed a deep-seated desire to see me dead, I'd sure as hell do something more than act all stone-faced and unaffected.

Eventually, Connor does do something more. He begins weeping and says:

"I wanted to kill myself, too, Terrence. I wanted to die and be remembered as the kid my mother thought I was, not the shit head you knew. I wanted to erase that day in the boys' bathroom from the world's collective consciousness, that day and everything that led up to it, but I couldn't. I want you to know I'm a very different person now, and I am so sorry I dragged you into my hell."

I need to sit down. My muscles yell at me. *I need my own wheelchair.* Instead, I spot the nearest wall, five feet away, and collapse against it. Connor follows me in his chair.

"Our kids love each other," I say, smiling up at him.

"I know." He returns my smile.

"Before today, Connor, I didn't want to *think* about forgiving you. Tom probably thinks I'm a jerk, I've been so tough on him." *You treat him the same way Beth's father treated you.* "All because I know who he is."

"Tom isn't me, Terry."

"I understand that."

I need to be better towards my son-in-law from now on. How can I do that? Drop the grudge you hold against Connor. That's a start.

As much as I want to drop this grudge, long-held and unhealthy, I am wary. *Would that mean I have to forgive him? I'm not sure I can get there... yet.*

But I *can* now say the words I've wanted to tell him all day. "Congratulations, Connor."

"And to you, Terry," he replies. "The two of us should go out for a drink sometime. What do ya say?"

It's as close to forgiveness as I can get. For now. But it's *something*. A first step. "Give me a call," I say, "and we'll figure it out."

We'll figure out where we'll have our drink. And the complicated logistics of who will get Connor and me to a restaurant. And when.

THE REVIEW

"We never had that drink," I say.

"Why not?" God is old Connor. We're back in the hospital corridor. I'm against the wall. He's in His chair.

"Connor never called, so I figured—"

"You could have called him."

"I could have. But I didn't. Because I could never rid myself of that grudge completely. I hated myself for this. And then, whenever I let that hate permeate my mind, I was allowing myself to be the victim all over again. I would blame the palsy for something *I chose* not to do. and I'd hear Chloe's voice: 'You're better than that, Terrence. I know you are.'"

FORMER NORMS REPLACED

Traditions take many forms
And turn into traditions
When they topple former norms.
Stay on Earth long enough,
Beat back life's sundry storms, and
Through many you'll be born.

But, as a child,
It's impossible to imagine any
But those unbreakable traditions with which
One has grown.

34

A CHRISTMAS TO FORGET

MATTIE MAILER MCDONALD IS 35. THE YEAR IS 2030.

Ten years. 120 months. That's what I have left. That's *all* I have left.

Am I sick? No. In fact, I'm anything but ill. I feel the healthiest I've ever felt.

I kind of wish God hadn't come to me thirteen years ago, hadn't revealed my end. (Most of my long-ago visit faded with the next morning, but that end… somewhere in my subconscious it lives, and I am its uneasy landlord.) But forgoing this seminal event would also mean having to forgo my life with Terrence and Megan.

Terrence is probably the healthiest he'll ever be as well. I may have ten years to go, but as far as quality years together, we've got just over five left. I want to change this fact, to fix it. There's only so far free will can go, though. I can do nothing but be prepared. Get myself and my pages of our story ready.

When the chart says it's time, it's time.

Yet to suggest I know what catastrophic event or illness will end Terrence's life would be inaccurate. When I had the opportunity to learn this answer, I came to the conclusion that I didn't want to know it. I remember thinking that seeing my own death described was one thing, and though it scared me a little I could handle it, but to see Terrence's death written out—though The Boss would surely have blocked the scene from my memory before I woke, leaving me with only traces of it—even the traces would be too much. *It would be like cheating.* Knowing when it would happen was enough for me.

This is why I never looked at his chart's final lines.

TERRENCE MCDONALD IS 40. THE YEAR IS 2030.

I enter the house in search of refuge from a driving snowstorm. One that reminds me of Megan's childhood. Back then, she rode the family sled down our backyard hill with neighborhood friends for hours.

Now that scene is a wisp of a memory, a snippet of a mind-song, and Mattie and I are empty-nesters. Grandparents eager to spoil the next generation, Emma. She's on the doorstep of her terrible twos and living just down the road.

"You want me to make some tea, honey?" my wife offers. "Something to warm you up?"

"I'd love some. Thanks."

Mattie knew—or she'd guessed correctly that—I'd appreciate a hot beverage now that I was finished shoveling our driveway. To call the task tedious and backbreaking is to be kind. Or naive. She would have done it herself, but I wouldn't let her. When she offered, I politely refused and said, "You do so much for me, Mattie. I *want* to do this for you." She hugged me and said thank you.

I will pay for the effort tonight, with the aching in my legs, the throbbing pain in my back. Both will persist for days. But it's one of the few things I can do—*don't be a victim, Terry; that's the well-trained victim within you talking*—for the woman who chose me. *She could have chosen any number of men, none of the others palsied with bad eyes. But she chose me. Late at night, or after I conclude an ill-advised snow-shoveling session, it isn't hard to get me wondering why.*

I peel off my cold-weather gear, drop it in our laundry room, change into a more casual outfit—an old gray sweatshirt and matching pants—and sigh down into a chair at the kitchen table. The tea will take a few minutes, but while the water boils, and then while we wait for it to steep, we can talk.

"A lot has happened in this house," I start, looking around, wistful.

"Yes. And a lot is *still* to happen." She tries her best to keep my spirits up. Since Megan left home, marrying Tom instead of finishing college, stretches of inclement weather and dark skies tend to depress me. Mattie knows this better than anyone. My calling was to be a father. The raising-a-child bit done, I am lost. Amid a cocktail of depression and the kind of wonderment no one wants—*Why did she pick me? How can she possibly be happy with her decision?*—I finally pose aloud the question that has haunted me for years.

"Mattie, I need to ask you something," I say, as a way of prefacing what's coming.

"What's on your mind, honey?"

"Do you ever wonder what your life would have been like without me in it?"

"Well, I… uh… yeah. Sometimes I do."

I lean forward towards her but do not leave the table. She stands over the stove and the teapot, but her eyes are on me.

I ask, "Do you ever regret marrying me? Do you ever wish you'd… chosen someone else?"

"Absolutely not. What kind of a question is *that?*" Her nostrils flare.

"You can't tell me it's been easy."

"That's true, it hasn't been easy, Terry. At times, it's been even harder than I figured it would be. Always having to be the one who drives, for example. Or thinking to myself, when I see other couples enjoying themselves, doing a physical activity together—hiking, biking, that sort of thing—*Hmmm… that looks like it could be a good time. But I'm not sure Terrence could do it.*"

"You could have chosen someone with money," I put in.

She ignores me. "But what you're asking me to do is to… re-imagine my entire life without you in it. I can't do that. That's *unthinkable* to me. You and Megan are my family. I'm Grandma Mattie now, and that's a title I'll answer to with pride. So, no, it hasn't been easy. But whoever said I wanted easy? I wanted a life with my best friend, and you've given me that."

THE REVIEW

Mattie-God and I wait for our tea. God stands where Mattie stood then, manning the kettle. Awaiting its shrill whistle.

"It's been so long since I've seen Mattie—and I've been living life in a fog—so I'd forgotten how she answered that question. How her nostrils *actually flared.* She knew I needed to hear her answer, but she was genuinely upset that I needed to ask the question."

"What did you learn that day?" God asks in her guise.

"That Mattie *actually* loved me. That her being with me wasn't a form of charity. I get that the whole thing started out as a favor to You, an answer to Megan's prayer. But, in the end, she loved me. She chose to spend her life with *me*. Her best friend."

MEGAN MCDONALD KOLB IS 29. THE YEAR IS 2036.

The snow is five and a half inches deep and getting deeper as we arrive at Dad's house, our windshield-wipers earning time-and-a-half holiday pay. Dad refers to the house as "our modest little place" and, in his more temperamental times, he'll go so far as to decry it, labeling it a "goddamn shack."

Which is sad, because I remember this house of his, and I treasure the memories made here. They formed the foundation for the person, and the parent, I am today. The birthday parties, seven of them. The last one rowdy and overcrowded and including a keg, unbeknownst to Dad. My first kiss with Brian Sasser, the locking of our lips awkward but beautiful. Getting ready for my senior prom with Doug Davenport, who showed up at the door an hour late and lobster-red. "I was trying for a tan," he told me. "I wanted to look good for you. The sun must've put me to sleep. When I woke up... I'm so sorry, Meg. We don't have to go if you don't want to, if you're too embarrassed." We went. We danced. We had a blast. At the end of the night, we stopped into a drugstore and bought poor Doug the largest quantity of Aloe Vera available.

Last—but far from least—was my wedding to Thomas Kolb. A celebration full of laughs, hugs, tears, and nervous apprehension.

It was never a shack to me. Nor was it modest. To me, in much the same way that my mom's apartment was a safe haven, this collection of walls, a staircase, and four bedrooms on the upper floor, two of them used for their intended purpose, the other two serving as commute-free offices for Dad and Mattie respectively—with the kitchen, a living room, and a bathroom below—was a home.

.　　　　　.　　　　　.

"Mom, do you think Santa came to Grandma and Grandpa's house, too?" seven-year-old Emma asks me. She is giddy with the Christmas spirit.

"I guess we'll have to see," I tell her.

"I bet he did. Santa is sneaky."

"Is he?"

"Mhmm."

"What gives you that idea?"

"Last Christmas, when I sat on his lap and asked him for a baby brother, he said he would do what he could. I didn't think I'd get one. Then, when I went to look under the tree Christmas morning, there he was."

"You mean Scooter?" I ask. She's referring to our year-old puppy, a lab-husky mix, colored black with patches of white that blend in and shade small areas of his fur gray. When we left him at home today, he looked like a cross between Yoda—with one black-furred ear perpetually sticking up—and a spurned lover. *Oh, fine, you guys just leave me here while you go off to have your fun,* I imagined him grousing. *I'll be here when you get back. Where else would I go?*

"Of course I mean Scooter, Mom." Emma's grin is missing a couple ivories. The tooth fairy has taken possession of them, and she has been handsomely compensated.

"Is Scooter your brother?"

"Duh."

Tom gives our daughter a dagger of a look. "Hey now, little one," he attempts to reign her in, "I know it's Christmas and all, but that doesn't mean you get to disrespect your mother."

"Sorry."

Before we can make our way inside the house, Mattie opens its wreathed front door. She wears an appropriate Christmas-red-and-snow-white Rudolph sweater. The reindeer's nose protrudes from the fabric slightly at stomach level and glows its own bright shade of crimson. (*How does that work? Batteries?*) Emma and Tom mount the porch steps and stand on either side of her. I hang back.

"I'm so glad to see you!" Mattie squeals when Emma gives her a hug.

Once the hug ends, Emma goes into her traditional, yearly query. "How is your Christmas, Grandma Mattie?"

"It's great now that you're here," says the woman who held our family—my father and me—together. She came to the rescue right when it could have splintered apart into a million unsalvageable pieces.

"Emma, you run inside with your dad, okay? Say hi to Grandpa, and take a look under the tree."

Mattie gives my husband a quick hug, whispering in his ear. He acknowledges what she's told him—an indication almost imperceptible—and she continues, her eyes never having left Emma. "I need to chat with your mom a second."

Uh-oh. What's she gonna tell me? Did the package containing Emma's big Christmas present, an Easy-Bake Oven, fail to arrive in time? What'll we do if this is the case? It's not like we can run to the store and purchase one. Not with every store closed. And even if all businesses weren't boarded up for the holidays, this snow is the kind of wet, slushy muck that gives rise to fender-benders and spinouts. We're not going anywhere for a while.

Her granddaughter safely out of earshot, Mattie climbs down the steps and meets me in the snow. "We need to talk," she says.

"About?" *And so begins The Great Easy-Bake Debacle?*

"It's your father."

"Dad?" *Or is it something worse? Something truly worthy of being designated a crisis?* "What's wrong?"

"He's forgetting things, Meg."

"Oh? What kinds of things?"

I'm trying to remain calm here, but it's not working. I can feel Christmas cheer and tranquility emptying out of me in a gush, like fresh blood escaping a crushed artery. My body embalmed by panic.

"Last night, for example, he was so excited Emma was coming over today… for her fifth birthday party. He asked if I would go to the store and buy the cake."

What? "He knows what day Emma's birthday is, doesn't he?"

Mattie is quiet.

"Oh, God, he doesn't? Maybe Tom and Emma and I should just go home. Or take Dad to the doctor. We could do that. All of us take him to the doctor. Or the hospital. Or…"

Mattie folds me into a Christmas hug. My tears soak into the Rudolph sweater. She's still holding me by my shoulders, and I see determination in her face when she says, "Meg, trust me… I have been crying for a week straight. I may look totally composed right now, but I'm not. I get how upset you are; I'm upset, too. There's so much we're gonna need to figure out. For starters, your dad absolutely refuses to see a doctor. I think he needs to go, and we'll have to convince him together. And, frankly, I'm not sure how much time we've got before we'll need to find him somewhere else to live. Somewhere safer. But all of that can wait."

"How long?" I ask. My nose is running from the cold, but I don't care.

"Not long. Just until the new year."

"Does Dad know today is Christmas?" If she says no, I might collapse.

"It took a lot of work, but yes, he does. Let's just get through Christmas for Emma, and we'll go from there, okay?"

"Sounds good." It doesn't sound *good*. That's the wrong word. It sounds like the best of a group of terrible options.

Christmas is—or appears to be—a blast for everyone involved. Those for whom it is not hide their troubles well. Emma opens more gifts than I thought could fit under a Douglas Fir, and she screams with delight when the Easy-Bake is revealed.

At the end of the night, a cold rain washes the streets virtually clean of snow, and we've gathered our gifts, preparing to leave. I tell Dad good-bye, and that I love him, and merry Christmas. He repeats my words exactly, but his have no meaning—no discernable *tone*—behind them. At the door, Mattie and I exchange knowing glances. Both of us accepting the hard truth. That, as of this holiday, our lives will never be the same again.

• • •

"I'm scared, Mattie," I tell her as we sit in the hospital's waiting room. I am thirteen again, thirteen in all respects but appearance and actual age; frightened by the trying twists and hairpin turns, the unanticipated forks life is certain to heave into my pot-holed path. Am I ready? Am I properly trained to be without my father?

.   .   .

I never told him, because I didn't feel it needed saying, but our phone calls—daily when I was a kid, weekly once I married—were the highlight of my week.

"How are you, gingersnap?" he'd always start.

I could be honest with Dad. I didn't have to pretend everything was great all the time. He knew it wasn't, and that was okay. That was *to be expected*. I'd tell him what the week had brought, in pleasant times and awful.

The two-week period following my honeymoon offers an example I never forgot. I went for a job interview on Tuesday of week one. The meeting—in a downtown high-rise that housed an office manager job I'd found advertised online, and for which I was sure I'd be perfect—went so well I was all but given the position. The lady who conducted the interview promised to get back to me. She actually said, "*I promise I'll get back to you,*" I told Dad when I called him that night. She didn't. The next week, when I was sure I'd been passed over, I related the heartbreaking news. News that meant yet another week of unemployment, of searching, with declining hope, for the perfect career. "I must have really messed up in that interview, Dad. Maybe they thought I talked too much. Maybe I didn't talk *enough*. I wish I'd finished college like you wanted. Then maybe this would be easier." I was lying on my bed in the dark with tears in my eyes, a cold washcloth wrapped around my head to combat a tear-induced headache. "Did I answer all of their questions the way I should have?" Dad could barely get a word in. He tried, a few times, but he must have thought it best to let me ramble until he could find the right place to cut in. "Hey," I said, "I have an idea. I'll tell you what they asked me—I remember exactly what the lady said—and then I'll tell you what I said back, and you can tell me if—"

"Let's not do that," Dad said.

"Huh?"

"You didn't get the job. It's okay. You'll get a better one. One you'll *like*."

"Do you like your job?" I asked him.

He didn't answer immediately. "No," he told me after the pause.

"Then why do you do it?"

"Originally, I did it so I'd have a little money to help raise you. Before I took it, I relied on Grandpa Carl, and the little bit of money social security bequeathed upon me each month. I just knew living on such a tiny amount wasn't sustainable. Not if I wanted to give you the life you deserved."

"That's why you took the insurance job?"

"It isn't insurance. I work with annuities. I oversee the contracts for—"

"Yeah, okay, snore-fest, Dad. I didn't get it when I was a kid, and I still don't get it today." The washcloth wasn't cold anymore, and my head wasn't pounding any longer. I reached up, unfurled the cloth, and tossed it aside.

"So what would you really want to do, Dad? If money was no object, what's your dream-job?"

"To write," he said, no hesitation. "I want to be a writer. I once thought I was *supposed* to be a writer."

"Well, maybe you are."

"No. Writing is Mattie's field, not mine."

"Who says?"

"Um… well, me. I guess I'm the one who says."

"Maybe you need to have more faith in yourself. You'd be a great writer."

"You think so, gingersnap?"

"I know so, Daddy."

After we hung up, I tried to fall asleep, but I couldn't. I kept thinking about Dad and how he'd dreamed of writing. So what did I want to do? Could I identify my own dream? More than anything, I wanted to see the dawn of knowledge come across the face of a child. I wanted to teach elementary school.

·　　　　·　　　　·

"You don't have to be scared, gingersnap."

She's using my dad's word—*gingersnap*—confiscating it from his library of terms. Should I be angry? She's never called me that before, always opting for her own invention: "Ms. Meg." Deep down, I thought gingersnap was off-limits to her. I let it slide. Today's not the day to quibble over minutia.

I ask, "Why shouldn't I be scared?"

"I didn't say you *shouldn't*. I said you didn't have to be. Whatever your father is dealing with, we'll get through it. You and me. Together. That's what a *family* does."

"Tom and I… we've never been sick." Not yet we haven't. Oh, dear God, let us stay healthy. "Not like Dad might be. We've never been tested like this."

"You will be. Someday. Unfortunately, I can just about guarantee it. But don't worry about that now. Focus on the present, and later will take care of itself."

Her nerves close to their end, nails down to their quicks, Mattie picks up and begins flipping through a well-read magazine on the table before us.

"God doesn't expect miracles of you," she goes on, eyes fixed to the periodical. "Just live your life, one moment at a time. Be a good mother. Be a good wife." Mattie shudders. "A good wife. That sounds so antiquated. What I meant to say was, be a good person. Take pride in the woman you are."

She's right. Later will take care of itself. I'd rather not think on what might happen in the coming years to separate Tom and me, anyway. What illnesses. What maladies.

Back to the issue at hand.

"You'll be here for him, Mattie? Really?" In a society littered with broken relationships, it's refreshing to see one stay strong.

"Through everything. It's what I promised. It's what I promised *you* at Christmas." I suppose she had, though I didn't know it then. "He would do the same for me," she says.

What a wonderful woman she is. A godsend.

"That's a load off my shoulders. Thank you."

"You're welcome. Where is Tom, anyway? I expected to see him here with you."

"Oh, he's at work. He's always working. It's the only way we can manage to make ends meet. He's beat at the end of the day, every day."

"And Emma?"

"With Tom's dad. He's watching her. You remember Connor, don't you?"

A spark of recognition. Followed by a look I can't read curling across her face. "Oh, yes, I remember him."

"Yeah. He kinda keeps to himself. Reminds me of Dad a little, in that sense."

. . .

We stand at the doctor's approach. He is a short man crammed into his coat. He is also almost completely bald, nothing on top, tufts of brown hair hanging on with what miniscule follicular strength remains, stray wisps sticking up at the sides; a forehead wrinkled with thoughts long forgotten. His manner is gentle but direct.

"I'm deeply sorry to say the news is not good, ladies. Mr. McDonald appears to be suffering from a case of early onset Alzheimer's."

"What? There's gotta be some mistake," Mattie pleads. "I've never even *heard* of an early onset version of Alzheimer's. Are you sure that you—"

The physician interrupts. "We've run all the necessary tests, ma'am. And we are as certain as technology allows us to be. This form of the disease is exceedingly rare. Only about five to ten percent of the patients who present with Alzheimer's show the early onset type."

He shakes our hands, says, "Again, I'm so sorry. If you have any questions whatsoever, feel free to call me anytime."

THE CABIN

When you ask him where it is,
He offers a location
That could not be.
The woods of his father's youth
Don't exist anymore.
There's just the odd bramble,
A single, sad tree.
It's an address
That would not meet
With success
If entered into a GPS.

Yet he is convinced,
Beyond a doubt,
That—were he allowed to wander about—
Outside the grounds,
He'd find himself instantly
Among untempered wilderness,
Which, on all sides, would surround.

35

THE LOG CABIN REST HOME

MEGAN MCDONALD KOLB IS 33. THE YEAR IS 2040.

I curse God. Who, as part of His big, sprawling plan, chose to use me as the vessel to steer my father into that God-awful rest home. What's the name of that place again? Shady View or Shady Meadows, or some other Shady variation of horrific that so valiantly tries to convey comfort. I have yet to commit its moniker to memory, though it can be argued I should have by now. In my phone, it is identified only as DAD'S. I'm not blaming the staff for my father's plight. They do what they can. It's the rotten circumstances at which I bristle.

I don't like making the trip out there. To be honest, I hate it. I'll go, twice a week, but I hate it. It takes an hour each way. Once I arrive, the smell permeating the halls makes me want to vomit. Old people mixed with piss. And, worst of all, he isn't happy. Dad. He's restless, a lost soul in a long-broken body.

Of course, he doesn't know he's in a rest home. When I first enrolled him (they called it *enrolling*, like a goddamn college; like he was gonna walk out of there someday with a degree in Why Life Blows), I'd arranged his things so that his surroundings looked as much like his fictional home as possible. His worldly possessions are few and include a small television and the miniature generator that would hypothetically power it. The latter is never put into use, never fueled up. It's a prop. The former is one of his only windows out onto the world. If you ask him, he'll tell you he lives in a log cabin. One he helped his father build, and he experiences life "off the grid."

To him, "going out to eat," which he proposes we do each time I see him (except on Mondays, when our meetings are theoretically elsewhere)—"Let's get outa here and go find ourselves a meal. I know a great place nearby. Mattie loves it"—means trekking to the anything-but-great cafeteria and choking down the wretched Salisbury steak. Every time I'm gagging on that flavorless crap, I feel like cornering one of the nurses and saying, "For Christ's sake, these people are old, not in prison. You can up the quality of their food just a skosh, can't you?"

The log cabin that wasn't. It has grown into a family-wide myth. So that, whenever I played with dolls as a child, I liked to imagine the figures weren't *dolls* at all. They were feisty pioneer women who lived and worked hard amongst the wilderness. I thought that, if given the chance, *I* might have been able to do what those women did in that harsh but beautiful land. Thrive in austere, rustic resplendence.

I envisioned my father and grandfather, pioneers in my eyes, out on a cool fall day, rain misting, chopping wood—my father never chopped a log in his life, but that didn't stop my imagination—and dreaming of *their* cabin.

"He always said we'd build one." My father remembered his father's declaration and was forever pained by his rescinding it. "A log cabin. But life got in the way."

I wondered what on earth had happened to steal a dream from this man I cherished.

He would never elaborate on that topic. "Time to go to bed, gingersnap," he'd say if my curiosity got too invasive. "I'll see your pretty self in the morning."

I knew then not to belabor the subject. It made him cry, even if he didn't admit to the tears.

.   .   .

I knock twice. There is a loud rustling behind the door, and then the only entrance into his room-—*his makeshift home*—swings open.

"Megs!"

"Hi, Dad."

"What brings you here, gingersnap?"

I step inside. He closes and locks the door that has no locks, while I survey the rubble of his *now*. It depresses me anew every time I see it, but I can't react outwardly, because I don't want to upset him.

God, this place is a mess. Is anyone looking after him? I know the answer is yes, but that doesn't mean the looking-after is being done with the care I'd prefer. He appears left to his own devices, by and large. This is not what I pay for.

I feel guilty, but it's the best I can afford. I wonder if I should say something, maybe lodge a complaint with Cheryl, the Shady director. She's become a friend. I trust her. If I can't be here for Dad every minute of every day-—and I definitely can't—I'm glad she, or a group of people she trusts, *is* here.

No, I decide. *I won't say anything. The sad event that brings me here today has made me hypersensitive.*

"Dad, I came to get you. We're going out today." I don't like having to treat Dad like a clueless child, but it can't be helped. *Don't tell him the reason we're going out. He's not ready for that.*

"You want to have a father-daughter day." He smiles. "I'm sorry I haven't been able to get away from work lately. But this morning you're in luck. I'm not all that busy. Where shall we go? The zoo? The aquarium? Watching the walruses is always fun."

Yes, it was. Twenty-five years ago.

"I've actually planned our day out, Dad. I hope you don't mind." Of course, he has no choice. I signed him out at the front desk.

Until we return, he is under my guardianship.

"You're an enterprising young thing, aren't you?" He hugs me to his chest. "I don't mind. Where are we headed?"

Don't tell him the truth. We're off to see Mattie for the last time. Saying good-bye to his beloved. Who lies comatose in a hospice bed. It's an encounter he won't remember, yet I owe him the outing.

Where are we headed? Think on your feet. Chances are he won't remember the lie I tell, either. Erased ten minutes after serving its purpose.

·   ·   ·

I drop the most important content of Mattie's safety deposit box—an unfinished manuscript—off at the rest home's front desk.

"This is for Terrence McDonald," I tell the woman, in her sixties, who's holding down the fort. Visiting hours are near their end, as is her shift, and she's getting antsy, fidgeting in her swivel chair. I hope she'll sit still long enough to hear me out. "Can you make sure it gets to him?"

The woman blinks. "Yes, ma'am, I can, but Mr. McDonald is very sick. He has—"

"I know what he *has*. I'm his daughter." She *must* be new here. Staff members are not allowed to divulge Dad's condition.

"You know, on second thought, I'll just run down and leave it at the nurses' station for his wing." I will make sure an orderly helps Dad open it before I leave; I don't trust the old lady answering the phones to make quick enough work of the task.

.   .   .

A note written in Mattie's stellar penmanship and left taped and folded on top of the box had my name on it. It strictly forbade me from peeking between the covers of the story.

Mattie wrote, *You will see what this story has to do with you in time, gingersnap, as you will be the next to take custody of it, when your father joins me. For now, however, it is his to do with as he chooses.*

"What do you mean, Mattie?" I nearly shouted when I first read the words. I was standing next to a startled bank employee. "He's too sick to choose."

Along with the story, Mattie bequeathed unto my ailing father her ancient typewriter. *He'll know what it's for.*

Aside from those two items, she wrote in her will, *I give my estate—and all possessions therein—to Megan McDonald Kolb, my daughter.*

TERRENCE MCDONALD IS 50. THE YEAR IS 2040.

My heart is heavy days clear of her burial. (When was it? A week ago? A month? Can't remember.) I have a vague sense of the event, of being there when it happened; a cool day, a drizzling rain, the white casket I'm told I helped pick out. Was there a graveside service?

And now I'm back home, and I am given a pile of pages and a typewriter. "One of Mattie's last wishes," I hear, but I'm not clear who says this.

And I discover that the plot of this manuscript has me at its center. *There was a story Mattie had hinted at since the day we met, wasn't there?*

"I thought you said this story was about your mother, honey," I say into the air, hoping she's there, in the vast expanse mortals cannot plumb. "It was a ghost story. What happened to that? Were you not telling me the truth?"

Her response comes to my mind. Is she actually responding, or am I just hearing voices, talking to myself? *How would you have reacted if I'd told you the night we met that God asked me to write a story about you, a man I'd never laid eyes on before?*

"I wouldn't have spoken to you again."

Exactly. So, you see, I had to lie. I had no choice. But I didn't want to. And, in case you're wondering, yes, my mother did actually ask me to write something beautiful for her, and you, Terry, are helping me do that.

"You knew you weren't going to finish this story, didn't you?"

It wasn't mine to finish. *It's in able hands. I'm not worried.*

"Well, I am." What-ifs run rampant through my thoughts. "I'm not a well man, Mattie. What if I ruin your life's work?"

That's your own insecurity rearing. Have faith in yourself, and everything will come easier. Give yourself a hard time, and it's going to be a quagmire. Trust me on that.

"I always did trust you, Mattie. I love you."

Prove it by finishing what I started. Fill in the gaps. Paint the parts of the picture I couldn't see.

"What for? No one's gonna read it, no matter how magnificent it might turn out to be," I protest. "They'll dismiss it as the ramblings of a distraught man."

So what if they do? We'll know it's something greater.

Suddenly Mattie's voice is replaced by my daughter's timbre.

"How are you holding up, Daddy?"

"Okay, I guess. I'm gonna finish Mattie's book for her."

A pause. A *what-the-hell* pause. A *he's-not-making-any-sense-but-just-go-with-it* pause. She thinks I'm nuts.

"That's… great. I'll be by to visit you next weekend."

"You're gonna come visit me?" I can't remember the last time I saw my daughter.

"Sure. Maybe I'll bring Emma this time, too. She always likes seeing you."

"Emma? Who's—"

She has to go. She always has to go. So busy.

Was I that way when I was her age? Did I look for any reason I could find to cut conversations with my parents as short as possible?

TERRENCE MCDONALD IS 53. THE YEAR IS 2043.

The book is a waste of my time. Why am I still writing it?

I mull the thought.

Correction: Why am I still trying to write it?

Internal dialogues like this one are commonplace. The only mechanisms keeping me sane. Slivers of sunlight in a valley of caves hewn from depression, deprecation, delusion.

You're still writing because you feel it's your duty. Something both Mattie and God trust you to see through. And because it's much more than your duty; it's your dream. Those are the only reasons why you haven't thrown that God-forsaken typewriter of hers against the wall for its final blunt-force trauma.

"What if I don't have the talent for it? What if Mattie's saying I did was a way of keeping my spirits up, but she knew all along I was hopeless?" Spoken aloud, the words sound pathetic. I want to return them to my mouth immediately upon their escape.

.   .   .

My body aches. Not just in specific areas treatable with quick doses of medicine—which it does—but everywhere, always. An ache attributable to the soul more so than to anything physical.

I want out.

My life's turned into nothing more than a sad commentary illustrating how handicaps *can* get in the way, if those handicaps are allowed to embed themselves deep inside the mind alongside unhelpful thoughts. Thoughts like: *What have you done with your life, Terrence? In all these years, what have you done? There's Megan. We'll give you that. But what else? A whole lot of nothing, that's what. What are you doing now? As always, nothing. Megan's gone. She's on her own now. She doesn't need you anymore. No one needs you anymore. Why are you even here? Wouldn't it be easier for everyone if you just left? Really left? Think about it. Then you wouldn't be such a burden on your family, on society as a whole. This pain you've been feeling for years could finally end.*

The commentary is honest but painful, and most people won't stand for stories exhibiting honest pain. They would rather be numbed to reality thanks to mindless dreck.

I am fifty-three, sitting alone in my secluded log-cabin home. My refuge.

For all intents and purposes, I am off the grid. I have a generator so that the TV located directly in front of the couch runs sporadically, when I choose to fuel it. I don't have a refrigerator; I eat out every night. You might think this odd for someone wanting to be left alone. But it's not as if anyone in town knows who I *really* am. They are acquaintances of mine by pen name reputation only.

It's interesting, and off-putting at times, how readers can fashion their own views and beliefs about writers based solely on the words they've scribbled down. In my case, they're not even my pen strokes, my scribbles; they belong to Mattie. I'm a caretaker of words, but they belong to her.

.   .   .

How I became a caretaker of words.

By the time she passed away at the age of forty-five, breast cancer the culprit, Mattie had garnered a rabid—albeit paltry—readership. What her publisher referred to in private as "a niche audience." The reference troubled me, as I thought Mattie deserved more credit than that. Yet it did not seem to faze her. "They're an audience," she said to me one night as we readied for bed. "More importantly, they're *my* audience. Outside of my family…" She poked me in my side at this, playful. "Outside of this house, they're the people I write for." *They* attended every talk, reading, or signing of which they got word via her social networking platforms, and they snapped up her newest books on the day of their release, if not before. These volumes consisted, at first, of short stories and essays. The kind of springboard material a burgeoning novelist saw as practice. In her more seasoned (I wouldn't call them latter) years, she graduated to well-received thrillers and collections of poetry, her real crowd-pleasers, and her most lucrative releases by a wide margin.

When Mattie died, I made a pledge to her. It was never spoken, but I thought on it many times and determined it was what she would have wanted. I committed to not only seeing her unfinished manuscripts published, a task with which I was assisted immensely by her friends in the business, but I would also continue her signings, readings, and talks—to the extent that I could.

.   .   .

One evening, as I sat in a small, independent bookstore in Charlotte, North Carolina, I saw her. Megan.

"Megs. What are you doing here, sweetheart?" I wondered. "Shouldn't you be home watching Emma?"

"Emma can take care of herself for a couple hours, Dad. She's sixteen now." Megan's eyebrows furrowed.

She had a point. "Even so, Charlotte is a long way from Seattle. More than a couple hours." My geography skills were impeccable. "Are you sure you should have come here?"

"I'm here to support you, Dad. And for Mattie. Emma understands."

"She does?"

"Yes."

"Okay," I gave in. "In that case, it's great to see you, stranger."

I don't think Megan cared for this term of endearment. *Stranger.* I was clued in to her displeasure by a frown.

"It's nine-thirty, Mr. McDonald." This was the store manager interrupting. A young man barely out of puberty, having just left his Burger King gig for greener—more literary—pastures. His parents' bookshop. He was whispering in my ear. "We're just about to close. You can sign for two more people, then we're gonna have to put an end to it." Message imparted, the kid stepped to the side.

I nodded in his direction, took a copy of Mattie's newest book-—her final publication before the cancer won its war—off the massive stack to my right and said to the next person in line, "Who should I make the autograph out to?"

"Make it out to Marcia," the woman requested. "Sir, I was one of your wife's biggest fans. I just wanted to tell you how much her writing meant to me."

I grinned. "Mattie would be pleased to know that. As am I." I signed the book and handed it over. "Here you go. You have a good night now."

MEGAN MCDONALD KOLB IS 36. THE YEAR IS 2043.

Dad has no idea.

He thinks he's doing the noble and honorable thing; carrying on her legacy, that legions of Mattie's fans come to see him in different cities every week. What he doesn't know—I thank God for his ignorance as to this matter—is that his "signings" are tacitly sanctioned by the rest home. The foyer (it's more like the smallest lobby in recorded history) is re-decorated every week-—Mondays from 7:30 to 9:30 P.M.—to reflect different cities, different seasons. I pay for the decorations, and I attend the "events."

I used to bring Emma, earlier on, when he was more himself. But there came a juncture when I realized she would always be seven years old in his mind. If she showed up, it would do nothing other than confuse him further.

My father's apocryphal sojourns all over the United States—like his Mattie-signings—are, in truth, carefully planned and managed farces, from start to finish.

At approximately seven P.M. Monday, either a nurse or an orderly, taking their cue that it is "Terry Time" from the home's always-cheerful director, will rouse him out of a nap, inform him how he should be on his way soon; folks are waiting; the limo is outside. At the mere mention of a place to go and people who want to see him, Dad jumps up and out from under the covers like his bed is infested with a colony of aggressive fire ants.

The "limo" belongs to the home's director. Besides being cheerful, Cheryl can also lay claim to being one of the most kind-hearted women I know.

The car is no limo but an antiquated Town Car. Beat up badly enough that it regularly sees a mechanic. Once my father is seated comfortably in-side, usually drinking a cream soda, the driver is asked to "tool around town for about twenty minutes or so, then come back." This time without Dad is used to outfit the lobby with the week's party favors.

When the vehicle returns, the well-known celebrity is ushered inside, seated at a table stocked with books, and he knows what to do from there. When it comes to these types of gatherings, to engaging with "bookshop management" and "readers"—employees well aware of the drill and often given scripts for any dialogue they may have with him. He never identifies them as employees; they're Mattie's readers and, when it comes to selling his wife's stories, Terrence McDonald is a natural.

He never questions how he travels to so many locales without the use of a single airplane. He does, however, wonder how *I'm* able to show up to so many of his tour dates, and this gives me hope that his mind is still somewhat intact.

THE ULTIMATE ARBITER

Time stands as the ultimate arbiter
Of who stays
And who goes.
Everyone's existence
Runs on a clock,
Whether a person spies
Their time-keeper or not.

Strive do well-meaning doctors everywhere
To search their countless tomes,
Common and rare,
For an antidote.

But even they,
If they listen close,
Will hear their clock,
Its ceaseless pendulum swinging to-and-fro.
At that sound, one can't help
But take stock.

36

TWO MONTHS TO GO

THE REVIEW

In the living room of the home I shared with Mattie (Mom's reproduction of the home, that is) God—as Grandpa Jack—occupies the love seat. Jack's big, once-an-umpire frame fills it full. I am in the overstuffed chair to His left. We both agree, without saying so, that Jack is the perfect person for disclosing one last bit of information to me.

"So what happens next?" I ask Him.

"You'll go back to Earth for approximately sixty days," God declares, "give or take a day here or there. Since we don't have time up here, I don't worry about details like that. The hands-off approach gives a little leeway for humans to exercise free will, and it allows us to alter the schedule or a particular chart slightly where needed."

"Why do I need to go back?" *I'm just getting used to the way things work up here.*

"You have yet to tell me the overriding lesson of your life."

"I'm sorry. I'm just not one-hundred percent sure, and I don't want to be wro—"

"It's okay to be unsure at *this* stage. But you *can't* be unsure when your panel meets to formally deliver a verdict. By then, you *have* to know what your life was meant to teach you. Otherwise—"

"No more me."

"Right. I would like to point out again," He says, "that this was not My call."

"No. I know. It was mine."

"I'm giving you another couple months to think it over. To work out whether or not you've come to the right conclusions. In those two months of Earth-time, your Alzheimer's will recede; it will not be gone or cured, do not misunderstand me. But your mind *will* be clear, and you will have the chance to say proper good-byes to both Megan and Emma. Treasure this opportunity. Very few receive such a gift. Near your life's true end, a fog will again descend upon your mind. Don't forget that, when you return Home, it will be time for your verdict, time for you to articulate your lesson."

"Wait. What about Mattie's book?"

"Oh, right. Can't forget the book. Prior to your return, you will be the guardian of Mattie's manuscript. Which is, in truth, your story as much as it is hers. Once you return, it will next belong to Megan. After her, Emma."

"Haven't I *been* working on that manuscript for two years now?"

He sighs a Jack-sigh. His whole body inflates on the inhale, deflates on the exhale, and He seems to get smaller. "No," He says. "Not even close. I was waiting to tell you this because… well, it's kind of awkward, but I wasn't sure how to broach the subject. The fact is, you *thought* you were working on that story, and everyone, including Me, *let* you think you were working on it, because the thought brought you a measure of peace. But the Alzheimer's was in control. Terrence, you haven't written a meaningful word in three years, and it's been three and a half since you last read a novel.

"Mattie left you that manuscript, that your mind might be kept sharp. No one expected you to write anything of consequence. Pressuring you… making you believe you *had* to write "Mattie's book"—you did your best, out of love for her, I understand, but it was a mistake to do that. A mistake made Up Here. A red-tape mistake, if that makes sense.

"That part of your life was clearly defined in your chart, as we had originally figured it would give you purpose in your last days, and no one thought to remove it. We should have been more thorough, more vigilant. We should have seen your disease had progressed to a point where what was being asked of you was no longer realistic."

"You don't think I can do it. You don't think I can finish *my* sections of Mattie's book."

"I didn't say that, Terrence." Jack-God leans forward, his eyes imploring me, *Calm down, Terry*. He wouldn't put his hand on my shoulder like his daughter used to do. To calm me down, he'd focus his eyes on me, and *they* would *implore*.

"You certainly implied it. That's okay, though."

"It is?" To surprise God is exhilarating, like taking the reins of an out-of-control stallion with full confidence that you will get it where it needs to go safely and no one will be hurt in the process.

"I don't need to calm down. I'm not angry or frustrated. Not anymore. But I won't stand for anyone thinking there's something I can't do, least of all God Himself—*especially* when there's writing involved. The thing I know I'm good at (despite the fact that I ended the last sentence with a preposition). You say I've got two months to go? Fine. Then, for the next two months, I am going to dive headlong into my life. I'm going to fully participate in it. I'm going to write that story. I'm going to say my proper good-byes. And I'm going to prove You wrong."

"Do it," Jack-God encourages.

MEGAN MCDONALD KOLB IS 38. THE YEAR IS 2045.

Dad's room isn't furnished.

It has furniture in it—one chair, plastic and uncomfortable; one TV, small but adequate; one hospital bed he'll often mistake for a couch, where he waits for the inevitable while downing barely edible courses at mealtimes and watching Seahawks football or Mariner baseball ("Come sit on the couch with me," he'll say, patting a supposed empty spot, to which I'll reply, "That's okay, Dad. I'll stand")—but it isn't *furnished*.

Why not? That seems cruel. And what does "furnished" mean to you, anyway, Megan? The term can mean different things to different people. The way I see it, to fully furnish his room would go against the whole log-cabin idea. It would also irritate him, which I'd like to avoid.

On an evening in late December, at around seven-thirty, the sky outside full-dark, a call comes from that room. Emma picks it up. She finds me in the kitchen and says, "Someone's on the phone for you, Mom. It sounds kind of important."

"They're on the landline?" Almost no one calls that number anymore.

"Yeah."

"Did you ask what they wanted?" I am reluctant to leave the stove. The water I'm watching is sure to boil the moment I turn my back.

Who did I give that number to? How many years have passed since I jotted it down?

"Yeah. She said it was about Grandpa."

The rest home! The house phone was a secondary number.

I sprint to the receiver.

"Hello?"

"Megan, it's Cheryl at Shady Grove."

"Hi, Cheryl." The hand in which I'm holding the phone shakes. I am sobbing, and my vision has blurred. "Is there something—"

"First and foremost, Megan, your father is okay."

"Oh, thank God." I put my hand to my chest. *You can slow down,* I tell my heart.

"But I'm calling to let you know he *did* suffer a heart attack this afternoon. The staff worked on him for quite a while, and he didn't respond. Things were looking pretty bleak when he suddenly started breathing again and sat up screaming your name, insisting he be allowed to see you. Again, he's fine now. I want to stress that you should not be worried, but I really would appreciate it if you could please come down right away?" She's been trying to reach me on my cell for hours, she says. In a frantic non-panic—the kind you might experience if you're ever told your dad had a heart attack but you shouldn't worry—I dig the phone out of my purse and confirm the battery needs to be charged. Then I apologize and thank her for being so persistent.

"I'll be there as soon as I can."

.   .   .

I arrive and find Dad sitting up in his bed. He is ecstatic when he sees me.

"Thank God you're here, gingersnap. You're hard to get ahold of these days. Did you know that? A man has to practically throw a conniption."

"How are you feeling, Dad? You gave the folks here quite a scare."

"I died, Megs. I came back... for now... but I'm still dying."

"What? We're all dying, Dad, if you want to get technical about it."

"No, you don't understand." His stare is purposeful, a magnetic gaze that won't let me go. "I was *told* I'm *really* dying. Soon."

"No, you're not," I counter. "Who told you that?"

He goes silent. Is this silence because he doesn't want to answer, or because, in order to answer, he'll need a moment to invent someone?

"Who told you that?" I repeat.

"Grandma Chloe. And God."

Grandma Chloe I'd buy. He dreams of her all the time. But:

"You talked to God? Like, in person?"

"I did."

That's a bit of a stretch, don't you think? Has the dementia we've been told to expect taken hold? If so, Dad may be right. The end could be near. Dementia often mingles with Alzheimer's in the final stages, or so the doctors warn.

"What did God say?"

"A lot of things."

The end may be near, but I am far from ready to accept it.

"You're gonna have to be more specific than that," I challenge.

"God told me my mind would be clear for the next two months," he shares. "So that I can work on Mattie's story and get my affairs in order."

"Is your mind clear?"

"As a bell."

"Prove it."

In order to prove it, Dad relates the story of his first meeting with Mattie. The blind date. A yarn that hasn't surfaced—submerged in the foggy harbor that shelters his fragmented thoughts—for close to three years.

As he finishes, my eyes moisten. "I like when you tell that one."

"I know."

"Does this mean you're leaving me, Daddy?"

"Oh, sweetheart, I've been gone for years. I just didn't know it, and it's been a burden on you."

"It wasn't a burden."

"Yes, it was." His words come with conviction. "Don't lie to me. This way, with me fully aware of what's going on, the two of us can organize a proper send-off. And make sure you bring Emma by to see me. It's been eons since I've laid eyes on the little angel."

"She isn't so little anymore, Dad."

"Well, it'll be nice to get to know her again."

The declaration is so honest and heartfelt. I'm pained by it.

TERRENCE McDONALD IS 56. THE YEAR IS 2046

I finally get to be the writer I'd always wanted to be. Part creator, part dreamer, part journalist. On the birthday-weekend I have accepted will be my last, with my beautiful girls in attendance, I am on a mission. I undertake a process I call "The Interviews." I tell them both, "This won't take long." *There's a cake baking in my honor. I won't let this take long.* "But there are a few things I'd like to know before…" They know what *be-fore…* means. I call them into my room separately for chats that will not only inform Mattie's book—I've got her mother's typewriter dusted off and clack-clack-clacking again—but should also give clarity as to my life's lesson. I start with Emma.

Since my return, the folks here at Shady Grove have seen fit to give me a writing desk (I'm certain Megan paid for this, just as she paid for all the book signings, but I can't prove it.). Emma is across from me at that desk.

"Hi, Em. I just have a few questions for you."

"Sure, Grandpa," she says, distracted, busying herself on a tablet.

"First of all, could you put that thing down, please?"

"Oh… uh… sure." She shuts it off and sets it aside.

"Emma, what would you say is the best thing about your grandpa?"

"The best thing? About *you?* That's hard." She thinks for a second. "I never knew until you came back to us how smart you were." *Until I came back to them.* "I'm glad I got to see that. And, when I was really little, you used to watch baseball with me on TV. We'd both sit on the couch, cheering, and we'd share a bag of caramel corn."

We would? I don't remember that. My memory is clear, yet it is no match for the fog of age.

"I thought that was pretty great," she says.

"It was," I lie. *No point in telling her that, for me, it's gone, irretrievable.*

I make notes on the typewriter. Then I place both of my hands on the desk and lean toward Emma. The way I do when I'm trying to indicate: What I'm about to ask is important.

"Okay. Good answer. The next question is… if you could change one thing about your grandpa, what would it be?"

"Grandpa… I don't feel comfortable answering this question. I wouldn't change anything."

"Don't bullshit a bullshitter, Em. What would you change?" *The palsy. She's going to say the palsy.*

"I was in second grade. I knew you were sick, but my class decided to throw a party for our grandparents at the end of the year, and I wanted you to be there."

"Yeah?" Clack-clack-clack-clack-clack. "Go on."

"Well, one of the things you could do at this party… if you wanted to… was the three-legged race. I knew, even if you were able to come, you wouldn't remember any of it afterwards, but I didn't care. The night before the party, I dreamed we won that race."

"Emma, we wouldn't have won. I would have slowed us down too much."

"You think I *cared* about winning? It would have been awesome, but it wouldn't have been realistic. The thing I would change about you, Grandpa, is your memory. I'd make it better. Maybe if your memory were better, you wouldn't be so afraid."

"You think I'm afraid?"

"Sure you are," she says, tapping her sleeping tablet, whose technological capabilities are supposed to far exceed those of anything I've *ever* held in my hands. "You won't let me show you how this thing works. I've been begging you to let me show you for two weeks, since Mom brought me by to see you, but you keep saying…"

"I've got bad eyes, Em. I wouldn't be able to see—"

"It would take *two minutes*. But you're afraid."

I sigh. She's right. "Thank you for being honest, sweetheart."

"Thank *you* for coming back, Grandpa. I missed you."

"I missed you, too." She gets up, and I embrace her for a good fifteen seconds. At the end of which I add: "Can you ask your mother to come in?" Emma says she will, and then she exits, wiping her eyes.

·   ·   ·

Megan is next. Today, she earns the title of "Suspicious Megs." Before I can invite her to sit at the desk, she launches into her own inquiry.

"What's this all about, Dad?"

"What do you mean, sweetheart?"

"My daughter came out of here practically sobbing. What are you up to?"

"I didn't mean to upset her. Will you sit down?"

"No, I won't. It's almost time for cake, which we are having in the cafeteria. And I'm not all that happy with you at the moment."

"I understand. Well then, I suppose the quicker I ask my questions, the quicker we can be overdosing on chocolate. So here goes." I set my hands over the typewriter, poised to bang the keys in my index-finger-only style. "Megan, what's the best thing about being my daughter?"

I figure she'll hesitate a moment, ruminate as *her* daughter had. She doesn't. Instead, she barely takes a breath before answering. "I knew from the very beginning that *different* didn't mean *worse* or broken. You taught me how different meant a chance to learn. A chance to see the world from a new perspective."

I did? Why hadn't I learned this lesson along with her?

The answer comes to me in a thunderclap. *Because that was her lesson, Terrence. Not yours.*

"And now for the big one," I preface. Megan waits, impatient. The smell of cake wafts in through my closed door. "If you could change one thing about me, Megan, what would it be?"

Will she say the palsy? No. My memory? Maybe.

"I wish you had been less afraid, Dad," she says.

"Afraid, huh?"

"Yeah."

"Did Emma tell you what she told me?"

"No," Megan replies. "She didn't say anything to me other than that you wanted to see me. Then she burst out crying."

"When you say you wish I'd been less afraid, what exactly do you mean?"

"I mean, you lived life on the sidelines, Dad. Always observing, but leery of *doing*. 'What if I make a mistake? What if I do it wrong?' You lived life like it was good enough for *everyone else*, but somehow you weren't worthy of it. Mattie could be a writer, and so could your friend Charlie, but not you. You dreamed of becoming a writer, but you never did one solid thing to achieve that dream... that I saw, anyway. The fact is, if it weren't for Mattie, I'm not sure if we'd be..."

"A family?"

"That sounds horrible, I know, and I'm sorry. But you were such... such a—"

"Victim? That's easy to be, or to let yourself be, sweetheart, when you think you're a mistake from the get-go, like I did. One big mistake."

She is startled. We haven't talked like this... maybe ever. "You weren't a mistake, Daddy."

I hold my hand up to stop her. "I let my palsy define me, Megs. On one hand, it was painful, but on another, it was comfortable, something *I knew*. I was wrong to do that, and I want to thank you for never giving up on me, and for seeing me through what is a difficult end for both of us."

"You *are* leaving soon, aren't you? I knew this wouldn't last." She moves towards me, her arms outstretched. She needs a hug, they indicate, I oblige her.

"I am. But don't be sad, Megs." Her face is buried in my emaciated chest. "It's time to celebrate! This is a birthday party! Get yourself together, and let's go have some cake. What do ya say?"

YOUR FATE

Funerals function
As melancholy junctions.
Going to a funeral
Is like putting life on pause
And momentarily reviewing–
Under a magnifying glass–
The fine-print clause
In our contracts with God.

"Just as it has
Befallen this body,
Once vital,
Death won't be late,
Is bound to be
Your fate
Whether you're active or perpetually idle."
This truth no one shall escape.

37

DEATH, PART 2: GOING HOME AGAIN

TERRENCE MCDONALD IS 56. THE YEAR IS 2046.

This is the way it's supposed to be.

Megan and Emma stand at the foot of my bed. Thank God I will not die alone.

"Is there anything you wanta say to Grandpa before he goes, Em?" Megan asks her daughter.

"I love you, Grandpa."

"Love you, too. Any news for the old man before he bites the big one?" I'm smiling, and so is she. My voice escapes in sharp, shallow breaths. Each. Word. A. Sentence.

Emma brightens. "There is one thing. I have my first boyfriend."

Weak as I am, I'm also pleased at this morsel. "What's his name, gingersnap?"

"Kevin."

"Does he treat you well?"

"Yes. Last Friday, when I forgot my lunch money, he bought lunch for me."

"Sounds like a good man."

"He is. He had to skip lunch himself, since he only had enough cash for one of us to eat."

"You remind him that you're a keeper, okay, Em? You're one of a kind. He'll never find another one like you."

She blushes. "I will."

"Good."

"Grandpa?"

"M-hmm?"

"When you get to Heaven, can you tell Grandma Mattie I miss her?"

Hearing her say the word—*Heaven*—reminds me how close to death I am. How far from the living I've wandered.

"Grandma Mattie loves you very much," I say. "We both do. Death won't change that. You can talk to us whenever you want. We'll listen. We'll hear everything you need heard."

A doctor takes Megan, who stands behind Emma, aside and whispers something in her ear. Enlightened but downcast, my daughter approaches the bed.

"Dad, your blood pressure keeps falling, and you aren't getting enough oxygen. The doctors are concerned. They want to hook you up to some machines to…"

"They don't need to do that."

"They don't?"

"No. I'm ready to go, gingersnap."

I'm ready to go, and she's asking God to take me, swift and painless. I know. I've sent up the same plea.

·   ·   ·

Five to ten minutes of tense quiet pass before my voice is heard again. Weaker. The soul commencing withdrawal.

"Is this it, sweetheart?"

We both know it is.

"This is it." Megan takes my hand under the sheet where it rests. Lying limp. Her upper-body convulses with quiet grief.

"I had a good life." I say this as a means to remind myself as well as to assure my offspring. "Thank you for being part of it. Thank you both."

"It was an honor, Dad."

"And you'll carry on the story for me, Megs?"

"I will."

"It's yours now. Take good care of it."

I hear Emma ask, "Story? What story, Mom?"

She's curious. Good.

Megan hugs her daughter close. "You'll find out someday. Hopefully not for a while, though."

The end is abrupt, my soul losing traction, its grip on the physical realm. I've got seconds left.

"Bye, gingersnaps."

The earthly world turns almost holographic once my last words are issued. My soul rises, and I turn in the air for one last look at the shell responsible for carrying me this far.

It's time to come Home, I hear my mom say. *You're ready now, Terrence. Come Home.*

.   .   .

I expect to see my mom and the beautiful Ms. Mattie. But neither of them welcomes me Home.

You'll see them soon, says someone I've never met. He's a slight man wearing a white robe and looking not unlike my panelists. Except for his clearly defined features—the small nose, the fat cheeks, the gray eyes. So I am not surprised when he tells me, *I am here on behalf of your panel. It's a pleasure to make your acquaintance, Terrence.*

Uh-huh. My mind is elsewhere, unfocussed. I don't even ask his name.

I'm supposed to let you know that you've got some important business to which you need to attend.

I do?

Yes. *First, there's the matter of your funeral. It isn't mandatory that you go. But most people enjoy attending their funeral. It reminds them how many friends and loved ones they had in life, how strong these bonds are still. Modern humans tend to forget just how much they matter to others.*

I'd like to go to mine.

We will arrange it. Immediately after you and I are done here. Then, when your funeral ends, you are expected at The Hall of Records.

The Hall of Records? For what? I ask.

For your final judgment.

Could you make the thing sound any more ominous?

I'm sorry. But that is what it's called. The final judgment.

Kinda cryptic. I shudder.

I suppose, he says, indifferent. *Here comes your funeral.*

. . .

With those words, I am swallowed into the scene. The stranger disappears, and I know I am present on a crisp Tuesday afternoon in mid-February, the ides just past. Winter—cruel and unusual with cold this go-around—maintains a strict hold on the Pacific Northwest. In the corner, a waiting Spring cowers. *Do not displease the old man, Spring's body language says. His wrath is not myth, nor should it be tested.* Those who attend the service are bundled up against the chill.

In another corner, Megan stands, pensive.

"You're gonna do fine, Mom," Emma tries encouraging her. "Don't worry about it. The people here today all loved Grandpa Terrence."

I observe the mourners from an empty pew. Filing in, steps deliberate and measured, and I have to agree with my granddaughter. Sure, there aren't *many* folks here, and the weather's kept some notorious homebodies where they belong. But those who did show—Grandpa Jack's sweet younger sister, Aunt Mildred, herself in mourning at her brother's recent departure and a real trooper, turns up; as does a bevy of Mattie's publishing associates and almost everyone affiliated with the Shady rest home—did so because some part of them loved Terrence McDonald. Maybe more than I did. *More than I do.*

The clock on the sanctuary's brick wall reads three-thirty when Megan McDonald Kolb takes her place at the podium. Atop it she sets a tiny sheaf of paper. It is from this sheaf that she reads.

"Thank you all for being here today. My father would be heartened to know so many people think so highly of him." She chokes up, clears her throat, and brushes an errant strand of hair out of her vision. "My father lived for his family," Megan continues. "For Mattie and me and, later, for Emma. The toughest years of his life were doubtless the last, without his steadying force, his rudder, his Mattie, by his side. He did his best to live those years well, though, and I think he succeeded, when you take into account the disadvantages dealt to him. For all his faults, he was a wonderful father.

"I remember baseball games, barbecues, snipe hunts, and so many Christmases. Ice cream when I was feeling down, popcorn and either Frank Capra movies or Casablanca, Citizen Kane, or To Kill A Mockingbird on lazy days and nights. I told him they were ancient films and that he should get with the times. He just shrugged and said, 'That's not the way I do things, gingersnap. I live in my own time.' He did.

"Then there's the first time I ever tasted a Puyallup fair scone. On my first bite, the strawberry jam went all over my pants and dried there in the sun. Dad laughed for ten minutes, then he bought me another."

Megan has deliberately skipped two pages worth of anecdotes, setting them aside; deciding she won't be able to get through their telling. Therefore, my eulogy is near its close.

"Do any of you recall the story he told of the first boy I ever liked enough to bring home?" she asks rhetorically. "Every Thanksgiving afterwards, you couldn't leave his house without being subjected to that story. Basically, the long and the short of it was that this cute boy I'd had a crush on since forever agreed to walk me home. Well, it was early September, and the weather was still summer-hot. He needed a drink of water, so when we got to the house I brought him inside. Dad began questioning him immediately, about everything from how he knew me to *how he felt about me.* The kid was so intimidated he nearly fainted." The room erupts with laughter; everyone knows her rendering is no exaggeration. "As you might imagine, he never spoke to me after that, and I was so angry at Dad I refused to talk to him for a week."

Here we come down the home stretch.

"In the end, perhaps he didn't live long enough. I would welcome the chance to make more memories with him; I'm sure all of you share this inclination. Emma told me just yesterday how she wished her grandfather could read her another chapter from one of his favorite books. Reading was something they did together, over the phone. An almost daily ritual before he got sick and she grew up. Perhaps my father went too soon, and our family should feel disappointed or angry with God, or whoever it is that has the reins of this crazy world. But I'm not angry. I feel blessed. Today, in the snow and the ice, we commit to the earth the physical remains of Terrence Griffith McDonald, and to the heavens we say, '*Be gentle with him. No man is perfect, but this man is good'.*"

•   •   •

The funeral dissolves into somewhere else. The Hall of Records. Full of onlookers. Including Mattie, Lisa, and my old college professor. I don't see Dad or Charlie anywhere in the crowd. The Hall's librarian reads a short monologue into the record. To be kept, not surprisingly, here in The Hall Of Records.

"Here in the Great Hall, the crossroads of all faiths, devout or shallow, we will now hear the final judgment of Terrence Griffith McDonald," the woman says. Every syllable perfectly enunciated. "The distinguished panelists tasked with this case are the souls most recently known on Earth as Charlie Ewell, Carl McDonald, PhD, and the panel is led by the doctor's wife, Chloe Cooper McDonald. It should be noted that Dr. and Mrs. McDonald are parents to the concerned, and Mrs. McDonald has volunteered to be incarnated as the eldest son of her granddaughter, Emily Madeline Kolb-Cassidy and her husband, Robert Jonathan Cassidy."

I am at the table I shared with God months ago. But the room is bigger. Wider. I'm sure of it. There are seats in this retrofitted room that weren't here back then. And, high in the air, a balcony is suspended in front of me. The balcony holds three seats of its own.

Do I look as flushed as I feel? Have I done enough to ensure I'll see my family again?

The librarian continues. "There are two distinct determinations the panel must make in this hearing. First, is Terrence Griffith McDonald worthy-—based on the life just ended, the lessons he learned therein and thereafter—of the rewards of the afterlife option Heaven as it is constructed in his personal beliefs, or will his existence end entirely? Or might said existence perhaps conclude, should he discover his main lesson but not its companion, in a slightly different fashion—with him haunting Earth indefinitely in a self-imposed purgatory?"

A companion lesson? No one told me about a companion lesson!

Purgatory: I latch onto the word. The concept. *Not just never seeing my family again. It would also mean never meeting the daughter Mattie and I lost. I'd much prefer ceasing to exist in any form to this hellish outcome.*

"Second, should the panel find the concerned to be Heaven-bound, they must then assign him a profession." The librarian folds the paper from which she's read and recites the rest from memory. "Those ground rules having been set forth, ladies and gentlemen, please rise and welcome our panel."

. . .

Welcome our panel the spectators do, with reverential applause. Reverential but not loud. I hear someone a few rows back from me say, in a noisy whisper, "I could never be a panelist."

Her conversation-mate, also a woman, agrees. "It would be a delicate tightrope to walk. After all, everyone, at one time or another, feels unworthy. You'd have to wade through the bull and find what's real about a person, their true worth."

"Quiet, please," the librarian admonishes.

The conference is stifled, and for the first time I get a good look at my panel in their true forms. The shimmering white robes gone, their identities no longer ambiguous.

My mom sits back in her seat, higher by a full foot than the perches of her colleagues, signifying her place in their troika. She dons a pair of glasses, speaks.

"Let me say, as we begin, ladies and gentlemen, that, while Terrence McDonald was my son, I will lead this panel impartially." She stares down at me, her glasses enlarging the irises of her blue eyes. "Now then, before this panel can come to its decision, we need to ask Terrence a few questions."

I know what's coming before she vocalizes it for the room. She has telepathically transmitted to me: *We're going to ask about your life lessons. This is the big one. You have to get this right or...*

She doesn't finish the *or*. That's okay. Get this right or... or there will be no more me.

I hope you're ready, Terrence, Mom thinks, as she asks aloud, "Terrence, please detail for us the overriding lesson of your life and any accompanying lessons you wish to share. You are clear on the consequences should you be unable to furnish this panel with your overriding lesson, are you not?"

"I am," I say.

"Good." *Stand up,* she adds without *saying* it. I do.

"You may begin, Terrence."

Despite the fact that I have no more use for lungs, I feel the urge to take a deep breath. "I came into my review," I say, "skeptical and angry. *God?* I said to myself. *I think not.* Even if He exists, He's far too busy to care about me. I was too flawed to matter, in His eyes. Too imperfect."

Mom holds up a hand, stops me. *Just like I did with Megan.* "Terrence, did you think Heaven was full of perfect beings?" she asks.

"More perfect than me."

Me... the mistake, I almost think, but I stop myself, because I don't want Mom to "hear" that from me. And because... while God can and does make them, I wasn't a mistake.

"You were wrong, it isn't. How do you think our imperfect God would feel if it were? You have to remember, Terrence, even God makes mistakes."

"I know that *now.*"

The librarian steps forward. "Mrs. McDonald, try to refrain from editorializing. Terrence... Mr. McDonald... has yet to offer his lesson, and we cannot have interrupt—"

"My apologies. Go on, Terry."

"The lesson I believe was meant for me sounds simple, and maybe that's why I doubted it *could* be my lesson. It's simple to say, but extremely difficult to put into practice. Here's the scariest thing. Before I returned to Earth a couple months ago, I thought my lesson might be something else entirely, something other than: *do not live in fear of failure, or you will never do anything productive. Living in fear of failure accomplishes nothing. For some people, me included, living in this way brings about a kind of self-fulfilling paralysis in the soul. You must always be willing to try. Know your limitations, and don't exceed them to the point where you put yourself in an unsafe situation, but always be willing to try.' My review showed me the results of not trying, or what happened when I too often gave up on myself too soon, and then I saw what really trying looked like.*

"Thankfully, two of my favorite girls weren't afraid to tell me the truth. They let me know *I* was afraid. That I'd lived my life afraid."

Dad and Charlie scribble down some notes, share whispered thoughts. Mom does not join in. She's focused on what she *has* to say next.

"That's very good, Terry, but there is one more thing," she says. "Most souls are provided with what is called a companion lesson. The panel would like to know: Do you believe you were given a companion lesson and, if so, what was it? A warning: If you *were* granted such a lesson and you don't relate it to us in full, we are bound to authorize the punishment of purgatory. You won't cease to exist, but you won't exist, either. You'll be fully separated from all those you hold dear."

You should know that you do have a companion lesson to impart to your panel, Terrence. Patricia's voice. My spirt-guide, guiding me.

I think I know what it is, I tell her, hoping our confab is private. Though I doubt anyone in this room would listen in, out of respect for me. *But what if I'm wrong? And how come no one told me, 'While you're busy trying to figure what The overriding lesson of your life is, be on the lookout for its companion, too?'*

No one is ever told of their companion lesson, Terrence. Not until their verdict is near. However, this companion should dovetail nicely with your main lesson. That's why it's called a companion *lesson. As for the if-you're-wrong part of your query… if you're wrong, you're wrong, and you would need to suffer the consequences. Of failing to find your companion lesson. The utter loneliness of purgatory. That's terrible, I know. But if you don't answer the question, Terrence, then that fate is yours, anyway. So you might as well try.*

"Do not hold grudges," I half-speculate. "They won't achieve anything besides ulcers. Forgive. You must be willing to forgive everyone you can."

"Have you done this, Terrence? Have you forgiven everyone who deserves your forgiveness?" Mom asks.

"No. Not *everyone*."

"Who haven't you forgiven?"

"Connor Kolb. We were supposed to have a drink years ago, and I was going to forgive him then, but I just couldn't…"

I can see him now, no wheelchair, his strides halting at best—as if he's still getting used to using his legs again. A squat man with wispy white hair and dreadful posture. *He's been here, in this crowd, since my hearing began. But how is that possible? As far as I knew, he was still very much alive when I left.* I get the answer telepathically. It comes from Mom. *He's asleep, Terrence, thinks this is all a dream. If I'm not mistaken, something similar happened to you once, didn't it?* My earthly self might have wanted to punch Connor, knock him on his ass, and stand over him victorious, but I'm far beyond that desire as he reaches my table. This is about healing. Healing both of us. I stand and look him in the eye.

"Connor, I understand why you did what you did. It's what you knew. Of course, I wish you *hadn't* done it, but there's no going back and changing it now. I do forgive you, my friend. I hope you can forgive yourself."

"I'll be able to now," he replies, swallowing hard. "I've been waiting for years to hear those words. Thank you, Terrence. Thank you so much." With that, he's gone, making his way back up the nearest clear aisle. *He'll wake up a new man! You did the right thing, Terry,* Mom cheers.

Even with the tough assignment of forgiving Connor out of the way, there is still one person to whom I know I need to show the same compassion. If anyone deserves my forgiveness, he does.

I tell my panel, "The final soul to whom I owe a measure of forgiveness is my own. Other people looked at me and said, '*He's so brave'* or '*He's an inspiration.*' That type of thing happened *way* too often for my taste. I learned to accept it over time. People say stuff like that because the palsy isn't normal to them, and they don't know how to react to it other than awe.

"Well, palsy *became* normal to me, and yet I blamed myself for the things—the simple things everyone else took for granted—that I couldn't, or *didn't know how,* to do. Thanks to the review, when I think back on the day I finally left my father's house for good, I do so with happiness that was not at my disposal then. I didn't know what was going to happen to me. My first night on my own, in my apartment, was the scariest night of my life. I was thinking irrationally. I was sure I wouldn't survive it. Something was going to *end* me, and it would be vaguely related to my palsy. I'm not sure what I thought was going to happen, *but* something definitely was. For weeks afterward, I was sure someone would see me walking the hallway, or in the elevator of my building, and they would immediately know: *He's lost. He doesn't know what he's doing here.* They might take pity on me, but—more likely, in my worried mind—they'd take advantage of me. Of course, none of that ever happened.

"Instead, on that first night in my new apartment, Mom convinced me I could preheat my oven without burning my apartment to the ground. I'd been sure I'd do something stupid that would put it—and myself—in mortal peril. 'It'll be fine,' Mom said. It was.

"The day I got my first job with Mr. Chambers. God, I was so scared of him as Dad drove me in to the newspaper building. Dad had built Mr. Chambers up, saying, 'He's a great man, Terry; taught me so many lessons I still employ today. You're getting this job because he respects me, and he believes that, even with palsy, even with your eyes, you can do the work, so don't let either of us down.' I was destined to fail. People expected I would fail. Not Chambers or Dad but *other* people. I knew that's what they expected.

"'How is he supposed to do the work a *normal* boy can do when he's crippled?' my colleagues asked each other.

"They thought they were whispering soft enough that I wouldn't hear them wondering aloud. On the contrary, I heard all of their comments and more. Though, I will admit, many of these comments were manufactured, put into their mouths—and made audible—by my own psyche.

"Of these manufactured thoughts, I can say with confidence they existed, at first, as an odd form of protection. They were with me to save me from failure. I wouldn't fail if I just sat on the sidelines. But what they really did instead of protecting me… they made me afraid of life itself. I became afraid to *try* anything."

Only with these words… *I became afraid to try anything…* only with this admission do I at last understand why my soul requested—and, when pressed, why I held to—such a draconian punishment for myself, to be meted out if I failed to come by the overriding lesson of my life (and, apparently, its companion, too) during my review. The Terrence who oversaw my chart-building *knew* he was entering the mind and body of a man who, at life's end, would find both compromised. He'd blame himself for this, think himself a failure on several fronts, and he would not like himself much. The Terrence who oversaw my chart-building knew it would be difficult but that my soul *needed* to be *changed* by the review, as I could not abide entering the afterlife unfulfilled and *still* broken.

"I forgive myself for not trying," I continue on. "I forgive myself for the things at which I tried hard and failed, anyway. Most importantly, I forgive myself for the numerous times I did not want to be me because, in my mind, I wasn't good enough."

AN ANXIOUS MAN

The entire room is silent
As the defendant rises.
He's done nothing violent,
And wasn't a slave to his vices.
Yet the worry that has him gripped
Is real.

While the scales of justice
Seldom tipped the wrong way
On all those cop-shows he watched,
He can't help but imagine
This most important outcome being botched.

38

THE VERDICT

When it's clear my statement is through, Mom turns to Charlie and says, "Mr. Ewell, I believe you had something important you wanted to add before the verdict is announced?"

"No, Mrs. McDonald," Charlie answers, too quickly. "Nothing to add."

Mom gives Charlie a glance. I can't read its meaning.

"Very well then," she tells him, and to the spectators she says, "This panel is prepared to make its decision known. Terrence, if you would please remain standing."

Yes, ma'am.

"The librarian will now read the verdict, in full, into the record."

This she does. "In the case of Terrence Griffith McDonald, we, his Judgment Panel, find merit in his life and the actions therein sufficient for a full and unmitigated entrance into Heaven, the afterlife option to which his soul has been committed, and we decree that, upon this entrance, he shall debrief and reunite with his spirit guide, Patricia, and his guardian angels, selected for their posts prior to his earthly birth.

"We further find that he shall take on the duties of the head curator at The Hall Of Records when the current head curators, whom Terrence met briefly as a child, step down. There is no time in the afterlife, but every soul can decide when they are through with a job and then can either petition for another, retire into a quiet existence, or enter a new body, returning to Earth. The curators are no exception. Terrence will apprentice under them until both feel their work is done.

"This vocation will require him to learn the location, content, and meanings of every article in this hall. Much of this knowledge will be delivered telepathically following the rendering of this verdict. Coming to know the most esoteric bits and pieces is the purpose of the apprenticeship.

"This decision was arrived at after much discussion, deliberation, and debate, since becoming curator in The Hall Of Records is an eminent honor. There have only been six—including the two co-curators currently in the post—since God created all things."

Only six? I am humbled. And I allow myself to believe something I wouldn't have when this journey began. I am good enough to be given—and more than competent to undertake—the task.

.   .   .

A small crowd has gathered inside The Hall of Incarnation. This moment marks the end. The true end of one existence and the inception of another. We are all honored to be here, to bear witness to it.

Mom's new chart is written, her contract signed. She's been allowed to inhabit and test out her future body, a courtesy afforded all who request it, and the same courtesy given to the adults my six-year-old self met so many eons ago. Now she's back to being her previous self again as we've come to the good-byes. The send-off.

"You don't have to do this, Mom. You lived a great life. *You don't have to do this.* You could stay *here.* Dad and I need you."

She shakes her head. "No, you don't. Not anymore." A similar phrase was uttered the day she disembarked from the physical world, am I right? "Emma and Robert need me now. And, heck, this'll be fun."

"Fun? You really think so? Knowing all that you know?"

"Sure." Mom defends her assertion. "I mean, it won't be *perfect.* What's perfect, anyway? Not even God. Don't worry about me, Terrence. I'll be fine."

"I'll be watching."

"We both will," Dad promises. He is behind me, his hands resting heavily on my shoulders.

A man in a white robe beckons for Mom. "Mrs. McDonald, it's time. We have to go now. The birth is about to take place."

"Alright," Mom calls. Turning back to Dad and me, she says, "You two be good. I'll see you when I get back."

"Eighty years, one month, two weeks, three days," Dad reminds us all.

"Yes. Give or take a week or two."

"Mrs. McDonald, please!" The white-robed man is near a frenzy. "We are in something of a hurry here. If you don't go now, I'm afraid—"

"I'm coming."

Mom kisses Dad and me each in turn, flashes us a thumbs-up, and—to the man orchestrating her entry—I hear her intone: "It's not Mc-Donald anymore. My name is Cassidy from here on out."

"Yes, it is. Good luck and Godspeed on your journey."

"Bye, Mom," I shout after her.

But by the time I get this sentence into the send-off's record, she is through the portal, the gateway connecting both worlds, and my beautiful granddaughter has given birth to my great-grandson, Tyler Robert Cassidy. His middle name belonged first to his father. The newborn is eight pounds, nine ounces, and a future force in the literary world.

I haven't had a chance to thoroughly review Tyler's chart, but if I'm not mistaken he'll spend a few weeks on the New York Times bestseller list, and he'll flirt, in his later years, with the majesty that is a Pulitzer. When asked where his talent comes from, he will state, "I believe—with all my heart—one has to nurture and nourish true talent to receive its full benefit, and true talent is found in two locales; one's passion and the genes they carry."

And he'll be right.

I'm turning to leave, in step with a few other well-wishers also headed for the exit. Suddenly, a woman I've never seen in life, death, or in between—a dark-skinned beauty—catches my eye and then my arm. She steers me toward a less-populated area.

"I just wanted to say thank you, Terrence."

"To me? You wanted to say thank you to me?"

"Yes."

"For what? I'm sorry, but I don't recognize—"

"I'm Clara," she reveals, "but my friends and my parents call me Clare. I'm Charlie and Patty Ewell's first-born. On behalf of my brother, Jessie, and myself, I wanted to thank you for being there in our father's hour of need, after our mother came Home. Without you, he might well have decided to join us too soon."

Is she referring to…? She can't be. Charlie would never think of…

"Suicide, yes. You may not have known it at the time, Mr. McDonald, but *you* were instrumental in saving my father's life. Thank you."

"You're very welcome, ma'am. I had no idea. But why are *you* telling me this? No disrespect to you, but why wasn't this covered in my review?"

A hologram forms on the floor between us. I see The Hall of Records prior to the holding of my hearing. My panel. They stand with God. He is an *entity* in that room, but not the God I've come to know. He's a collection of atoms, white-blue as the fieriest flame, a collection that pulses when He speaks, remains still and attentive when He's spoken to.

"I'd like to be the one to tell him," Charlie says, his lip quivering just enough to be noticeable.

"You don't have to do that," says God.

"I know I don't *have* to. I want to."

"We have a procedure in place for situations like this. They are exactly *why* the review was put into use. Why do you wish to circumvent that process?"

"I *don't* wish to circumvent anything." Charlie chucks God's words right back at Him. *You go, old buddy!* "But this is *my life* we're talking about here. If Terry is going to learn he saved my life—and we can all agree that he must learn this, yes?—then I want to be the one to tell him… to thank him."

I don't see God's reaction. The hologram ends and disappears, so I'm not sure He *had* a reaction, other than to agree. Because here stands… not Charlie but Clara, Charlie's first and only daughter.

"It was supposed to be in your review." Clara picks up where our conversation left off. "And it *was*, in part. You remember when God replayed that first meeting between you two in your café?"

Yes, I do. He told me to keep it in mind, and I did.

"Originally, that's where God intended to cover my father's aborted suicide attempt. But my dad insisted—and he convinced God—he should be allowed to tell you how grateful he is."

How grateful he is. For his life?

"That's right. When he couldn't bring himself to do this at your hearing, he asked me if I could step in and help. That's why I'm here. The night you invited him to the café was the night he'd finally convinced himself, after an inner-struggle that lasted years, the world would be better off without him in it. My mother was gone, my brother and I before her, as you know, and he couldn't see that he had anything more to live for. Your invitation to share breakfast—the tenuous connection you forged with him—was the beginning of a turnaround for him. Your friendship gave him a new purpose after he felt he'd lost all purpose."

"I'm so glad you told me that, Clare," I say. "I know that can't have been easy for you." These words are not nearly enough to convey how honored I am.

We shake hands. Then, her thanks given, she walks away.

I saved Charlie's life. This new and wonderful nugget exposed, I can now state that, while God may be imperfect, He doubtless has a plan. I'm *still* not sure of its overall scope, even being Home—and anyone on Earth who purports to know the full scope is either lying or misinformed. However, in the course of helping to execute the small plan portion entrusted to me and the people I know, I saved Charlie's life. In this same course, he, Chloe, Megan, Mattie, and countless others—in many ways and instances, through a communal effort—saved mine.

·   ·   ·

Mattie materializes in front of me. She's wearing the same red dress she wore on the night she met Megan. Her hair is in the neat bun of that night, too, the one she must have worked for half an hour to get just right. This vision has me frozen where I stand.

"You figured it out, sweetheart," she says.

"I figured it out."

It happened during the review, somewhere in among Megan's birth, Mom teaching me how to operate my household appliances, and watching Lisa agonize over whether or not she should call me. But I didn't *realize* it happened until after my return to Earth. Until a life lived impatiently was at last awash in a peace I might have laughed or scoffed at before I met God.

It's a misplaced peace, I would have argued.

It wasn't any one thing in my review that brought about my enlightenment. Rather, it was the review as a whole. The knowledge that, if I couldn't find the answers I was meant to find, I'd be doomed. Ended altogether. I would never see my family again. No Heaven. No Mattie. No Megan (when she returned Home), no Emma (when she followed). And no baby Chloe. I'd been waiting to see our baby for decades. The sweet cherub we lost. I had to get this right.

I can do it. I know I can, I told myself, when my chances seemed bleakest, and even as the part of me who feared failure most wanted to vociferously dispute this claim. That: *I am not the body I inhabited on Earth. The palsy. The bad eyes. I am now—and I have always been—a worthy and capable soul.* The overriding lesson of my life came into sharp focus once I allowed this thought to form and crystalize.

"You wrote those poems, didn't you, Mattie?" I ask her, changing the subject.

"I did," she says. "After I came back Home and went through my own review, once I knew more about the *why* of it all. I wasn't even sure you'd ever see the poems, but I figured, if you did, they might help you somehow. And, if you didn't, I knew at least they'd helped *me.* I was honored when the curators came to me and told me *my* poems would be included in what they called our 'big book.' Because this meant the poems would always be preserved, not just separately but *together,* as part of *our* story. Did you like them?"

Her question is fragile. It is as though I could reach out and shatter its brittle, unseen exterior with a mere swipe of my afterlife-hand. Or the query might creak and break apart like an icicle under the weight of an inartful utterance from me; the word no. A syllable which has *no chance* of finding purchase on my lips as we stand together.

"You did a wonderful job," I tell her. "They helped me understand. I read them after my review, as I was settling into my new job. And, as one of the curators, I will make sure they're included in our big book."

Mattie doesn't tell me thank you for this favorable critique. But there is something new—something near relief—in her countenance, and I imagine our two visages could be mirrors of one another. Only one question remains for me. *What's next?* I wonder, and I ask this of Mattie telepathically. *What comes next?*

"I am so proud of you, Terry," she says. She chooses to give physical voice to these words. Then, via telepathy: *Let's go meet our daughter. Our Chloe. She's waiting for us.*

ACKNOWLEDGMENTS

The idea that a solitary writer left alone with his thoughts can produce meaningful work has always sounded a tad bit nuts, to my ears. Writers must live life well to write well, as they are, at the heart of the profession, chroniclers of life itself. Living life well means being *with* other people, taking in the human condition. Even those who revel in fantasy are chronicling lives, however much they may differ from reality.

I do not pretend I took this writing journey alone. Instead, I give thanks to those who went on the ride with me. (It was long. It was bumpy. At times, it almost broke me. But, in the end, it gave me something special to share with the world.)

·   ·   ·

To my siblings: Ben, Katie, James, Delaney, who have always been there for me in their own unique ways.

To Luke, who is the best friend a guy could ask for.

To my parents. My dad's the writer. My mom's the reader. My upbringing taught me to do both. Love you guys.

To Brad and Doyle and Harkness. Two are good doctors. One is a heroine you root for. One is a wonderful friend.

To Carol J. Bova, who edited and fought for this thing and encouraged and cajoled. Carol was my own personal Max Perkins on this project, which is the highest compliment I could pay her.

To Lauren Sweet. When Carol was done, the book went to Lauren, who assisted me in deepening the story to an extent I hadn't thought possible.

To Amanda Ryan, beta reader. Your thoughtful critique came to me at a time when I didn't know what I had in this book. Your words buoyed me up.

To Amy. With all my heart, I am so grateful to have you in my life.

LOVE, ME. (My Papa used to sign all of his cards to my grandmother in this way, capitalization and all. I love to sign notes to you in the same fashion, as another way of keeping my grandparents in my heart.)

To Papa Dick, traditionally my first reader, who never got to read this book, but he surely has since his passing. Pop, you're as alive today in my memory as you ever were on Earth.

The same is true for Ilene Rhodes. You once told me, in an emotionally charged moment, "We have a special bond." It is my hope that this book gives reason and purpose to your life beyond that which you ever knew in the physical world.

As to a special bond, the same goes for Scoot. Love you, buddy.

Grandma Ilene's father, my great-grandfather, was Edward "Babe" Seidenverg, the man who paid for the surgery that allows me to walk. When he was told of the surgery and how it could help me, and how my parents needed money for it, Papa Babe said, "If it's for Derek, I'll give you whatever you need." Or something like that. I can't quote him for certain. I wasn't there.

A giant thank-you to the man who performed that surgery, Dr. Leslie Cahan. Sir, you are the reason I'm walking today. There are no words equal to the task of expressing to you what this means to me.

To Jenny Bocko. Ducky says, "I did it!"

To Jenny Milchman. Friend, supporter, and great writer in her own right; and her husband, Josh, who once said something along the lines of: "He really knows how to make you *feel,* doesn't he?" in reference to me and my writing. Thank you for that.

To all my teachers, who knew I could do this before I knew I could do this.

And, last but not least, to Jill Marr, who believes I know what I'm talking about, which is nice of her.

It should be noted this thank-you list is far from complete. I would also hate for anyone to feel I'd left them out. If you don't see your name here, and you think it should be, you're probably right.

.   .   .

Now that I've reached the end of Terrence's long and twisting writing-journey, an end that once verged on unforeseeable, I admit to a measure of sadness. Terrence has been with me, has been mine–and only mine–for so long that to see him journey out into the world is a strange experience, to say the least. I want everyone to love Terrence as much as I do. To join him on *his* journey. I *know* this is unrealistic. And yet I must remember . . .

This story has enriched my life. It has made me not just a better writer but a better person. I am grateful for the minor but important change it has brought upon me.

Often, people say they'd like to be a part of change for the better in this world. But those same people, in their next breath, will say, "I'd like to be part of changing the world, sure. But I wouldn't know where I'd start."

Start with what you do best. That's my advice. In my case, that's writing. May this story be a small part–among so many other small parts–of changing this world for the better.

If it can do that, Terrence–and his entire family–will be proud.